Family Ties

A John Seraph Mystery

By

C.G. Eberle

Published by
Melange Books, LLC
White Bear Lake, MN 55110
www.melange-books.com

Family Ties, A John Seraph Mystery ~
C.G. Eberle ~ Copyright © 2013

ISBN: 978-1-61235-577-1 Print

Cover Artist: Lynsee Lauritsen

Family Ties
A John Seraph Mystery
C.G. Eberle

John Seraph's life is jeopardized when he begins looking for a missing woman and learns she was involved with one of his brothers and a New York State Senator.

Family Ties recounts how John Seraph is asked by a former classmate to help find his missing sister, because John's father is Stefano Angelo, head of the local organized crime family. John has not seen or dealt with his family in over three years since he walked away from them over moral differences about the criminal organization. John agrees to help and in the course of his investigation he learns a disturbing secret about the missing girl which leads him to her workplace and confronting New York State Senator Kingsley Addar and then his own brother Michael. As John digs deeper his life becomes endangered, but he is determined to learn the truth and see justice served.

Dedication

I want to thank some good people for believing in me and my writings;
My parents, George & Dottie, who have never stopped supporting me
through the bad times as well as the good.

My family including my cousin Mark who in reality is my older brother.
And my brother Mike who, even though we haven't always seen eye to
eye, we're there for one another.

My friends and associates in my Mystery Writers Critique Group.
Rosemarie, Mark, Ron, Nicole, Norma, Paul, and everyone else who has
helped me sculpt my story.

And last, but certainly not least, Janet Evanovich, Sue Grafton, & Robert
B. Parker. This trio of the best has been an inspiration to me and even
though I've never met them I consider them all mentors in a sense,
especially Evanovich who's been a major help and kind enough to
answer all my writing questions over the past few years. Thanks Janet.

Prologue

"If a man is not rising upwards to be an angel, depend upon it, he is sinking downwards to be a devil." Samuel Taylor Coleridge

My name is John Seraph and I'm recovering in a private-room at Buffalo General Hospital. I was shot in my left shoulder, and cracked a bone in my leg. This happened because I helped out an old college buddy, but before I get ahead of myself its best if I start at the beginning.

First, the name my parents gave me is Giovanni Angelo. If you recognize the last name, it's understandable, because my family doesn't have the best reputation.

I legally changed my name more than six years ago because of problems with my father and most of my family. This has been going on since my late teens because my old man is boss of the Angelo Crime family—an 'arm' of the Magaddino criminal organization—and its claws are sunk into almost every major illegal operation out of Western New York. Some activities the 'Arm' engage in are, prostitution, smuggling, hi-jacking, extortion, blackmail, the unions, arson for hire, and most recently, they've entered the world of hi-tech cyber and financial crimes. The only thing my old man won't deal in is narcotics. He's still old school when it comes to certain things, which is the nicest thing I can say about him.

I'm keeping this journal so I'll have some kind of record before I forget everything that happened, partly due to the pain killers my doctors have me taking. At least my conscious lets me sleep because I helped a family in need and exposed the truth for them. Hopefully my actions brought the Tillis family some peace and me some redemption.

Chapter One
~ Thursday ~

Last Thursday I got a phone call that surprised the hell out of me, because I barely remembered Sebastian Tillis from our college classes a few years ago. I'm a student at Buffalo State College, working towards my Bachelors in English Education, which can be frustrating beyond words at times.

When I got home, my answering machine was flashing, so I tossed my book bag on the loveseat in my small living room and pressed play. There was a message claiming I won a contest and all I had was call them back. Before it finished I pressed the erase button.

Next, my sister, Constance, called to see if I was coming to our parents' estate for Sunday dinner. As soon I heard Connie's voice I thought *Dai nemici mi guardo io, dagli amici mi guardi Iddio!* Which is Italian for *I can protect myself from my enemies. May God protect me from my friends!* I knew I couldn't ignore her as much as I wanted to because she'd keep calling and irritate the hell out of me. Finally, there was a desperate message from a Sebastian Tillis.

It was simple, but effective. I heard the worry and felt the panic in his voice. "I'm looking for John Seraph. My name's Sebastian Tillis, I don't know if you remember me, but we were in the Honor's Program at Buff State. I need some help finding my sister Dana and didn't know whom else to call. Please call me as soon as you get this. Thanks." After he finished his plea Sebastian ran off his work, home, and cell numbers so fast I had to replay the tape three times to make sure I wrote them down correctly, then stuffed the notepad sheet in my shirt pocket as a reminder to call him after dinner.

This was a major shock because Dana Tills had been missing for almost three weeks, and had been in the news almost nightly. I'd no idea she was Sebastian's sister and his call left me wondering what he wanted.

* * * *

My day had been a bitch, sandwiched between school and the rush hour traffic from the north side to South Buffalo. I had to deal with insane drivers on the 190 and the Skyway. Normally the half hour drive wasn't bad, but there'd been a major tie up thanks to a car accident on the 190 South, on top of which drivers around here treat Route 5, the Skyway and the 190 like it's a NASCAR race track and they're Dale Jr.

I was tired and hungry since I didn't eat all day and knew I'd have to get something in my stomach before dealing with Connie or Sebastian. As I scrounged around my small kitchen to see what I had for dinner, I tried to remember Sebastian as best I could.

We weren't that close, but we were both in the Honor's Club so that meant we shared some of the same English classes, other Honor's courses and took part in fund raising when we served as club officers. Sebastian always seemed like an all right guy, but like I said, I never got very close to him. Then again, I don't get that close to anyone really, by nature I'm a lone wolf.

I kept looking around, and finally realized my fridge and cupboards could've belonged to Mother Hubbard and I'd have to order in, go shopping, or go to a restaurant. My direct-deposit wouldn't kick in till Saturday, so I knew I'd have to be careful with my money and decided I'd have to go shopping at a small convenience store around the block from me.

I live in the Steeple Bay Apartments, which isn't bad for one or two people. There are 24 apartment buildings on both sides of Arbour Lane. Each building holds four apartments, two uppers, two lowers. I'm in a lower, close to Eden Street, which anchors a winding Arbour Lane to McKinley Parkway and there's many things I like about this place. Off street parking, laundry facilities, it's within walking distance to a number of stores and pizzerias in the neighborhood, and I'm a short walk from the Abbott Plaza, which is where my gym is located. All in all, it's a great South Buffalo neighborhood.

I grabbed my suede jacket, locked up and headed toward the rear parking lot. I could see two of my neighbors' cars in the tiny lot beside my car, and I went behind them to the fence that had a hole knocked into it as a short cut. Over time a number of my neighbors expanded the hole, making the walk to Abbott Road easier. I cut through and came out in the rear of the convenience store parking lot, which is owned by friends of mine.

I came around to the front and going in I saw two cars in the parking lot, and once inside I smelled the chickens on the rotisserie at the deli counter, and they had my mouth watering instantly. The girl behind the counter was one of four kids the owners, Charles and Dixie Baxter, hired to work in the store. I recognized her from my frequent visits, but I never bothered to learn her name. I didn't see Charles or Dixie, so I headed to the cooler and grabbed myself a turkey, a chicken and a Salisbury steak T.V. dinners, a package of dinner rolls, a quart of milk and a bottle of Diet Mountain Dew then headed straight for the counter.

I saw Charles coming out of the back and, once he saw me, I got that same big, bright smile he always has for me that makes me feel welcome. "Hey there, Johnny, how you doing, son?"

"Hiya Charlie, not bad. Where's Dix?" I asked because I knew she never left before five thirty. He answered as he began bagging my stuff after the girl ran them over the laser scanner.

"Her sister's not feeling that well and she went back home to help her out some." 'Back home' was Atlanta, Georgia. Charles and Dixie moved to Buffalo after they got married in the sixties, because they thought it best to move to a town that was more open-minded than the segregated south where burning crosses could become part of one's landscape, especially with Charles being white and Dixie black.

After I moved to South Buffalo, the Baxters sort of adopted me in their own way, and they knew about my family issues.

"Oh man, is this her older sister?"

"Nah, Mazy's still strong as an ox, this is Ella, and she's the baby. Ella's a bit high strung and their mother always fussed over her too much. She expects Mazy or Dix to come running when something's wrong. It gets to be a real pain in the ass." I laughed out loud at Charles' by-the-way attitude some things flew out of his mouth. One thing we have in common is we both realized life's too short for bullshit. The cashier just glanced at her boss and sort of blushed, but I figured she was used to his manner. "So have you talked to your mom?" I paused because this was unlike Charles, he normally never brought up my family, leaving that job to his more tactful wife, but I understood his concerns and I didn't hold anything against him.

"Ahh no, I haven't talked to her since last month and I haven't spoken to anyone else in about six or seven weeks. Actually, Connie called today. I got to call her back." Almost mercifully, the girl said my total was thirteen dollars and forty-eight cents and I gave her my debit card. I was grateful for the interruption to an uneasy topic. After I signed the receipt, I said goodbye and headed home, being careful not to snag my plastic bags on the damaged fence, and came into my building through the back door that opens onto the parking lot. There were three more parked cars and knew it had to be getting close to five thirty.

Once inside I checked my answering machine and there weren't any new messages so I put the chicken and Salisbury dinners in the freezer on top of my ice trays and next to the week-old banana-split ice cream. The milk went in the fridge, and I opened up the turkey dinner. Having made a thousand T.V. dinners I knew how long to set my microwave's timer for, without reading the instructions so I tossed the empty box in the trash. I headed into the living room with a glass of ice, set it down with a knife and fork on a T.V. table, and turned on the news. In a few minutes, I heard the microwave ding and I went back into the kitchen and grabbed dinner.

I knew what the rest of the night held for me after I ate. I'd call Sebastian, then Connie, and start my homework. Somehow, I knew my homework would be the easiest job of the three.

Chapter Two

After dinner and the news, I brushed my teeth, and had time to think things out and decided and it was better to get the bullshit out of the way. It's kind of like knowing you got to have an excruciating tooth pulled. Welcome to the world of dealing with the Angelo family.

I muted the T.V., picked up my phone and dialed Connie's number. My stomach tightened up, just like before you puke your guts out. As I dialed, everything flashed back on me. The problem with memories is once they start, you can't stop them.

Don't get me wrong, I love my family, especially my sisters, Constance, Maria and Alidia the baby. Almost everyone in the family is fine with our father being involved in organized crime, not to mention my brothers, and Beau, Connie's husband. I'm the only one who took a stand against the family and the Arm, which is the criminal family and my walking out shocked everyone.

Six years ago, the old man finally told me he wanted me to become the next Boss of the Arm. My brothers Peter, Paul, Michael, and Anthony all proved themselves working their ways up in the business, but our father said I was 'The One'. He knew I saw things differently than most folks, and this 'gift' he claimed I had, would be a benefit for the Arm. He also claims I'm smarter than my brothers and he didn't want to kill me. It's not unheard of, and I know this is an issue I'll have to deal with sooner or later.

By this point in my life, I'd already moved away from my family and their lifestyles, and made my own plans for my life. I promised my mother I was going to make something of myself, something I could be proud of and actually be a benefit to others.

In reality my troubles began when I was in high school, back then I wasn't far from following in the old man's path because of the money and the lifestyle, never considering how he made his fortune or who got hurt. I was wrapped in my own crap, and nothing else mattered.

Finally, in my senior year, about two weeks before the prom, I was cruising around with my best friend, Fred Mathis, in my first car, a black, Mustang convertible, which was any early graduation gift from my father. The first week I had the car I showed her off to all my classmates and Fred and I cut classes that Friday and went cruising instead. We were able to pick up a couple six packs and ended up at Woodlawn, a suburb south of Buffalo near the Ford Stamping Plant. The roads turn, twist and curve all over, looking like a pair of mating octopi. I was driving, lost control on one of the turns, and rolled my car several times, crashing somewhere between Lake Shore and Hoover Roads. I was drunk, going way too fast, and the accident was my fault absolutely. I know how lucky I was to have walked away with only a couple cracked ribs, a damaged left knee and severely sprained ankle. Sometimes my knee still bothers me, but all of this is nothing, Fred got the worst of it. He received a number of broken bones, some sort of neck injury, a major skull fracture and a punctured aorta from his broken ribs.

I walk out of an accident that was my fault and my best friend ends up as if someone ran over him with a bulldozer, life sure ain't fair.

By the time the Fire Department got us out Fred didn't look good, but made it to the emergency room. He was strong and made it through the night but died the next day. Facing Fred's family after that was the hardest thing I ever had to do and I'd rather die than go through that hell again.

His parents couldn't talk to me, and his sister, Melody slapped me across my face as hard as she could. She called me every name in the book, including murderer, and I couldn't blame her. Melody was pulled off of me by hospital security and she swore I'd pay. Guess I'm still waiting for judgment day. I know I have a lot to answer for but I'm doing my best to make up for my past.

As bad as everything was, the worst came when the old man fixed things to make it look as if Fred drove. Thanks to our family lawyer Aldrich Kaufman, bribes were made to the right people, reports were altered and for those few who refused to cooperate some associates of my father's 'discussed' the matter with them. Officially, Fred drove my car and the accident was his fault. Thanks to the old man's money and power I was cleared legally, but morally I'm guilty. The Mathis family tried suing me for wrongful death but their case didn't stand a chance when matched up against the falsified account that had become a matter of legal record.

I try to not think about what happened, focusing on the here and now, but there isn't a day that goes by I can't help but think of Fred or his family and the hell I caused.

It was while I was recovering in the hospital my mother talked to me. She told me how disappointed she was of me and that hurt worse than the wreck. I let her down, I let Fred down, and I let myself down. I thought I knew it all like most teenagers and I had to learn the hard way I didn't know jack-shit. She told me she knew enough men who had potential, waste their lives by getting what they wanted by hurting or killing. They may have been successes, but they weren't doing anything with their lives. It was here my mother made me swear a blood vow to make something of myself, to help others when I can, and that I'd make her proud of me again. After the accident, I finally realized there is right and wrong, in most areas there cannot be areas of gray. There must be justice for all.

Six years ago when the old man and Aldrich told me they wanted to become the Boss, I told them my decision to leave. Because of the situation and the feelings of my brothers and sisters I thought it best to distance myself from everyone. I moved an hour away from the family estate in Niagara County, in Newfane to South Buffalo, and started my new life by legally changing my name and not looking back. The last time I saw everyone was about three years ago, at my Grandmother Justine's funeral.

* * * *

The phone rang once, twice, and finally on the third ring a male voice say, "Hello?" My voice stuck in my throat, finally I answered back.

"Hey Beau, is Connie there?"

"John, that you man?" He was clearly stunned.

"Yeah, been awhile I know. Your wife left me a message, she around?"

"Yeah, yeah, she's here. Hang on." I heard him put the phone down and walk away. Knowing I caught him off guard, I was positive he asked Connie why she called.

A moment later, I heard running footsteps come closer and finally my sister's voice chimed out in excitement. "Gio, that really you?" using her nickname for me that she's used since we were kids.

"Connie, you know that's not my name," I answered back in frustration.

"Sorry, hon, I know that, but you'll always be Gio to me. It's hard to call you anything else."

"Well I'd appreciate it if you'd try. What did you want?" I asked switching my tone to let her know I wasn't in a pleasant mood.

"I was talking to Mama and she wanted me to ask you about Sunday dinner, again. So what do you say?" She emphasized 'again' just to let me know how long this has been going on, as if I needed a reminder. For the past six years, almost once a month, my sisters and my sister-in-law, Valeria tried to play peacemaker and get me to come back to the fold.

"Sorry, Connie, I've plans Sunday. I got to get a major report done for school next week and…"

"Bullshit, Gio. I always know when you're lying to me."

I thought, *Yeah just like Mama.*

"You can make it out. Mama really wants to see you."

"Fine, tell her to drive out here, unless she thinks she's too good for South Buffalo."

"Hey you're her son and you should make the effort to reconcile."

"Yeah, and maybe you hypocrites, who claim to be good people, should walk away the from the old man's businesses." Connie may have been quiet, but I heard her breathing hard and knew I hit the bull's-eye. Connie was one of 'the favorites'; our father could never do any wrong in her eyes, especially when he paid for a wedding or a house or three so far. "You going to say something Connie, if not I got stuff to do." I wasn't lying and figured I should've only called Sebastian back

"I don't get you, Gio, I mean everyone wants to see you and you're still being so goddamn bullheaded."

"All right, little sister, I'll explain for the very last time. If I go along with the old man, act like the rest of you, join the Arm like our brothers and Beau, I'd be saying that's okay, and I can't do that."

Connie's voice rose up in anger and I knew I hit a raw couple of nerves, "So you're saying my husband I are bad people?"

"You said it kid, not me. My conscious is clear, how's yours?"

Again, angry silence, then finally she erupted "You really are a bastard you know that?"

"Maybe so, but I learned from the two of the best, Grandpa and the old man." It was the way Connie slammed her phone down I could tell I really pissed her off. I thought *La lingua non ha osso ma rompe losso,* which means *the tongue, has no bone, but it breaks bone.*

I hit a massive nerve mentioning Beau like that. Connie can't stand to hear the truth when it comes to our father or her husband. Besides sharing our mother's olive complexion and black hair, the one thing my sisters all have in common is they love being Mafia Princesses. Connie knew there was no way I'd come out for Sunday dinner and would tell Mama. What Connie or nobody else knew was that I get together with Mama about once a month for lunch. As much I'd love to reconcile and see everyone, I couldn't. Connie was right about one thing, my stubborn streak. I once heard, "You got to stand for something, or you'll fall for anything."

Fortunately, I had other things to distract me from my family problems. I pulled out the paper with Sebastian's numbers on it and tried his home first. After two rings, I heard a young boy's voice say, "Hi there, Tillis residence." I instinctively smiled. I love little kids, they are honest and innocent. I always thought they're like little sponges that pick up so much from adults.

"Hello, can I speak with Sebastian Tillis, please."

"Sure, hold on please." Then I heard, "Dad, phone!" I laughed aloud at the sound of little feet running away.

While I waited, I thought about Sebastian before he graduated. We played poker a few times when some of the honor students would get together after class on Fridays. Sebastian stood out from the rest of us because we were mainly English or Art Majors. Sebastian was a Political Science Major with his sights set on Washington D.C. someday, so he said. I had no idea what his ultimate goals were or what happened to him in the past two and half years and, to be honest, I hadn't thought about him in a long time.

A moment later an adult's footsteps came closer and a familiar voice came on. "Hello?"

"Hello, Sebastian, this is John Seraph. You called me?"

"John. Thanks for calling me back so soon. I'm glad you remembered me."

"It took me a little time to recall, so what did you want to talk about?" I knew he mentioned Dana, but I figured it was a good way to get him talking. Sebastian's voice changed just a bit, but I could tell something was really wrong.

"You know about Dana, right?"

"A little, what's the latest news? I hadn't heard anything in the past couple days."

"The police are still looking into her disappearance and her background, but to be honest I doubt they have a goddamn clue." I heard the pain and frustration coming through in his voice. Sebastian really loved his sister and wanted to know what happened to her. I couldn't blame him. I'd always heard it was the not knowing that really was the true nightmare in missing persons' case.

The nightmare started three weeks ago and Dana's story was still relevant in the news. All of Erie County and Western New York knew the story by this point and it was looking grave. Dana worked in the Downtown Buffalo campaign office of New York Senator Kingsley Addar. She came to work like usual on a Friday and at end of business that afternoon she said goodbye again just like normal. When Monday morning came around and she wasn't at her desk, nobody panicked, but a couple of her co-workers asked questions because Dana was usually on time and a professional at her job. By lunchtime, most of the office knew something was wrong and the office manager, Sean Bruden, called Sebastian since Dana hadn't called in sick.

"I checked out her apartment, spoke to Dana's landlord then called the cops. I got the usual forty-eight hours missing then report bullshit they're required to give in these cases. What was upsetting was Dana was last seen on Friday around five, and I called the cops Monday afternoon after two o'clock. Technically it was almost seventy-two hours."

I could only imagine how insanely frustrating it had to be for Sebastian and his family to have to wait because of some bureaucratic rules and regulations. I couldn't imagine myself in this impossible situation and remain as cool as Sebastian was. I figured either he was barely keeping it together and was wearing a mask for his family, or the whole thing hadn't hit him yet, but when it did, I'd hate to see the man crash. Either way, when he let himself explode I knew it'd be ugly.

I also knew he needed more help than he was getting. "What did the police do?" I asked.

"Took my report, gave me a copy, and then began their investigation. They sent out some detectives from missing persons to Dana's apartment and her office. They talked to her coworkers, neighbors, girlfriends; even two of Dana's ex's were questioned, a couple beauties there."

I could hear the contempt in Sebastian's voice rising mixed with anger over those who were sworn to serve and protect. Finally, I asked him straight out, "Sebastian what did you want from me?"

"I was wondering if you could help me find Dana."

"What, I'm not cop or a private investigator."

"John, you're a natural detective, don't you remember you were able to figure out who the real thief was?"

"Yeah, believe me, I can't forget that." I had an immediate flashback to when we served as honor club officers Sebastian was President, and I was the Club Secretary. During some fund-raising, money vanished and it looked like our club treasurer was the embezzler. He had a pretty good motive and was just short of being expelled and arrested. Something in the way he swore his innocence hit me, especially when he was escorted by security out of class one day and taken to the Dean's office. Then I started to poke around. I didn't exactly believe him, but things didn't add up and something kept bugging me. I became like a bulldog with a bone. Finally one night when I was having dinner with Charles and Dixie, a spark of intuition went off in my head. It was like a flash from a camera, and like that all the pieces fit together.

I figured out our Vice President's girlfriend stole the money and framed someone else. When I talked to the Dean, we confronted her about her actions. Eventually she admitted her guilt and was ultimately expelled and arrested.

"Sebastian, I just got lucky, I figured out things."

"Yeah, that's my point. You made things come together for Eddie, otherwise he'd be doing time now. You always had that thing in your head John, those instincts are a gift."

"Alright I'll give you that, I'm good at figuring out things, but I'm not a trained investigator. Why not hire a real P.I.? I mean there's plenty around."

"My family already did, thought it would help."

"What happened?"

"The guy took our retainer and was on the case for about a week then I get a call from him saying he didn't find anything out of the ordinary, except for a bus ticket receipt to Santa Fe, New Mexico."

"What?" I asked, as I felt my face turn into a question mark.

"Yeah, I know the story was total bullshit if I ever heard one and working in the mayor's office I've heard plenty. He sent me a report which pointed toward Dana going to New Mexico, but there's no way she'd go."

"Why's that?"

"First, my wife's expecting again, soon. Dana wanted to be here for the birth, second she loves playing aunt to Toby and Chelsea." As Sebastian said that I felt like I was hit by the Buffalo Bills' defensive line because I thought of my nieces and nephews. "Second, Dana's a beach-bunny. She hates the desert and mountains."

I was intrigued. It was almost as if a spark was lit in my head, but I felt he was holding back. "There's something else, isn't there?"

Sebastian was hesitant and for a moment, a very uneasy silence filled the air. "Yeah there is, when I remembered how you figured out about the money I also remembered you may have some contacts most folks don't have."

Oh shit! He was talking about the Arm. I really didn't want to have this conversation. "Sebastian, I don't have any contact with my family and I was never involved in my old man's business."

"Listen, I know you haven't been in touch for a while,"

"You got that right!"

"John, please wait. I thought you might be able to ask someone if they'd heard or know anything. Believe me I know what I'm asking you, but I wouldn't do it if I had any other options available." It was here Sebastian's attitude changed. He wasn't angry or upset, he was begging for my help. He was desperate and scared, not that I could blame him. "See after my dad died I took responsibility for my family. I kind of replaced him, made sure my sisters got into college and became a second father of sorts for them. Right now, I don't know what else to do. There's nobody else I can turn to, John. Please just ask around, maybe your family has some contacts or knows someone who can help, or anything."

My first instinct was to tell Sebastian I couldn't do it. Too much bad blood had built up between me and my family, I was too busy or I was positive there was no way anyone would know anything about what looked like a simple case of a girl leaving town for a fresh start across country. I couldn't do it. God help me, there was something in this situation that kept me from lying to the man.

It's funny. I can bullshit my sisters and brothers, but I couldn't lie to a former classmate I hardly knew. Here he was, by all accounts a decent husband and father, looking for answers and nobody seemed to give damn about. He turned to all the normal, available channels and there was nothing they could do for him. I couldn't be another brick wall to Sebastian and his family, they deserved better than this. They deserved the truth.

"Alright, I'll ask, but I can't make any promises."

The relief in his voice was immediate and his gratitude was crystal clear. We made plans to meet the next afternoon at City Hall, since I only had two morning classes and Friday afternoons I was usually off campus by 12:30. He'd bring me the reports and anything else he thought would help.

* * * *

After I hung up, I began pacing back and forth along the hallway past the bathroom, and to the two bedrooms, trying to burn off my nervous energy. I turned around and headed back to the living/dining area. I was restless and started trying to figure out how the hell I was going to approach my family, especially after talking to Connie. Any way I looked at things, this cake was going to taste like shit. On my final pass to the living room, I stopped in the hallway at my oval hanging mirror. I looked haggard and said to myself, "Into the valley of death rode the six hundred." Then I just shook my head in disbelief and went back to the living room for the routine of my homework and evening TV.

Chapter Three
~ Friday ~

Friday began like every other normal school day. I got up early, shaved, dressed, brushed my teeth and hair and drove out to school via the Skyway and the 190 North. I got to the campus around six twenty, found a parking spot in the small lot behind the library near Elmwood.

I was at Bacon Hall so early I practically had the building to myself; except for the janitorial staff, I was the only one there. I settled into my classroom and took out the new Janet Evanovich novel I just started. I had about two hours to kill before my first class and this was a routine I'd gotten used to. Get to school very early, skip breakfast, go through my day and grab some lunch later after school. It may not be the best thing for me, but neither was pissing off a mob boss. By contrast, this was easier and safer.

* * * *

On Fridays, my classes are back to back and by noon, I was ready to get out of there like most students. After my last class, I tossed my book bag in the trunk of my Plymouth Breeze and headed down Elmwood toward downtown Buffalo. Eventually I crossed over a side street, then over to Delaware Avenue and reached Niagara Square about fifteen minutes later.

One of the funny things about downtown is right in front of City Hall, there's a landmark called Niagara Square, but it's a large circular path with a park like lawn and a miniature Washington Monument I never understood why. I found a parking spot after I circled the Square a couple times, got out and fed the meter. Not being sure how long I'd be there, I stuffed in eight quarters giving myself a two-hour window. I grabbed the paper with all of Sebastian's numbers on it and called his office number on my cell, hoping I wouldn't have too much trouble getting a signal downtown. A minute later a voice that sounded like it could melt butter answered, "Director of Communications Sebastian Tillis' office. May I help you?"

"Mr. Tillis please."

"May I say whose calling?"

"My name's John Seraph. Mr. Tillis is expecting my call."

"Just a moment please." I was put on hold and heard Air Supply playing over the phone. A minute later Sebastian picked up the line.

"Hi John, I've been waiting for your call." I could hear the excitement in his voice and the last thing I wanted to do was let him down, but I had to be honest with the man.

"Like I said I can't promise anything, but I'll try."

"Anything you can do, my family will appreciate. Where are you?"

"I'm in front of City Hall."

"Come up to my office, its Room 1458."

* * * *

Downtown Buffalo always struck me funny because it always seemed to be a real contrast. On one hand the older buildings of the 1930s were of an art deco style. City Hall and the Ellicott Square Building were symbols of the past and the hard working founders of the city, who were able to build up the industries that were the backbone of Buffalo for decades. On the other hand, the modern buildings like the First Niagara Center, the M&T Banking tower, and the Main Place Tower were clean-cut straight lines and edges with very little in character or style. To me they seemed to represent the decline of the economic picture of Buffalo and Western New York.

Actually, my family has historical connections to the older buildings. My Great-Grandfather Giuseppe Angelo was an architect and stonemason back in Sicily, but when he became a U.S. citizen he was forced to work his way back up from being an immigrant bricklayer to that of a respect designer and builder. When I see his work still standing it gives me a feeling of pride, something I never got from my Grandfather or the old man.

After I signed in and showed security my I.D. I headed to antique elevators that looked like they were made of tooled brass, in the style of the building and the lobby, which still has the original black, white and tan tile work still in place. I lucked out and had the car to myself, pressed the button for the fourteenth floor, the doors creaked shut and up I went.

I got there in no time. Mounted in front of the elevators, was a directory on the wall showing the offices on the floor, who occupied them and the direction they were in. I found my way to 1458 and entered. The only person in the outer office was Sebastian's secretary and man she was a looker. She had to be in her mid to late twenties, with short chestnut brown hair, blue eyes and a nice figure. The girl looked up from her computer and the clicking at her keyboard stopped. "May I help you?" she asked in that same sexy tone I heard on the phone.

"Yeah, I'm here to see Mr. Tillis. The name's John Seraph, he's expecting me."

"Just a moment please."

I stood there looking around at the sepia-tone pictures on the wall of past Buffalo politicians and the books on Buffalo's history lined up on the three book shelves as she spoke to Sebastian on the phone,

"Mr. Seraph," she purred, "Mr. Tillis will see you now." She slid out of her chair and opened the inner office door then shut it once I stepped inside. As the door shut Sebastian got up from behind his desk and I got to admit I couldn't place the face; if I didn't know who this was there was no way I could've picked him out of a police lineup.

Sebastian's blond hair had begun to recede and was thinning near the top, his face had grown a bit fuller and I could see his stomach had gotten a little plump too. I guess being the Director of Communications didn't leave him much time to hit the gym and of course, the stress of Dana's situation didn't help. He reached out his hand and instead of just shaking mine it felt as if he were about to rip off my arm.

We sat down in front of his desk and Sebastian asked how things were going. "So how have you been?"

"Pretty good, been busy with school, still working towards my B.A. in English Education, eventually I want my Masters, but that's still a few years off." After a couple minutes of getting reacquainted, we got down to business. He pulled out a manila envelope and dumped the contents on his desk. "These are copies of the investigator's report and the police report." Then he shoved a single sheet in front of me. "This is a receipt from the bus ticket and I have a list of Dana's coworkers and neighbors here too." Sebastian then brought up a sore spot, "I want to thank you again. I remembered how bad things were between you and your family.

I know this won't be easy for you."

"I'm not going to lie and say things are any better. As a matter of fact it's been about three years since I last saw my most of my family."

"Well, either way, I'm grateful for any help you can give me and my family."

I put the reports away in the envelope. "I've an idea of who to talk to and I'll call you in a day or two with anything I dig up."

He pulled out his wallet. "I want to give you some money for your time on this, I know..." I held out my hand to stop him from pulling out what looked like three one hundred dollar bills.

"Whoa, man, that's not necessary. You asked for help and I don't mind doing what I can. Keep your money."

He slid the cash back into his beat up wallet. "Okay, but if you come up with any expenses let me know."

"Sure no problem, but I doubt there'll be anything like that."

Just then there was a knock at the door. It opened quickly and I have to admit I was blown away. I felt my eyes expanding and my mouth went slack jawed as Mayor Byron Brown stood there, smiling. We both got up and just stood there as Buffalo's first black mayor came in. Not missing a beat Sebastian introduced us. "Ah...Mr. Mayor this is John Seraph, a friend of mine from Buffalo State College. John, I think you know Mayor Brown?"

We shook hands and for a moment, I really couldn't believe I was meeting the Mayor like this. "Of course I do. It's a pleasure, Mr. Mayor." Then Mayor Brown stopped and got a funny look on his face then smiled broadly

"John Seraph?"

"Yes, sir, that's me."

"I'm sorry to interrupt, Sebastian, but the meeting scheduled has been moved up to about ten minutes from now."

"Don't worry," I said. "I have to get going anyway." I sounded a bit apologetic, but Sebastian stepped in.

"John's here to help look into my sister's disappearance. He was just picking up some information."

The mood shifted, but Mayor Brown gave us his reassurance, "Well, if there's anything I can do to help please call my office, Mr. Seraph. We're all very concerned and have been praying for Dana's safe return. I'll leave you two to wrap things up."

"Thank you, Mr. Mayor, I appreciate that. I've a feeling I'm going need all the help I can get."

After Mayor Brown left I turned to Sebastian and told him that was something. "Yeah, I know, but Mayor Brown's a really decent guy to work for. I mean I never thought I'd be part of his Administration Cabinet when we were in school."

"You've come a long way, bubba." I had a feeling Sebastian could use an emotional boost, so I added, "Your dad would be proud of you and what you've accomplished."

"Thanks."

We walked out and as we stepped into the outer office Sebastian told his secretary he'd be at the meeting with the Mayor then walked me to the elevators. "I don't mean to rush you, but this is a big deal. Mayor Brown's meeting with me, the Commissioner of Community Services, the Director of Citizen Services and the Director for Division of Youth."

"No problem, I'll get started on this idea I have. Like I said I'll call you in a day or so, but it might not be till Sunday night, that okay?"

"Hey I'm just glad to have you on my side. It's like I said somehow I always knew there was something different, special about how your mind works."

We said goodbye at the elevators and I could tell Sebastian was already starting to feel better. Even though I knew what this would mean for me, I felt compelled, as if I had to be involved in this situation, but I also knew there was nothing I could do to avoid it.

Chapter Four

After leaving City Hall, I headed for my car and the meter told me I still had over ninety minutes left, so I figured it was time for lunch. I grabbed a jumbo Italian sausage, a soft pretzel and a can of Diet Pepsi from a street vendor. Since this was the first bright blue day in a while, a lot of folks had the same idea, to eat outside and enjoy the nice weather. The temperature was mild, there was a gentle breeze coming off Lake Erie and the grass was dry enough to sit on without worrying about getting wet, but still I opted to sit on one of the benches surrounding Niagara Square. I sat down to enjoy lunch and said "Hi" to a pigeon, which looked like he was hoping I'd toss him some crumbs. "Sometimes there's nothing better than meat that's been grilled by fire, this is definitely man food." He just looked at me, sort of.

While my feathered friend pecked near my feet, I ate and skimmed through Sebastian's notes and read the police report. It was taken by a Detective Laila Bishop, and then followed up when she and her partner went with Sebastian to Dana's apartment and began to look into her disappearance. After that, they headed to the campaign office, talked to Dana's co-workers and didn't find anything. Next, they contacted Dana's ex-boyfriends, both of whom had airtight alibis and the detectives didn't believe they had any motives, since one was married and the other now had a boyfriend.

I figured I'd have to call Detective Bishop, maybe meet with her. Before I left, Sebastian indicated to me he thought Dana's disappearance could've had something to do with either work or her neighbors, so that'd mean I'd have to check out both and go over the same ground the police and the P.I. did.

If the police dropped the ball, I'd like to think it was due to the fact they're overworked and underpaid. I can only imagine how many other active cases Bishop and her partner must have, or how many missing people there are in just the city alone.

I was convinced if anyone didn't do their job it had to be this P.I., Charles Lee. I knew I'd have to talk to him too but I knew I might piss off somebody if it looked like I was examining their work. Nobody likes their dirty laundry aired in public or getting second guessed but I didn't give a damn about that or anyone's feelings. I gave Sebastian my word I'd look into this and I've never broken my word.

After I finished eating and satisfied my feathered friend with some hot dog bun and the last bite of pretzel, I got back to my car, pulled out my cell and dialed a number I never dreamt I'd call again. I was anxious and I figured my best bet was to ask some casual questions and ease into the search, but not by calling the old man or my brothers.

If anyone could get a lead, or any piece of information, it'd be Aldrich Kaufman. He always seemed to know what was going on. I thought *A mali estremi, estremi rimedi,* or desperate times calls for desperate measures.

I took a chance and called his downtown office first. Aldrich's secretary told me he was working out of his Sheridan Drive office in Amherst today. I swore under my breath because I hate driving to the Northtowns.

I drove up to the thruway onramp, got onto the 190 North heading back towards school, went past the campus and kept on going until I reached the 290 interchange and wound up on Sheridan Drive.

I knew where Aldrich's three offices were and being one of the best defense attorneys in New York State he could afford them all. On top of his defending a large number of criminals, most of whom were associates of my father, Aldrich had been the old man's personal lawyer long enough to know everything he was into.

* * * *

When I got to the offices of Kaufman & Heyman: Attorneys at Law, I was blinded by the shimmering cement of the office building and had to stop a moment to give my eyes a chance to adjust. I also used this time to brace myself for what was coming.

Aldrich had an interesting background because he came from an Irish/Jewish family. His mother was third generation South Buffalo Irish and his father, also a lawyer, was originally from New York City.

Aldrich worked his way up in the mailroom and as a stock boy in his father's practice, and eventually made it to Harvard and found his niche in criminal law. He saw the life style some lawyers made for themselves thanks to their clients and wanted a lot better than his father I guess.

Aldrich was first hired as a defense attorney for some associates of the old man's, who were caught in the act of doing an arson-for-profit job. Somehow Aldrich convinced the judge the arresting officers were derelict in their duties and it was a case of false arrest. Of course, there was speculation he bribed the judge too. The old man showed his gratitude and hired Aldrich full time as his personal and professional lawyer. That was over thirty years ago.

Aldrich was always around my family and treated us kids like his own. He didn't do this out of fear the way some of the old man's employees were when around. In many ways, Aldrich was more of a father to me than my own father was and I give him a ton of credit for that. He and his wife, Wenona, couldn't have their own kids so we were sort of adopted by them. They were always over for holidays, parties, birthdays, and get-togethers, so when I broke my ties I walked away from them too, this was the one the relationship I severed that really hurt. One of the last things Aldrich did for me was to help me legally change my name.

* * * *

The lobby was modern and clean with black tile floors, textured plastered walls, large potted plants neatly staged. At the check in desk I told the security guard, I had business upstairs. Being that Kaufman & Heyman was the only business on the second floor of the two story building, he didn't bother asking who I was going to see. When I got off the elevator, I walked over the secretary and told her I was there to see Aldrich if he were available. I gave her my name and sat down while I waited for his answer. A minute later the gray haired fifty-something year old told me Aldrich would be out in a minute. A moment after that I saw a face I hadn't seen in over three years rush out with a huge smile on his well-tanned face. "Jonathan, my God, son, it's been too damn long!" he yelled in excitement, with his arms outreached in an attempt to give me a hug.

"Aldrich, how you been?" I said with my best fake smile. I got to say, though, he was looking pretty good. He had more salt and pepper in his hair, leaning towards graying, but he was still very polished despite his face being a little fuller than I remembered. "I think we better get out of here before people start talking," I said, as a couple of folks including the secretary looked at us funny.

"Come with me," he said as he wrapped his arm around my shoulder leading me back to his private office and told his secretary to hold his calls. The funny thing is I've seen Aldrich in court in action, under fire with questions from the press, and deal with the old man's temper when it erupted, and he never loses his composer. Now he seemed like an overexcited kid at Christmas waiting to see Santa Claus.

As we walked towards the back, Aldrich began to ask me all sorts of questions, firing them out like a machine gun. "So how are you doing, son? What have you been up to?"

"Nothing much, still in school, but I'm still a few years from graduating."

"Wenona will kill me if I didn't ask, are you seeing anyone?"

I smiled, somewhat embarrassed and shook my head. "Nope, there hasn't been anyone since Kim."

"I know that was brutal for you, but I am positive the right woman is out there for you."

"Well, I'm too busy with school and work to worry about that stuff."

He stopped walking and looked me in the eye, "A word of advice, son, do not let too much time pass on this. Before you know it, it will be too late, and you do not want to wind up alone." At times Aldrich may have been an arrogant, smug, likable bastard, but he was right about a lot of things.

After we got caught up, I told him I needed to talk to him about something really serious. Once inside his private office Aldrich hung up his suit jacket on his coat tree and headed for his brass and glass wet bar. "Can I get you something?"

"No thanks." I could see his curiosity peeking through and got to the point.

"So what is so important you finally broke your self-imposed exile?"

"Do you recognize the name Dana Tillis?"

He raised an eyebrow, showing a puzzling interest. "Yes, she's been missing for about two or three weeks, correct?"

I told him the whole story and when finished Aldrich took a hard swallow of his scotch n' soda and just looked at me "You realize what you are asking, right Jonathan?"

As if I didn't know I was sailing into dangerous waters, I paused a moment, "Yeah I do, but I told Sebastian I really doubt anyone the old man knows would be involved in Dana's disappearance. I mean she's a civilian, an innocent., I told him I'd look into things but not to get his hopes up." One advantage of being who I am, is when it comes to dealing with anyone involved with my father they can't bullshit me since I know the truth.

"I certainly cannot blame you for wanting to help your friend, but I haven't heard anything from anyone involved in the business." It always struck me funny at the number of euphuisms people used to describe or talk about a crime family. Almost as if not saying the truth made things any better.

"You think…you think anybody else might know something?"

Aldrich just shook his head saying no. "This does not seem like anything anyone would be involved with. Would you like me to make some inquiries?" Aldrich already knew what my answer would be.

"Yeah, I'd appreciate it. I figured it isn't the Arm's business, but I promised Sebastian I'd do what I could." Aldrich knew what it meant when I gave my word.

"Let me make some calls and I will see what I can find out," he said as he reached for his gold pen and notepad on his desk.

"Sounds like a plan." I gave Aldrich my cell and home numbers, but suspected he already had them. I got up to leave, shook his hand and asked for another favor. "There's something else I need to ask you." My voice got stuck in my throat as I looked Aldrich square in his eyes.

"Let me guess, you would like me to keep this between us?"

"Yeah, I'd be grateful. I don't need anyone to know what I'm doing. It's none of their business."

He gave me a reassuring smile."Alright, Jonathan, and I'll get back to you as soon as I can."

"Thanks Aldrich, I appreciate everything." As I turned and left his office I heard him reaching for his phone and spoke to his secretary to call back someone. *What the hell did I get myself into?*

Chapter Five

The drive home was quiet and uneventful. I made good time getting back to South Buffalo, but in spite of this, I couldn't get my head around what was happening. Diving into the snake's pit for someone I hardly knew, to find someone I didn't know was insane. At least that's what my head told me. *Why did I have all the luck?*

I got home around three, but stopped off at Charles & Dixie's store first. I grabbed a couple bottles of Diet Mountain Dew and Diet Pepsi, some microwave popcorn and a big bag of ranch Doritos. I didn't see Charles so this turned into a quick snack run.

Once home I set my school bag and the groceries down on the kitchen counter, which doubles as a breakfast bar, and went to the front of the hallway to get my mail. From the deafening music echoing from upstairs, I knew my neighbors' teenage son was home early. His music, if you can call it that, felt like it was being shot through my skull by a rivet gun.

Inside the sanctuary of my apartment, I sorted through my mail and since there wasn't anything needing immediate attention, I tossed it onto my secretary desk in the corner of the living room. I needed time to figure things out, so I did what I usually do in these situations, I put on the Chairman of the Board, Frank Sinatra. As shitty as any day can be, once I hear Old Blue Eyes my troubles seem to vanish and my batteries recharge. I turned on the stereo, poured myself some Diet Mountain Dew and opened Sebastian's envelope so I could sort through the information more clearly.

I read both reports carefully and knew I'd be calling both Bishop and Lee probably before the weekend ended. Something bothered me about both reports, but I didn't know what. I changed my mind and decided to call them right away. I had a feeling I was going to piss off someone else, but I didn't care what anyone thought.

When I called Detective Bishop's phone number, I learned she worked out of the main precinct on Franklin Street across from the old courthouse. The officer I spoke to told me Bishop was out of the office so I left a message that I was calling in regards to the Dana Tillis case, and I'd like her to call me back at her convenience. It was a repeat when I called Charles Lee's office and left the same message with his secretary. *So much for that*, I thought.

After I examined Sebastian's notes, I wasn't sure what else to do and thought it was a good idea if I knew who the people in Dana's life were. I had the idea to take my own notes and write down any questions I might think of. I didn't want to lose track of anything and knew this was too important to trust to memory. So I grabbed an extra steno pad and jotted down whatever came to mind.

I already knew Dana was working for Senator Kingsley Addar's office, which was across the street from the Buffalo Convention Center, in downtown, so I had an idea of where it was. Sebastian's notes went on to tell me a little about Dana's coworkers. Sean Bruden, the office manager, Angie Eden and Crystal Bell, were Dana's coworkers, but Crystal was marked as a good friend of Dana's. I figured she might be a source I could talk to. There were others who had been at the office for the past two months that I thought I should speak with. Chalmer Bernard, the senator's campaign manager and strategist, Hope Abdi, the Addars' social secretary, Tyrone Caleb and Akiro Hondoa, were bodyguards hired away from Executive Defense, a firm which specializes in providing bodyguards services for royalty, politicians, celebrities, the idle rich and, on occasion, provide backup to the Secret Service.

They've all been here since Senator Addar, and his wife, Desiree, bought a new home in the Northtowns to maintain New York State residence, even though they still had their antebellum estate in West Virginia. Maybe the Addar's were worth talking to, then I realized I probably couldn't get a meeting with them, but if I played my cards right who knew.

I hadn't made any brilliant deductions and thought Sebastian made a mistake calling me, I admit I'm not Robert B. Parker's Spenser. I had to remind myself I wasn't used to this stuff and just started. I figured I'd done all I could for now since I had to wait for Aldrich to call back, hopefully with some good news. I looked at the clock and realized it was already past four thirty, no wonder I was hungry. Not wanting to screw around with anything, I ordered a fish fry dinner from Pat's, a local sub and sandwich place that delivers and has one of the best damn fish fries anyone could ever want. It really is one of the few dinners that will leave me stuffed. I knew from past experience I'd have it in less than a half hour, which relieved my appetite, and was the easiest problem I had to solve all week.

* * * *

After dinner I re-read the reports in hopes divine providence would give me an insight I lacked before, no such luck, so I fell back on Plan B, veg out in front of the T.V. with a family sized bag of Doritos and Diet Pepsi, and by eleven o'clock I was ready to turn in since I had to be at work in the morning. I locked up, showered and brushed my teeth, and still felt like I hadn't done enough. I couldn't think of anything else.

Once in bed, my mind raced thinking about how much Sebastian loved Dana and the hell his family was going through and the irony of our situations hit me. In many ways, he was luckier than I'd ever be.

Chapter Six
~ Saturday ~

I got up around six and dressed. After washing up, I toasted a bagel, added an egg and melted some cheese, all that with a large glass of orange juice was breakfast. After eating, I headed back to school because on top of attending classes, I also work at the Butler Library.

I was lucky enough to get the job two years ago and enjoyed it most of the time. Usually I man the check out desk, except when I reshelf books. With the library being three stories, there's plenty for the employees to do. After books are checked in, we sort them on carts then shelf them in the appropriate places.. One of the nice things about the job is it gives me a lot of time to read, and sometimes I can get some homework done—until work interrupts me.

For the most part work is peaceful except for the occasional student needing help here or there and of course checking books in or out. This was one of the slow times for the library. Spring Break was in a couple weeks so the students hadn't reached what many call 'Crunch Time'. That's when students are rushed to do final reports and projects. Generally, the insanity begins right after Spring Break, until then the library was active but nothing like what was coming. Basically, it's the equivalent of Black Friday at a mall.

* * * *

After I sorted the overnight returns and put them on the right carts, there wasn't much to do. Occasionally, a student or visitor came by to check out a book or ask how to operate the copy machine, but generally Saturday mornings were like a graveyard. It's when I had a rush of people that came up at once like a herd of gazelles that I hated.

I thought I could be productive by doing some research on Senator Addar and his staff. I figured it couldn't hurt to learn more about the players, so I used the library's data research computer to run a search on Senator Kingsley Addar and there was plenty to read up on.

Kingsley Addar was currently in the middle of his second term, having worked his way up the political ladder, which began in his hometown of Rome, New York sometime during the late eighties. After his career began, he married Desiree Langley, heir to the massive Langley tobacco fortune from Richmond, Virginia. Eventually he made it to Washington and served on the Homeland Security's subcommittee of Intelligence Information Sharing & Terrorism Risk Assessment.

After working on the subcommittee and proving himself Addar moved over to the Judiciary Committee and chaired the sub-committee on Crime, Terrorism & Homeland Security, which is where the man's career really bloomed. In the past decade he's lead the charge for major improvements in protecting the Country's borders and airports.

At the same time, the Addars began co-chairing a new foundation on helping those who've struggled with drug and alcohol addictions, and helping addicts and their families turn their lives around. The foundation also works with gang members and has been able to help some folks get out of that life and turn themselves around as well. I guess it'd be too much to hope they'd also be involved in an anti-smoking campaign.

The Addar Foundation began in New York City and the group's work spread throughout New York State and was about to reach out into Pennsylvania, New Jersey, Vermont, Massachusetts and Connecticut. Spreading into nearby states seemed to indicate Addar might have been sniffing around to see how people would respond to a possible Candidacy for the Presidency. A number of celebrities and the super wealthy have publicly supported the Addar Foundation and Addar had been gaining support from all the right people in Washington D.C. thanks in part to lobbyists from the tobacco industry. The senator would still need a ton of political support, even though he hadn't announced anything officially.

I found and printed fifteen promising articles on the couple, the media called the second coming of John and Jackie Kennedy so I could read them after work. During my break, I checked my cell and saw Sebastian called to see what progress I'd made. He sounded understandably anxious and I couldn't hold that against him. I called back and told him there wasn't anything new to report, but I was glad he called. "I was wondering if you had a key to Dana's apartment."

"Yeah, why?"

"I thought it might help if I took a look at things there, if it's okay."

"Not a bad idea. You have a time in mind?"

"How's after two, I'm working till then."

"I can be there. You know where Great Arrow is?"

"Yeah, I'm up at school now." Nice, because Great Arrow is only a few blocks away from the campus.

"I'll meet you around four thirty because I'm meeting with some city workers about some upcoming political/media events."

I was glad Sebastian agreed to let me look around since I was going nowhere fast and to be honest I had a few questions for him that I didn't want to ask over the phone. I needed to see his reaction and find out if he was telling me the truth about what he knew. I'm no human lie detector, but I've learned some tricks to tell if someone's deceitful. One method is the way their eyes go when they're lying as opposed when they remember the truth. It's kind of like a poker tell, when someone shows they're playing a good hand.

At two o'clock, I headed over to the school's cafeteria, which was open on weekends for students who live on campus and grabbed a cheeseburger, fries and a Diet Pepsi. I had time to read the printouts and, as I sorted through the pages, I thought, *Oh goody, pictures.* Hey, I admit it. I'm a compulsive smartass, which is about ninety-eight percent of the time.

After lunch, I strolled around a bit and it always struck me funny how deserted the campus was on the weekends, except for the library. Finally, I headed toward my car and I noticed the chill in the air, it may have been spring in Buffalo, but I've seen Old man Winter kick up a lake effect storm well into May. That morning may have been clear and sunny when I left, but now the sky was four different shades of gray and it was colder. I wondered if this was a sign, I may have been right.

* * * *

I got to Great Arrow just before four thirty and found a parking space on the narrow street a house away from Dana's apartment. Most of the buildings were single family, one-floor houses, but there were some two family split-levels and Dana lived in an upper apartment that was brick on the bottom and red on top. There was a group of kids playing street hockey where the street turns on an angle behind me. It was about ten minutes later Sebastian finally showed up. When we shook hands I picked up the sickening stench of cigarette smoke, which I didn't notice in his office. That told me he smoked outside of the office and being so strong I suspected he smoked in the car on his way to meet me.

Dana had the whole apartment to herself and I had to admit I was impressed because she had more space than I did. I wondered how a girl working in a senator's office could afford this place because the rents near Buff State and UB were disgustingly high. Most college students in the area either had two jobs, and a roommate or two, or both.

Everything was neat, clean, and seemed relatively new. Considering Dana had some stylish furniture, I figured this had to set her back a bit. While I looked around, I asked Sebastian about her car. "Does Dana drive?"

"Yeah…" he told me as he seemed to stay a couple feet behind me, almost appearing as if he didn't want to get in the way of my 'investigation', like I knew what the hell I was doing. "Dana drives a 2012 Prius. It's the red one on the street."

I went to the windows that overlooked the street and could see the kids still playing. Alongside them was a fire engine red, nearly new Prius just sitting there. *Shit!* While I was waiting, I could have scoped out her car instead of wasting time sitting on my ass waiting for Sebastian. "I want to take a look at it after we're done here."

"Sorry, I don't have a key to the car. She just got it about three or four months ago."

"Really?" I felt the wheels in my head start to spin. Something wasn't right, and I made a note in a small notebook I started carrying in my shirt pocket.

"Does that mean something?"

"Maybe, but to be honest I don't know." I turned back, looked for her phone and found it on an end table. I didn't need the phone, but it was the phone book I was interested in. I figured this would be something worth going over, even if the cops did so too.

I flipped through the pages trying to find anything that looked like a clue, and figured now was a good time to ask Sebastian the questions I had for him. "I got to ask you, besides Dana's two exes, do you know if she was seeing anyone else?" I glanced up from the book and watched as he just shook his head with a blank stare on his face. So I asked again, knowing I might get my ass kicked, "I don't care if they could've been serious relationships or one night stands."

I've learned if you want to piss someone off you don't talk about them, mention their mothers, sisters or kids. After that watch out, it's game on. I expected Sebastian to yell or take a swing at me, but he surprised me. He just stood there like a toy soldier, broken and hollow, and the color drained out of his face.

Very quietly, he just said something that made me feel for the guy more than I did. "To be honest, John, I don't know who Dana's been seeing, or what she's been into for almost two years now." He almost collapsed into the rocking chair next to the love seat in front of the fireplace. "I don't have any idea what changed in her. I knew something happened, but I couldn't say what." Sebastian seemed to stare off into the distance, through the yellow walls of the living room, almost as if he were looking into another time and place. "I guess I was too close to her as a 'father' and not a brother, like we were when we were kids."

I put the address book down and looked Sebastian in the eye, not sure what to say, kind of faking it, hoping I'd stumble onto the right combination of words. "Listen, Dana and the others, even your mother, needed you to step up in your father's role for awhile and that's exactly what you did. I don't know, maybe you did the job too long, out of your feelings of responsibility and loyalty. Maybe you got too comfortable in the role, either way the thing to remember is, it's true there are things Dana felt she couldn't tell you, but that doesn't mean you did a bad job or you two ever stopped loving each other. You helped raise her, but she had to become a woman on her own and that meant discovering herself."

"Yeah you're right, but still it's hard…"

"Hey, it's no harder than when your mom had to let you go."

"I know." Just then, Sebastian looked kind of weird as he felt around himself, as if fire ants were Salsa dancing inside his boxers. He pulled out his cell, which was set on vibrate. From what I overheard, I figured Sebastian was talking to Nicole. He began to get up, but I got up first and motioned for him to stay.

Giving Sebastian his privacy I started to look around and strolled into the kitchen, which didn't seem all that different from mine, until I reached the fridge. Next to the milk, juice and eggs there were three bottles of champagne laid out in a small pyramid. I reached for one and the label read Bollinger. Pricey stuff I thought. I also found a couple tins of Beluga caviar.

After I finished snooping in the kitchen, I headed for Dana's bedroom and could still hear Sebastian talking. I noticed the wind was beginning to pick up and the windows were rattling as if they were going through an earthquake. Through the rear window in the bedroom, I could see the neighbors' trees swaying like Hula dancers, with some real force.

The bedroom was small but classy, with pricier furniture than I expected. Dana's bed, which I figured to be a queen, was a four-poster job with what looked like solid base that held the box spring. There was a white wicker rocker that looked as fragile as glass and the walls were in a light blue with white stenciled border at the top and matching curtains hung from the windows. The carpets and bedspread were both blue and white with a flowery pattern. Next to the dresser was an old fashioned, antique Hope Chest.

After finding the light switch I opened the closet, still not sure of what I was looking for. It was here I was stopped cold. There were cocktail and evening dresses in a number of colors and lengths, from sequins to satins to silks. A sign something was up with the labels. I opened the plastic garment bags that held two or three dresses apiece and immediately I thought of my sisters. Prada, Chloe, and Chanel were the names that repeated through most of the dresses.

In the rear of the closet, hanging all by itself in a clear garment bag was a long, black mink coat, separated from the rest of her wardrobe. Stylish furniture was something of pride. A new car could have been leased. I could even buy the champagne and caviar being on hand for guests, but Dana's wardrobe astounded me.

Finally, Sebastian came back to the bedroom and told me he had to leave right away to give Nicole a hand with the kids. I told him I was hoping to stay a little longer because I wasn't done looking around. He said I could stay as long as I liked and gave me his duplicate set of keys to the apartment. "Just lock up."

"No problem, thanks, and don't worry I'll leave everything alone. Hopefully I'll be hearing from my contact tonight or tomorrow. Once I know something I'll call you, okay?"

"Sure, and thanks again." We shook hands and Sebastian took off leaving me alone to try and figure things out. I went over the facts again as best from memory and looked around Dana's room and tried to get into the head of a girl I didn't know at all.

I was convinced Dana was not only involved with someone, but that person was paying for some of these goodies. Hell, the old man has had a few 'girlfriends' on the side while married to my mother, just another reason I hate the bastard. A lot of guys I knew from the Arm were the same way. I figured this benefactor had to be paying for part of her wardrobe, maybe the car too. I strolled around the bedroom and looked at Dana's makeup mirror circled with sixteen clear bulbs. I never understood why women needed such things.

There were photos lining along the sides of the mirror. Some were decades old and looked like they were taken when Dana had to be six or seven with her family, before her dad died. A couple pictures looked like they recent and were taken in a photo booth, maybe at an amusement park, because Dana and a cute girlfriend were squeezed into a booth together. I could only see their faces and it looked like the snapshots were taken within the last year or so because Dana looked almost the same like she did in pictures seen in the papers and on T.V. Her girlfriend was attractive, with dark hair and glasses. To be honest I don't care what Dorothy Parker said; I would be happy to make passes at this girl with glasses. I'd remember this face.

It seemed like they were close I thought, scanning the strip of photos. They were laughing at something and had made silly faces in one picture. In the second they tried to put on serious faces, were talking in the third and in the fourth Dana surprised her friend by kissing her on her cheek. I thought I might need a recent picture of Dana once I started asking around, so I grabbed the strip and made a mental note to put them back when I was done. I looked over at the other pictures and nothing jumped out at me. In the family photos, there was a nice big one with her siblings and another with her niece and nephew. Sebastian was right about how Dana loved his kids. I couldn't see her skipping out on them. Finally, I noticed there was space on the other side of the mirror, but there was some pieces of tape left so I knew there were some pictures taken. It looked like there were about four pictures. Things didn't add up, somehow I knew something happened to Dana. The more time that passed the more I was convinced Sebastian was right. To be honest I was worried for her, because I never heard of these cases having a happy ending.

I took a final look around then locked up. As I headed out something nagged at me, as if I forgot something Sebastian told me, but couldn't remember what it was. I knew once I stopped thinking about it, it'd hit me. Before I left I stopped to talk to the folks downstairs. Turns out, I was in luck and the Nichols family was concerned for Dana as well.

The Nichols were a retired couple in their sixties and the landlords. Their twenty-something daughter Susan, and her four year old son,

Toby, lived with them. I quickly explained that the Tillis family asked me to look into Dana's disappearance, without giving them all the details, which I guess led them to believe I was another investigator. I didn't have a problem with this since they were happy to answer my questions.

Mr. Nicholas invited me in and immediately I was overwhelmed by the smell of Sheppard's Pie baking in the oven. It smelled superb and my stomach suddenly was awakened, rudely.

We sat in the living room Toby played with his cars in the adjoining dining room so everyone could keep an eye on him. After we got acquainted, the Nicholas's told me Dana was a great tenant. "She keeps her place clean, pays her rent on time and even babysits Toby," Mr. Nichols said.

Susan told me, "Dana loves watching Toby, but there was a problem sometimes." Susan held back for a moment then continued. "Dana has frequent overnight company and from the noise it sounded as if she had more than one visitor more than once."

Unfortunately, nobody saw Dana's visitor so I don't have a description of any of them. *Figures* I thought.

After the family told me what they could I thanked them for their help and gave them my phone numbers just in case anybody thought of anything else later on. Before leaving, I asked if the police had stopped by, then they told me something that almost knocked me out of my cowboy boots.

On the day Sebastian showed up with two detectives, he was upstairs with Detective Bishop, but the officer the family talked to was Detective Jethro Berriah. *Oh Shit!*

This meant I might be going to war with a dirty cop who was nothing more than a cacasodo. That's Italian for someone who doesn't think their shit doesn't stink. God help me.

Chapter Seven

The bile in my stomach flared up on the way home. I felt sour, as if I chugged rotten eggs and spoiled fish heads, and I knew I was going to hurl big time. Acid and anger churned through me and I knew I'd need something to settle my stomach or I'd never get any sleep.

Hearing Berriah's name brought back difficulties I thought I could avoid. I don't have problems with police officers, actually I've a great deal of respect for them despite the fact I've seen a lot of them cross the line and go on the take. Berriah was the type who gave all cops a bad name and should be doing hard time as somebody's bitch. I first heard of him when I was still living at the estate and from what I heard, like some city officials or other cops, he could be bought off.

My problems with the man started three years ago at my grandmother's funeral. Representatives from the Five Families, and the Rizzuto crime family, a.k.a. the 'Sixth Family' from Montreal, Quebec attended, to pay their respects. The Organized Crime Unit showed up as well and filmed everyone. I didn't think it was appropriate, so I asked them to respect our privacy. Berriah got bitchy and mouthed off, he didn't care for my rebuttal, in which I compared him to what a hooker does, and I admit bringing his wife and mother into it wasn't my best move. He took a swing at me, I ducked, and then I broke his jaw in one shot, then got arrested for assaulting a police officer. I was out that night thanks to Aldrich.

One of the officers testified how Berriah started the trouble and I was defending myself. The judge let me go and cleared my record. I lodged a civilian complaint against Berriah, which was added to his record. Nothing he can do will get rid of that, but after his hearing, he swore he'd get even.

* * * *

36

I got home around six. The sun had been hidden by clouds for most of the afternoon and the chill in the air made it feel like winter still had its clutch on Western New York. Then suddenly I'd felt very tired and knew once my stomach settled down I'd be alright.

I hung up my jacket and sorted my mail, again nothing important so I tossed it all onto my secretary. Any appetite I had was shot to hell and I hated to admit it, but I knew I needed an Alka-Seltzer. Trust me if I'm taking a medical martini, I feel like shit. I got a glass of cold water and dropped in the tablets. As I waited for them to dissolve, I checked my answering machine for messages. Just one, it was Aldrich.

"Jonathan, I reached out to some associates I know and no one knows anything about the Ms. Tillis' disappearance. Sorry. There is something else though, your father somehow got word we talked, and he wants to see you. He told me he may have some information and is willing to help. He also told me to tell you, you can pick the time and place, but you are more than welcome to come out to the estate tomorrow for dinner. After everything that has happened, he is willing to forget. If you want to call me later you know my home number."

As I listened I closed my eyes in complete disbelief. My nausea increased by a factor of a hundred. I braced myself against my loveseat. I should have known better than to trust that Sonuvabitch. I knew who the old man's 'source' was, but I was desperate and needed the help. It may have been reckless to trust that oily lawyer and I'd make sure he got his someday for lying to me, but that would have to wait.

Right now, I had two choices and I didn't feel good about either one. I could either lie my ass off to a family who was extremely desperate to find a daughter, or I dive head first into the serpents' nest. I didn't know what to do. I wanted to sneak away to Canada and hide.

I slammed down the Alka-Seltzer as if I were in a chug-a-lug contest. As I swallowed hard, I gripped the glass so tight I could feel the pressure building and knew I came close to cracking it. I headed back to the living room unsure of what to do next, so I fell back on Seraph's First Rule. 'When in doubt, Sinatra helps out.' I put on one of the 'Rat Pack' and crashed onto my love seat. I closed my eyes and tried to drift away at the sounds of Dean Martin, but his comedy and music didn't help me. Finally, I got up and went to my bookcase looking for a book of poetry.

I'm an avid reader and love a number of classics and contemporary writers, including Shakespeare, Frost, and Byron. From time to time, I try to find answers in their works the same way a religious man would look to the Bible or the Torah.

I sat back down and flipped through the pages searching for some sort of an answer I didn't have before. The pages blurred as the words and passages seemed to fuse together. I couldn't make any sense of things anymore. Finally, when I heard Old Blue Eyes belt out *The Best Is Yet to Come,* I came across one of my favorite pieces written by Lord Alfred Tennyson. *The Charge of Light Brigade* always seemed to recharge me, and after reexamining the words and their meanings I knew what I had to do, I'd go for it.

It's not like the old man would fire cannons at me as I drove up the driveway. It was going to be a major kick in the balls, especially with the way Connie and I left things, but I gave Sebastian my word. As a wise man once said, "Nothing to it but to do it." Christ I hope he was right.

Chapter Eight
~ Sunday ~

I didn't get much sleep, maybe two or three hours. My nerves kept me up most of the night, every time I closed my eyes, I imagined what would happen when I got to the estate.

I finally woke up around noon and wasn't in any real hurry since I knew dinner wouldn't be until around four o'clock. I took a long hot shower to help me relax and it gave me the chance to let my mind drift away. Even though it felt really good, I didn't feel any better. I figured I'd dress a little classier than my usual blue jeans and pullover, so I opted for one of my dress shirts, black jeans and black cowboy boots. Not exactly on the same level as the Brooks Brothers and Armani suits the old man and my brothers dressed in, but I was comfortable in my clothes. I mean who the hell needs to spend a car loan for a suit really.

After dressing I saw there was a message on the answering machine, Detective Bishop called back. "I understand you wanted to discuss the Dana Tillis disappearance. I'm sorry I hadn't gotten back to you sooner, but you can call me today anytime before six." She ran off her cell and office numbers, which I wrote down, then called her cell phone first. After the second ring, she picked up, and after my introduction, I explained that I was now looking into Dana's case. "Excuse me, Mr. Seraph, are you a licensed investigator?"

"No, why?"

"I'm wondering why Mr. Tillis contacted you."

"We were classmates for a while and Sebastian thinks I may be able to help out."

"I see. Is there some specific reason why he chose you?" I could hear her wheels spinning and understood why. I wasn't sure how she'd react to me doing my own investigation. For a minute, I considered lying, but I couldn't think of anything and besides I thought it best to play it straight with her and see what this would get me.

"Well, Sebastian thought some…of my family's contacts might be able to help out."

"What sort of contacts?" Here's where I figured the shit would hit the fan.

"Does the name Angelo mean anything to you?" There was a brief pause and I guessed she was trying to recall it, which didn't take her long.

"Yes, why?"

Finally, I said what I'd hoped I'd never have to say in my life again. "Stefano Angelo is my father. He's head of the Arm." My stomach whirled around and I prayed this wouldn't be a problem. "Now I don't have anything to do with his business, as a matter of fact I haven't seen him in three years Detective, but Sebastian thought, since nobody else knew anything, maybe…" as I let my voice trail off since I knew she'd get the picture.

"I see."

"One other thing."

"There's always something else."

"I'm the one who broke Detective Berriah's jaw a few years back."

She surprised me as she started laughing.

"That was you? Ohmigod!" I have to admit, that wasn't the reaction I was expecting.

"Uh, yeah that was me."

"You know he still has trouble eating steak?"

I started laughing and tried to explain the situation, but Bishop was ahead of me. "For a while that's all folks were talking about throughout the department. There are quite a few who thought he had it coming and wished you'd done more to him."

"When did Berriah move over to Missing Persons?"

"He didn't. He's still with Organized Crime, but we were shorthanded when Mr. Tillis called us and he was subbing for my partner who was out sick."

"I hope my situation isn't a problem for you?"

"I understand why Mr. Tillis called you, and I never heard of you being involved illegal. Tell me Mr. Seraph, what were you planning?"

"Playing things straight, I spoke to my father's attorney Aldrich

Kaufman to see if he could find out anything. He called me last night and told me he struck out, but my old man may know something. I'm…I'm going to see him later and find out what he knows."

"Okay, since you may be in a position to get some information from a source that would be hesitant to talk with me I don't see a problem with you helping out Mr. Tillis, but if you get any kind of information call me, understand?"

"Got it Detective."

"And don't worry. I'll keep this under wraps, there's no need for Berriah to find out."

"To be honest I'm not worried about him."

"I understand, but he can make things difficult if he hears about this."

I told Bishop I'd call her later with any information I got. She told me she was going to be in the office until around six and if I learned anything, I was to leave a message on her voice mail. After we wrapped up, I tried to imagine the old man's face when he found out I was willing to work with the police. I figure he'd have a coronary on the spot, but I knew I wouldn't be that lucky.

* * * *

I left around three and the drive to the estate was surreal because I made a blood oath to myself I'd never come back, but on the upside at least the weather was with me and it was a nice drive. The only thing that would have made it perfect is if this was in mid October, during the peak of the foliage change. The skies were bright and clear with sunshine and very few clouds, but the chill was still there. It warmed up a little bit, and as I drove to the thruway, I had my window down. Once I sped up I'd have to roll it back up a bit, otherwise my hair would've looked like I tongue kissed a light socket. Before leaving the city, I topped off my gas tank because the drive would almost take me an hour.

The estate is in Newfane, all the way up in Niagara County and that meant I'd have about an hour's drive ahead of me. Originally, the old man lived in Buffalo, from the West Side, but after he became Boss, he wanted something more private, secluded and secure had the estate built way up there.

When I walked away, I packed my things, took some photos and left a letter saying goodbye. I told everyone I'd be okay, but there was no way I could go on living like this with the family the way things were. It was my hope someday things would change, but there was no sign of that happening so I wasn't all that optimistic.

There are eight of us, with me being the oldest, and after I was born things really got interesting for my folks. Mama had the first set of twins, Peter and Connie, two years after me, Paul the following year. Maria and Michael, the second set was born two years later. Anthony was born a year after them and finally Alidia, who was a definite surprise. Is it a wonder why the old man needed an estate with eight kids?

The place is massive and probably more secure than the Erie County Holding Center with a nine-foot stonewall surrounding the property, cameras are mounted on all sides that gives a live feed to a pair of armed security guards at the guardhouse, which also controls the electrified gate. If anything, the old man takes his privacy beyond seriously. I always suspected he was a bit paranoid and had confirmation of this when my mother told me last year he had the property installed with some sort of anti-bugging devices that made most spy gear unusable on or near the property.

I admit the estate is amazing. With almost twelve thousand square feet, there was room enough for all. The main-house has nine bedrooms, eight baths, a music room and a billiards room with a library on the main floor, and a second library in the walk out basement. There are two guest rooms, which were originally two of our bedrooms, a gym with a sauna, a home theater, and a very large open area on the top floor known as the ball room with a next-door 'tower room'.

Mama worked with the decorators and contractors for weeks to design the perfect mansion. Custom cherry stained wood workings, a custom made spiral staircase and the jewel being a birdcage style elevator, which climbs through the open middle of the staircase. The place is beautiful and has the taste and style Mama has always had. It struck me funny how a woman from Riverside, who grew up almost dirt-poor can have more class and taste than some folks who have always had money their whole lives. A person can have all the money in the world, but that doesn't mean they have any class, style, or taste. To be honest this is one thing I am glad I got from her.

The one thing I always wondered was how much blood money paid for everything. I mean how many people suffered so my family could enjoy the good life.

* * * *

I reached the estate just before four and parked on the side of the road, with a clear view of the main house. It looked like a castle ready to repel invaders. For some reason it seemed a lot bigger than I remembered and was a lot more imposing.

On the one side of the house where the yard spread around I saw my nieces Kelly, Sandra and Catherine running around playing some sort of game and thought *Christ they got so big.* I started kicking myself over how much I lost out not being a real uncle.

After I cleared my head, I started back to the main gate and pulled around toward the guardhouse. The two security guards who looked like they belong on *America's Most Wanted* stared at me kind of funny at first and finally one with a pronounced brow and resembled the missing link, came over to my window. "Whatcha want, pal?"

Without removing my sunglasses I stared down the guard, "Tell Mr. Angelo he has a visitor out here. He'll want to see me."

"Sorry, but he's not taking visitors today, family party only. Why don'tcha call and set up an appointment?"

"Well I guess it's a good thing it's a family event. Call up to the house and tell him his son John is here."

Chapter Nine

At first, it looked like the guards were going to give me shit. I knew it was their job to protect the old man and Mama, so I wasn't going to hold that against them. After a huge, black fellow who I figured was at least 400 pounds, called the main house and learned who I was, he turned white and I thought he'd stay that way. He flipped a switch, waved me through as the guard I spoke to looked on in amazement, surprised and confused.

As I watched the black gates swing inward on to a two lane paved driveway I felt like I was going to blow chunks again. On either side of the road were rows of neatly trimmed small trees separated by small lights that were all on timers and the driveway was the only major change I could see, everything else looked the same. When I left, it was all white pebble stones.

In front of the main house was a large circular driveway that could double for a helicopter-landing pad. I felt a little self-conscious about parking my '99 Plymouth Breeze against all those luxury cars and SUVs.

I got out and froze as I looked up at the main-house. This had been my home, and to walk away from the people inside was one of the hardest things I'd done.

I strolled up to the front door trying to look and feel confident, but my guts felt like a raw egg ready to crack apart. I knew I had to stay strong once I was on the other side of those large mahogany doors. I pressed the doorbell and the familiar chime sounded.

The door opened up and there was my mother Sophia, looking as beautiful as the last time I saw her, with a deep olive complexion, black hair with some gray highlights, and few more worry lines surrounding her green eyes. Tears welled up and a sad smile coming across her face. She was wearing a dress I hadn't seen before, a violet and black floral print number. "Hi Mama, how you doing?" We walked toward each other and hugged. She placed her hand on my face. "Aogni uccello il suo nido e bello," which translates to 'To every bird his own nest is beautiful' or 'There's no place like home.'

She smiled. "Showing off again? Out of all you children, you always spoke Italian the best John.", then she squeezed the stuffing out of me. "I'm glad to see you, baby. How are you? I never thought I'd see you here again."

"I'm okay, Mama. I know what you mean, but he reached out to me."

"I know a little about what you're involved in, but not the whole story." Then she smiled her beautiful, sweet smile that made me laugh when she ran her hand through my hair. "When did you get your haircut?"

"Last month."

She just shook her head. "I didn't think you would ever cut off your ponytail."

"Well, it was time, besides it's a lot easier to manage now." I smiled broadly. As we headed over to her library we walked arm in arm and I told her the whole story of how Sebastian asked for my help. "I hate to say this, but the main reason I came was to find out what he knows about Dana Tillis's disappearance, nothing else has changed."

"Has there been anything new on Miss Tillis's case?" Before I could answer her Alidia, Maria and Anna came in chattering away, but stopped dead in their tracks when they saw me. The girls sacked me like a couple defensive players from the Bills, but they were so tiny I stood firm as they pushed against me. It was great to see them and I hugged back as hard as I could. Too much time had passed and seeing my family gave me a feeling I can't put in words. Three years is a long time, longer than one might think.

The girls cried and I admit I was a little choked up too, being their older brother I've always had a special protective relationship with them.

Alidia and Maria dragged me to the kitchen with Mama and Anna following us, as the girls talked up a storm. They asked me the same questions Aldrich did, and once we reached the kitchen we found the old man there and I wasn't surprised to find him slicing up fresh tomatoes and adding the pieces to a big brass cooking pot, that was sitting on the island stove cook top. This was one thing that always struck me funny that for such a dangerous man he could cook better than almost anyone I knew.

His back was to us as he was talking to Peter and my brother-in-law Beau, and all were drinking wine. The guys became quiet the second I walked into the kitchen and they looked past him, right to me. The old man continued talking and to be honest I doubt anyone knew what he was saying.

Finally, when he realized they weren't listening, he turned slowly, as if he knew something was going on behind him. I have to admit I was surprised by his reaction. I looked into a set of dark eyes that had a few more wrinkles around them and they started to tear up, upon a face etched with worry lines. As he saw me, the old man dropped his knife onto the cutting board sitting on the island, took a few stunned steps, and wrapped his arms around me.

"Hiya, Dad," was all I could say as I hugged him back. Even though nobody was saying anything, volumes were spoken and I thought *Acqua cheta rovina iponti.* Or Silent waters run deep. I admitted to myself I was glad to be home.

Just then, Connie came into the kitchen and her eyes widened when she saw me. She didn't say anything, but the look on her face screamed bloody murder at me. I didn't care what she thought because I had more important things on my mind.

"How's it going, Connie?" I asked and tried to hug her, but she just stood there pissed off with arms crossed and face flushed, looking like a younger version Mama when she's furious with any of us kids. There's one trait the whole Angelo family shares, we can hold a grudge like you wouldn't believe. I didn't push things with her and looked Connie square in the eye, telling her I wasn't backing down from her or anyone else.

After everyone finally settled down Alidia went to get me a drink and I settled for a soda. I never developed my family's tastes for wine and I didn't want any liquor because the old man may have extended the olive branch, but I've learned when dealing with him it was best to keep a clear head. We talked around the island and I did most of the talking, answering questions about what I had been up to, how school was going, but I kept quiet about Dana.

Things went on perfectly with the family gathered around the kitchen talking as the old man continued to make his homemade spaghetti sauce, the way it's done back in the old country. This'd been a tradition since I was a kid and I got to admit he makes an amazing sauce.

Dinner started with appetizers of toasted garlic bread with mozzarella and either diced tomatoes or diced green peppers, a pasta e Fagioli of red and white beans with ground beef, tomatoes and pasta in a savory broth. This was followed by veal parmesan with a side dish of spaghetti and for dessert, a chocolate gelato topped with caramel sauce and dark chocolate pieces. Everything was great, except for one thing, I don't eat veal. I wasn't worried about that since when it came time I just pushed it aside.

What was funny to see was the old man, the head of the Arm, a man who I knew was guilty of so many numerous crimes, he'd get twenty-five to life, looking like a kid at Christmas with a rosy look to his plumped out cheeks and heavy face.

We didn't have a full house since Paul and Michael were out of town on business, and Maria was on vacation in Palm Beach with her newest boyfriend, one of the Buffalo Sabers. So it was me, the folks, Peter, Valeria and their kids, Connie and Beau, Anthony, Anna and their two kids, Alidia and her husband Michael and Aldrich and his wife, Wenona, who arrived about ten minutes after I did.

To be honest, I wasn't looking forward to seeing Paul or Michael. Before I walked away, and word spread the old man wanted me to head the Arm someday, it made things difficult because both Paul and Michael saw themselves in that position. Now let me set things straight, most of the time they're alright usually, but Mike is immature and still needs a lot to learn. He doesn't use his head as much as he should. His biggest problem is, he doesn't think, he reacts. He's pure emotion, no logic and in the Arm's business that can lead to bad decisions, maybe it gets you killed.

As for Paul, he's someone who wants to be involved but doesn't have the potential or brains for the job. He'd make a great store manager, but he's no mobster. Paul just doesn't have the skills needed for leading a criminal organization. I always suspected the two of them were jealous of me while equally pissed off that I got offered the very thing they wanted and rejected.

* * * *

Dinner was amazing, nothing like a home cooked meal. We finished around seven-thirty and we all chipped in and began clearing the table, even the kids, and at one moment out of earshot of everyone I leaned over to the old man and told him we'd need to talk soon; he agreed and the mood of the night changed.

After the dining room was cleaned up I worked off dinner by strolling around the house by myself going from the dining room through the kitchen and into the breakfast nook. I looked over the backyard and watched as the sun began to slowly go behind some clouds. I really had forgotten how beautiful it was out here. I got some fresh air outside, and I was overwhelmed by the memories that raced through my mind. Finally, I realized my stroll down memory lane was sentimental but not productive. *Time to get to work,* I thought.

Inside, the kids were watching a movie with Beau and Anthony in the billiards room and they told me the women were having coffee in the living room and Aldrich, Peter, and the old man in the study and were ready to talk business.

I'd forgotten how incredible this room was; there were three wall-to-wall bookcases that ran ceiling to floor, loaded with books of every conceivable subject. The old man was an avid reader on almost everything from history to science to ancient cultures to true crime. Just about everything except fiction. When I was a kid, I spent hours in here reading most of his library, about as much time as I spent reading from Mama's library, which was mostly fiction. This is where my passion for the mysteries and reading came from. I think it's how I developed my so-called talents for deductive reasoning.

The old man sat behind his large mahogany desk, with Aldrich sitting in one of the leather high backs and Peter played bartender. I stood to the left of the desk looking past the books and large wooden globe and everything that was really window dressing in my opinion and stared into my father's gray eyes.

"As great as this has been," I said, "I need the truth now. You boys learn anything about Dana?"

The old man took off his wire rimmed bifocals, then rubbed his eyes finally resting his arms on the arms of his leather chair and began swinging back and forth a bit which was a habit he'd never been able to break when talking with people.

"Giovanni, it is admirable you are looking to help your friend, but I can honestly tell you we," pausing to wave his hands around in an all inclusive gesture "do not have anything to do with this girl's disappearance. I had our friends go through their records and Ms. Tillis has no dealings with our people."

I looked down at the hardwood floor in disappointment. It wasn't that I thought my father or any his men had anything to do with Dana's situation, but I'd hoped they'd know something I could tell Sebastian. "So Dana didn't need a loan shark, place a bet with a bookie, or was the target of a protection or extortion racket the Arm is involved in, is what you're telling me." The old man got up, came over to me and put his hands on my shoulder. "I wouldn't have put it quite like that, but yes you are correct. This does not mean we will stop asking, right Aldrich." I knew that last part more telling than asking.

After taking his scotch and soda from Peter, Aldrich took a sip and confirmed what the old man said. "That is right, Jonathan. Even though we were unable to learn anything new since I called you, we put the word out to our people and even feelers out to our associates in Canada. If anyone knows anything we should learn about it within a week." He took another sip. I noticed something odd; Aldrich wasn't looking me in the eye. Usually, when he talked to someone, he almost always looked them square in the eye, part of being a lawyer I guess, but now it was a different story. I didn't know if it was because he could be lying again or may have felt a little guilty lying to me the first time.

Peter handed the old man a glass of bourbon neat and tried to hand one to me, which I turned down, although part of me wanted to slam it down. "Come on, Gio, it's a special night."

I felt my eyes tighten up, focusing, looking at my little brother like a hawk eyeing a mouse, "I said no, and you know my name." I had to admit I was getting tired of retelling everyone my name. The tone in my voice told everyone I wasn't in a fucking around kind of mood. "Besides I've got to drive back to Buffalo. Rather do that clear headed."

The look in my brother's eyes told me he got the message loud and clear. "Alright man, I gottcha." Peter took the bourbon he poured for me, "Waste not want not."

"Okay, when you hear anything I'd appreciate a phone call."

"Of course we will, Giovanni." This was the only time I'd let the name issue slide as the old man placed his hand over my shoulder again. "Now I want to talk to you about working with Paul and Michael because they need some supervision and…" As soon as the words oozed out of his mouth, my stomach sank like a fucking anchor. I hoped he wouldn't ask, but I knew he'd try something like this. That's the thing about dealing with a mob boss; sure he'll be happy to do you a favor, but man you are going to pay for it sooner or later. I should have known better than hope for the best out of someone. If there's one thing I've learned about people in general they'll always let you down.

I peeled his hand off as I took a step away from him and I just stared at him. "That's not going to happen. You know I'll never walk that path." I got heated and lectured them all. "This maybe the life you've all chosen, fine but it isn't what I want. I'm working to make something of myself. You all want to be goons and mobsters that's fine with me," and I turned to leave and thought *Cambiano i suonatori ma la musica e sempre quella,* which means the melody's changed, but the song remains the same.

"Giovanni, wait!" the old man ordered. I didn't know if I stopped out of respect for my father or due to the possibility of giving him one last chance. "I know you have made your own choices and I would never force you to do something you would not want to do. I am asking you to help out your brothers because they lack your skills. I want them to learn from you and perhaps…pick up some of your better traits." I hated to admit it, but the old man made good sense, like he usually did, just one of the things that made him dangerous. Perhaps if my brothers did get some of my qualities it might not just help them save their lives someday.

"I'll think about it, that's all I can promise right now."

"I understand."

* * * *

We talked some more and by the time we finished up it was going on nine thirty and I had to get going so I said goodbye to everyone. I told them I'd be in touch and promised it wouldn't be in another three years. I think in part my folks wanted me to stay the night, in my old room upstairs, but that was from a different lifetime ago, and I was anxious to get home.

* * * *

On the ride home I thought about the similarities and differences between Sebastian's family and mine. Not the numbers, but the way things were. I thought of how Dana's life seemed to parallel mine in certain ways. Sebastian said she loved playing the aunt, but something kept her from being part of the family wholly, and I knew where she was coming from in a sense.

Halfway down the thruway, I thought of other parallels we shared and our beds were similar came to mind. A major difference being I knew she had frequent company in hers and mine might as well have had a monk using it. Then I thought about our box springs; my box spring support was hollowed, a bar frame with supports, but I used space under the box spring for extra storage and I began to wonder if Dana did the same. I doubled checked the time and it was still early enough, so instead of heading home I went back to Dana's.

Chapter Ten

It was almost ten o'clock when I reached Dana's and I parked in front of her building. On the drive from the estate I realized I needed a complete picture of who Dana truly was, what she was into and I finally comprehended not only didn't I have all the pieces of the puzzle, I wasn't even sure what the picture was suppose to look like.

Once upstairs I turned on the lights and the light hearted atmosphere I felt before with Sebastian was replaced by a more solemn, somber feeling I couldn't shake. Nothing had been touched since Sebastian and I were there and I wasn't certain if this was a good or bad thing. Secretly I think I hoped there'd be a sign Dana came back for something she may have forgotten. It was then I thought of the possibility of Dana being kidnapped. This was one option Sebastian and I never discussed. Now I had item number one hundred and one on my to-do list; talk to Sebastian and Detective Bishop about a possible kidnapping aspect.

I strolled around the living room taking another look around, and finally noticed Dana and I were more alike than I realized. On her pale yellow secretary desk, I saw a number of outgoing bills all ready to be paid. She had a movie stand toward the front left of the living room, next to the TV and a DVD player. Most of her movies were romantic comedies, a few dramas and some standup comics. Her CDs were limited to Sara Bareilles, Mariah Carey, Leona Lewis and Madonna. Not my particular brand of scotch.

In the bathroom, I found everything still in its place. In the medicine cabinet, there was toothpaste, mouthwash, deodorant, shaving cream and razor, and definite proof Dana had a social life, her supply of birth control pills. For me this was more proof she didn't plan on leaving town. Finally, I headed back to the bedroom and without Sebastian, I felt like an intruder, creepy and sleazy are the best ways to describe the sensation.

For some reason I picked up on another kind of emotion from Sebastian, almost as it was he didn't want to know the whole truth about Dana and her 'hobbies'. No brother would want to know about his sister's sexual relationships, I sure wouldn't want to know, it's bad enough I read about who Alidia is dating in the gossip columns. But since Sebastian and I started talking, it felt like he needed to know everything. Although it seemed as if there was a part of him that was holding back and couldn't face the truth. After a while, I couldn't tell where the brother ended and the father began.

In Dana's bedroom I turned on the light, and again I saw nothing had been touched since yesterday. This time my interest was in Dana's box spring or more to the point if anyone bothered to look under it. I didn't read anything about it in either of the reports and I doubted Sebastian checked.

I looked around her room but didn't touch anything because I was trying to figure out what was the last thing Dana's did here. *What she was doing, what she could have been thinking or planning. Was she happy, sad, upset, or scared?*

The bed was made up perfectly with a large pink and white comforter on top, and from the height, I could tell there were at least four pillows underneath. There was a white/gray curly teddy bear with button eyes and nose sitting on her nightstand. It looked old, as if Dana got it back when her father was still alive, and I began to wonder how much of the girl was still inside the woman. I looked around the bed as to figure out the best way to move the mattress without bringing the canopy down on my head and I quickly figured it out. I bent over to lift the mattress up, but something caught my eye before I could move anything.

There was something hidden in the shadow of the mattress itself, just alongside the edge of bed almost next to the box spring. It was small, silver—a wisp of a chain, the type a girl might wear as a charm bracelet or on a necklace. The only way anyone could see it was to almost be right over it at the proper angle which is where I was at. I snatched it up and on the chain was a tiny key, almost so small I couldn't think of any lock it could fit. The chain been snapped, as if ripped off someone. I felt my wheels begin to spin, when this happens I glance around like a hyperactive ferret on a triple espresso. It almost looks like I'm not focusing, but my mind is trying to figure things out. I knew I'd seen a lock this key might fit. *Where?* I asked myself. I glanced around the bedroom again and the answer was right in front of me, Dana's hope chest.

I could see how everyone could overlook the key, it was dumb luck, not skill at finding it. I slid the tiny silver key into the lock and at first it didn't go in and I thought *Oh Shit.* I tried it again with the key turned around and it slid in perfectly, *God I love being right.* After I pulled the white, lace cover off the top and lifted the lid my mind went blank. Inside looked like a combination of a Victoria Secret's and an Adam & Eve's store. Dana had something for every occasion, scented oils, special candles, and paddles. There were vibrators of different sizes and doubled headed models for multiple women. She also had anal beads, riding crops, sex slave kits, a sex sling, and lingerie with some expensive labels inside.

I needed to clear my head for a second and sat on the edge of the bed looking at a part of Dana's life, the part she kept hidden. I'd no idea how I was going to tell Sebastian about this, and I wasn't sure I wanted to. I looked at everything in the hope chest I wondered what the hell Dana could have been hoping for, then noticed a book in the corner on end. I pulled it out and saw it was a wire bound diary.

I rode the fence of whether or not I should read it and for the moment I tossed it aside, because behind the book there was a small bag of pills that were half dark green and half bright yellow. I'd no idea what they were or what they did, so I left them alone.

This was serious and suddenly I got very nervous. I felt like an intruder digging into the girl's privacy and it made me feel like scummy. Then I reminded myself her brother asked me.

I closed the hope chest, replaced the lace cover back in place and the key in my shirt pocket. I got to it, pulled the mattress off the box spring and slid it out of the way then I hoisted the box spring up. It was here I stopped dead when a whiff of decay hit me, sending me back a foot and forcing me to close my eyes in repulsion. A black body bag was stuffed under the bed like a winter outfit was put away in storage. I saw someone inside it, and I didn't need three guesses at who it was.

I held my breath out of reflex, as I held the support up I had to close my eyes again in total disgust. I knew no matter what I did this would haunt me as much as Fred's death. This was literally the last thing I expected and I was suddenly overrun with nausea, but fought the urge to vomit.

I eased the box spring down and took my cell out from my pocket, then reached for my wallet and pulled out Detective Bishop's numbers. I tried her cell and called it, but could only get her voice mail and left her a message of what I found. I figured she was busy so I called 911, and told them what I found.

I left Dana's room and tried to calm down in the living room as the fresh air cleared my head. My heart pounded so hard I thought I might have a stroke and I actually felt like I couldn't breathe. My adrenaline was pumping like crazy. Finally, I settled down and when I got hold of myself, I realized I'd have to be fingerprinted since I touched a number of items. I was okay with that then realized I'd better call Sebastian right away. This was something I really didn't want to do because as bad as everything had been this was just going plain suck. I considered letting the cops contact Sebastian, but that would be the chicken shit thing to do. I wasn't sure what to do, and suddenly felt like I needed fresh air.

I felt panic run away with me, but then forced myself to calm down. I began pacing back and forth like a wolf trapped in a cage at the zoo wanting to get away. I couldn't go anywhere and thought it best not to touch anything else, because if I screwed anything up I could ruin any evidence the police came across and that was literally the last thing I wanted. I knew something else at this point. This was no longer a missing person case, it was a homicide.

I made a blood vow to myself I'd help find the killer no matter what and old saying came to mind. *Chi di spada ferisce di spada perisce*, which means He who lives by the sword, dies by the sword.

Chapter Eleven

It took less than ten minutes for the police to show up with their lights and sirens waking up the neighborhood, but it felt like hours.

Before they arrived, I went downstairs to let the Nichols family know what was happening. I figured the police would talk to them again. Fortunately, Mr. Nicholas was still up watching TV and I told him what I found.

I went outside to wait by my car. As I sat there waiting I tried to organize my thoughts, but it didn't work. A cold wind had picked up and I could smell Lake Erie's icy waters all the way from across town. The chill of the night, the cold air howling and with a slight haze hung over the city, all conspired to make me feel hollow inside. Even though I didn't look inside the body bag somehow I knew it was Dana. I also felt this way because it wasn't just finding her. I felt like I let Sebastian down, and his family, even Dana herself. I had a bad feeling Dana may've died before Sebastian called me. The fresh air cleared my head of the decay I could pick up on, but I was still queasy.

Just then another thought occurred to me, I knew was there was a dead body upstairs, but it might not be Dana. She might be the killer herself, on the run, then changed my mind and followed my instinct and called Sebastian back. I knew it was my job to tell him what I found. "Sebastian its John."

"John, have you heard anything?"

The words got stuck in my throat like I had a turkey leg crammed down there. "Sebastian, I need you to meet me at Dana's now!"

"John what did you find out, just tell me!" he demanded. News like this was better in person than over the phone.

"Just get out here." I put my cell back into my shirt pocket then stared up at Dana's apartment in disbelief, trying to figure out how I was going to tell Sebastian. It was then I remembered what I forgot. "Oh fuck!" I yelled at myself when I remembered the diary.

I ran back upstairs, flew into the bedroom and paused a moment to look at the bed and thought of what this room now represented—knew it would mean to everyone. I was careful not to touch anything else. I reached in and grabbed the diary. I knew the police would want it and I should have left it alone, but I wanted to take a look at the book first. The answers could be in here and I needed time to go through the journal first. I'd let the chips fall with the police later on, if they came. I knew this would be a massive invasion of privacy and normally I'd never do this, but this whole situation wasn't normal.

I ran back downstairs and could hear the sirens drawing nearer I ran to my car, and tossed the diary inside as the first police car turned onto Great Arrow. By now the sirens were deafening and the cop inside shut it down. I headed over hoping she didn't see me hide the book.

As the officer got out of her patrol car I told her who I was and that I called them. She took my information and as I explained things, two more blue and whites showed up with their flashing lights giving everything a disco-like red and blue aura. "I've been in touch with a Detective Laila Bishop from Missing Persons." My heart still pounded from running around and I finally caught my breath. I was afraid the first officer might have seen me acting suspicious, but hoped they thought I was reacting to finding Dana.

"I'll need you to tell me everything you know, from the beginning, Mr. Seraph." The responding female officer took down my information as she sent the two male officers upstairs to Dana's bedroom to see for themselves. By this point Mr. and Mrs. Nicholas had come out but saw I was busy with the officer and waited on the cement patio at their front door. I could see them out of the corner of my eye, then saw some movement from the curtains and saw Susan looking, watching the action. Some of their neighbors were also looking out their widows, or some were braving the chill of the night and came out to see what was happening.

As I told my story, a few more cars pulled up and I watched as an eye-catching, fair-skinned African-American woman got out of her car with a guy who looked like he could have doubled as a pro wrestler.

"Officer, I'm Detective Bishop, this is my partner Detective Tyger," she said while they both showed their badges and hung them on their outer coats. She turned to me. "Are you John Seraph?"

"Yeah, nice to meet you, Detective," I said while I shook her hand, "I just wish it was under better circumstances."

"I know what you mean. So what can you tell us?" I told her everything that happened and reviewed everything one more time. While the huge Detective Tyger headed over to talk to the Nicholas.

Afterwards, the Medical Examiner showed up with the Crime Scene Unit van, which pulled up right behind him. By now the crowd of neighbors grew, which is why at least four more squad cars came rolling in for crowd control. Almost immediately news vans from all the local stations pulled into the street. Finally I saw Sebastian park across the street and run out of his car.

He tried to get past the yellow tapeline the police set up and when Sebastian tried to push his way past two beefy cops they held him back and told him couldn't come in. "Detective, that's Sebastian Tillis."

"Officers, let him through," Bishop ordered. She pulled Sebastian aside over to the Nicholas' driveway I saw the hell Sebastian was going through. In the flashing lights of all the vehicles, I could see his eyes welling up and the lump in his throat was clear. He already knew the news was bad when I called him. While Detective Bishop spoke to Sebastian, her partner finally came over with one of the officers. Detective Tyger just slowly nodded with a grim look scrawled across his face after verifying my story.

As Bishop told Sebastian the news, I couldn't look at the man, but forced myself to and all I could say was how sorry I was. "Sebastian I…I'm so sorry man."

"Jesus, John, what the hell happened?"

"I don't know." It was very surreal and nobody knew what to say. I felt like I drank too much, as if I was working with a fog hanging throughout my head. "But we'll find out Sebastian, I promise you that."

"Actually, Mr. Seraph, we'll find out what happened to Miss Tillis." Bishop stressed, telling me in her own way this was police business and I wasn't invited to the party. If I have one major hang up with people it's this, I hate being told what to do. Twelve years of Catholic school makes you obedient or obstinate, want to guess which I am.

* * * *

The M.E. was upstairs doing their preliminary investigation and I don't know how much time passed from when Bishop and Tyger told Sebastian about Dana to when the M.E. and his people brought down her body in the oversized body bag on a gurney. As soon as they came out of the front door, Sebastian yelled out for them to stop and broke away from us. He ran over to the gurney and tried to grab at the bag. I ran as fast as I could with the Detectives a step behind me. I grabbed Sebastian's arms to keep him from opening the bag. This was something he didn't need to see. Besides I figured the bag had to be evidence as well.

"Mr. Tillis you don't want to see your sister this way!" Tyger yelled out as he pulled back on Sebastian's left arm, while I grabbed his right.

"Sebastian, he's right." I said not sure what the hell I was saying. Finally, Sebastian eased up and he fully realized his sister was dead. The truth hit him hard and he started crying.

It's funny living in the world we're in. Men are always expected to wear some sort of 'armor' to hide our feelings. As if we're expected to constantly keep our feelings bottled up and have a 'John Wayne attitude' all the time, where nothing can get to us and we're invulnerable. That isn't the case. Men like the old man and those of his generation give this impression that nothing gets to them, for a time I had it too. Fortunately, my mother was able to balance things out for me, and I came to learn that real men let their feelings out when the time is right.

For Sebastian the time was now, not only had he lost a sister, but in a sense, he lost a daughter and I felt for my friend because I couldn't take his pain away. Nothing I did would ever make things whole again. All I could do was help any way I could.

Sebastian almost collapsed in my arms as he continued to cry and I helped him over to my car. He was in no shape to drive so I took him home.

As we walked to my car, the press rammed their cameras and microphones in our faces, asking their questions all at once. Fortunately, the police blocked the vultures from us, but one cameraman got to close invading our space, and I pushed the camera back, hard. The cameraman was lucky I didn't give him a right hook. The mood I was in, it wouldn't have taken much to push me over the edge and duke him.

Bishop and Tyger followed us and said they still had a number of questions, but knew this wasn't the time. They knew Sebastian wasn't in any shape to think clearly and I was glad I didn't have to argue the point with them. They knew how to reach us and Bishop told me they'd be in touch sometime tomorrow or Tuesday. I also got the feeling they were cutting Sebastian slack because of his position at City Hall.

I poured Sebastian into my passenger seat, as Bishop asked me "What made you stop here tonight?"

"Don't know, Detective. Sometimes I'll get some sort of bright idea, and thought I'd check on it. When Sebastian and I were here yesterday something about Dana's bed kept bugging me. I use my frame for extra storage and thought Dana might have done the same. What I'm wondering is why nobody thought to look under there before."

"Because at the time Ms. Tillis was a missing person and nothing was out of place. There weren't any signs of a struggle or robbery, so it isn't something we would consider at the time."

"Right," was the only thing I could think to say, besides Sebastian needed me more than the detectives did.

* * * *

After I dropped Sebastian home, I made sure he got inside okay and that's when I saw Nicole at the door. She looked about to be eight and half months along, but was frazzled like the rest of us. I hoped she could handle the stress alright. Sebastian made the long walk from my car to his front door okay but what made the twenty-four feet such a stretch was that Sebastian walked it extremely slowly, as if the man was in his nineties. I told him I'd call tomorrow and I wasn't finished. I don't know if he heard me or even cared at this point.

* * * *

When I got home, it was almost one-thirty and all I wanted was my bed. The strain I felt was awful, my eyes felt as if they were being pulled from their sockets. I parked in my usual spot, grabbed the diary and headed inside. No messages were on my machine, so I turned out the lights and locked up. I needed a shower before I turned in. The hot water felt good, but it didn't help me shake the cobwebs that were clogging my mind. Too many questions flashed through my mind like the paparazzi's camera. My curiosity fought for control with the anger I felt. I knew people died every day in accidents, from diseases, suicides, acts of terrorism, medical conditions, even Acts-of-God if you believe in that sort of thing. The one thing that always pissed me off was murder. At what point does someone think taking another's life is a solution to a problem? The only thing I could think of was whoever was guilty had one fucked up mind.

I finished up, brushed my teeth and got ready to turn in, but before I did, I picked up the diary and skimmed through it. My eyes were opened to a world I barely knew existed, and part of me wished I didn't know anything about it.

Dana was a girl who'd had serious problems, and these troubles could've led to her death. I read of encounters with men and women, strangers in private clubs, and in her apartment. Turns out she'd been seeing a doctor for help in dealing with this problem, because her doctor described Dana as having a sexual addiction. I then thought the doctor may be a lead I could tap into.

Chapter Twelve
~ Monday ~

I woke up later than normal, just before eleven. I don't remember when I fell asleep, but I know it was after three thirty. Even though I was tired, I became obsessed with reading Dana's diary, but only got a third of the way through.

I was late for school, but I knew I wasn't going in. I was too tired to really stir myself to get up and to be honest I really didn't care that much because of what was happening. I was too wrapped up in everything going down and knew I wouldn't be able to let this go. When something bothers me, I've a tendency to become like a dog gnawing on a bone.

I called the library and told them I wasn't going to be able to come in for the next few days because I was sick. It was the truth, sort of. I needed time to figure things out and as important as school was, helping the Tillis family became a higher priority.

I threw on my blue dress shirt, a better pair of my jeans and my suede cowboy boots. While I toasted a bagel and poured myself some OJ, I checked my machine and found two messages. One from Sebastian telling me everyone was all right and he was grateful for my help. It sounded as if the spirit was whipped out of him. Sebastian went on, "Dana's autopsy is scheduled for tomorrow morning. Once I hear anything, I'll call you with what the M.E. finds out. You can give me a call later tonight. Thanks." He sounded half-dead and I figured his family was the only thing keeping him going.

The second call was from Detective Bishop. "Mr. Seraph, I need you to call me A.S.A.P. Detectives from homicide are taking over the case and want to meet with you. My rotation on the stake out detail is over and you can reach me on my cell." This gave me some time to plan my next move.

It was almost noon when my raisin-cinnamon bagel was done to a crisp, golden perfection and I lathered on a healthy amount of butter and let it melt in. Frankly, I could never understand why folks opted for cold cream cheese when real butter melted beautifully into a perfect toasted bagel.

I turned on the TV and waited for the news. I wanted to see if there were any reports on Dana's case yet. While I waited I flipped open the diary again and picked up where I left off, still in a state of disbelief over what I was reading.

Dana started her diary more than a year and a half ago when she started seeing psychotherapist, Dr. Jennifer Irons, who specializes in the treatment of sexual addictions. Irons recommended Dana should keep a diary as part of her therapy, to monitor her progress and Dana was serious enough to follow doctor's orders. Which included but wasn't limited to keeping the diary to record her feelings, thoughts and the days' events, and entering Sex-Addicts-Anonymous, which is a twelve step program and a form of group therapy. Dana started seeing Irons because she was trying to fight her addiction that led to her risky behavior. This told me Dana wanted to change and fought her demons daily. Some days she won. Others she lost.

As I read each page, I became more depressed and felt sorry for Dana. We all have things we keep from loved ones, but I can't imagine how she would've even begun to tell Sebastian about her obsession. Dana wrote Dr. Irons was a having a difficult time treating her, because Dana had been a self-admitted addict for at least four years. She was also bisexual and had numerous affairs with men, women and couples. Finally, at some point, almost two years ago, she realized her addiction was dominating her life. Dana wrote she knew she wouldn't have much more of a life if she didn't do something about her problem, which is when she started seeing Dr. Irons. She also admitted she had problems with attending her meetings because she had seen a couple members of her group outside of the sessions and slept with them, which is a major no-no. It was clear Dana was fighting a losing battle and may have come across the wrong people.

On top of everything else, Dana began seeing people from work, but she didn't write down their names. She used initials or nicknames, but the icing on the cake I learned was someone recently gotten Dana onto poppers, a.k.a. amyl nitrite, which increases a person's sexual desire and arousal. I figured the pills I found were her poppers. Later on, Dana was into ecstasy, mixed with ketamine, which is known as kitty flipping, and ecstasy mixed with phencyclidine a.k.a. elephant flipping, but her favorite drug of choice was the straight up poppers.

The lead story on the news was some legal fallout from a former Erie County Executive's term where county workers were working on a county employee's home and yard. Dana's story was next, but there wasn't anything new since last night, although Channel Seven's cameras did catch a few glimpses of Sebastian with me in the background, some of the cops I talked to, and Bishop was interviewed briefly after Sebastian and I left.

All Bishop said was that the body of Dana Tillis, who had been missing two weeks had been found, and right now the investigation was beginning. The reporters mentioned Sebastian was there but unavailable for comment. There were also a few shots of me shoving a camera away giving my best 'Stone Cold' look, as the anchorwoman mentioned that John Seraph was seen at the victim's apartment. I swear I heard the old man hit the ceiling from my place.

There was no mention of Dana being murdered and I know it was early for me to assume this. I knew one thing, there was no way she could've sealed herself up and stuffed herself under the bed. Even if Dana died in some sort of accident, someone packed her away like Christmas decorations and went on with their day as if nothing happened. The idea somebody could just disregard a human life like this made me sick.

The report wasn't even thirty seconds and that pissed me off too. When Dana first vanished there was massive coverage on her case and search for her, but now she was reduced to the latest homicide in the Queen City.

After the story ended I turned off the T.V., finished eating, then called Bishop back and she told she needed me to come in and give my official statement to the homicide detectives. "That's no problem. When do you want me in?"

"The sooner the better."

"Okay, how in about an hour?"

"That'll be fine, Mr. Seraph."

"Listen, Detective, since we've gone this far you might as well call me John."

"Alright, John," she said, but there was a slight hesitation and I thought it may have been from her thinking that wasn't professional. "We'll go over your statement with Sergeant Yagel and Detective Wolfe from homicide."

"That'll be fine. I should be there before one-thirty."

I thought about what else Bishop and the police would want to talk about and I was really hoping nobody figured out I took the diary. If that happened, I was going be in some real trouble. I may have felt a little paranoid, but I figured better safe than sorry, and hid the diary in my linen closet under a pile of bath towels and washcloths. It might've been silly, but I didn't want to take any chances. I grabbed my notes, the info Sebastian gave me and the articles I downloaded and put them into a folder then locked up.

In the hall, I could hear my neighbor's television and knew at least Mrs. Duffy was home. According to their daughter, Marcia, the poor lady was almost bedridden and Mr. Duffy did most of the household work, which was another reason I helped them out. I wanted to look in on them, but parking in downtown could be a bitch so I wanted to get down there A.S.A.P. so I'd check in on the Duffys later.

When I left it was partly sunny, but by the time I got downtown, it was clouding up again. What took a while was trying to find a decent parking spot near the police station. I circled Franklin a couple times and realized this was going to be a problem. I had to go around onto Church, past a closed down nightclub, and a few small offices, and come back onto Pearl Street, headed for Franklin. There was still no parking because all the spots were reserved for the police on the left side of the street and on the right, there was no parking, period. Back at Church I made a left and was able to pull into the parking lot next to the police station. I was allowed to stay there since I was there on official business.

I headed inside and noticed it felt cooler than before and was suddenly overrun with the smell of chocolate chip cookies. That only meant one thing, the General Mills grain mill was making Coco Puffs right now and I had a sudden craving for chocolate-chip cookies and a cold glass of milk.

Before heading into the main entrance, I stared across the street at another prime example of Buffalo's history, the Old County Courthouse and felt sentimental. The courthouse was built in 1872 and was designed in a Victorian Romanesque style, standing tall and proud with its clock tower in the front and four sentries standing post surrounding the clock faces. The four story, gray building made some feel as if it were outdated and stood in the way of the modern age, as did a number of other buildings in downtown Buffalo like City Hall, the Ellicott Square Building, the Old Post Office which was now Erie Community College's downtown campus. Every time I see the Old Courthouse, I think of my family. My Great-grandfather Giuseppe, who had a hand in doing repair work to the clock tower, and my Grandfather Marcus, 'the Hammer' Angelo, was arraigned and tried there. His nickname's 'The Hammer' and believe me he didn't earn it in shop class.

In the old days, Grandfather made it a point to beat some folks to death with his sledgehammer-like fists. I got my oversized hands from him. He always said, "If I'm going to make a goddamned point, I want it to stick, so I beat it into their heads." He made his point by beating in the heads of at least four mobsters, and two eye witnesses. Sometimes I'm amazed I'm not a basket case with my ancestry.

* * * *

I left my sunglasses on as I stepped inside for a pair of reasons; first, I didn't want too many people recognizing me. It's not that I was afraid of being confused as a police informant, but there are folks on both sides of the law who wouldn't be happy to see me there. Secondly, I hate fluorescent lights that are in a lot of buildings like the police stations use. They bother my eyes, kind of, like when some idiot uses his high beams when they're not needed.

Inside, I headed upstairs from the lobby doors, and bounced up the eight steps and found the Sergeant's desk a hornet's nest. A pair of officers restrained a loud drunk who I think was Mexican or Latino. The guy yelled like a maniac about cutting his ex-wife's tits off when he got out, which was the only thing I could understand. He smelled like a backed up septic tank combined with a bar after last call. I was glad I didn't have to deal with shit like this because I knew I didn't have the patience to deal with guys who hit their wives, girlfriends or children. I've zero tolerance for assholes that think hurting others is a recreational activity and I knew if I had been a police officer a guy like this would have an 'accident'.

A third uniformed officer helped pull the drunk to the back of the building, and everyone watched as he kept up his temper tantrum. He spewed out every swear word in the book, using combinations I never thought of before, but most I didn't recognize because he was yelling in Spanish. The arresting officer told him to calm down or he'd be maced.

To be honest I was hoping they zap the jerk and I could see it.

The desk that was about a foot higher than me, there was a man who was white and a black woman dressed very well in business suits, carrying briefcases and asking where they could find someone. They passed their business cards on to the desk sergeant and identified themselves as lawyers from Mattar & D'Agostino looking for a client of their firm. The officer told them where they could find him and the Detectives who brought him in.

As they started to head down the same hallway the husband-of-the-year was forced down, the lady lawyer turned and smiled at me asking if I needed representation. "No thanks, my firm's Dewey, Cheatum and Howe." It was her puzzled look that told me she didn't get the joke. I just rolled my eyes.

When it was my turn, I told the Sergeant who I was, showed him my I.D. and that I had an appointment with Detectives Bishop, Tyger, Wolfe and Sergeant Yagel. The older officer called up to the detective's squad room and a moment later told me to head on up to the third floor, then handed me a visitor's badge which I clipped to my shirt pocket. Before I headed up he asked me one question, "Hey kid, you really John Seraph?"

"Yes sir, I am. Why's that?"

A smile widened across his round face. "Oh, just curious." and he started laughing as he turned away from me to get back to his business.

Chapter Thirteen

I caught the small elevator, which made the ones at City Hall look and feel roomy. I figured four people was the maximum load, and I held my breath as I headed up to three. I'm claustrophobic and can usually keep it under control most of the time, but I'm not crazy about small areas or being crowded. If I'm with a girl curled up on the couch that's one thing, but if I'm shoved into a packed room I can quickly turn into a really pissed off caged animal. It's nothing you want to see, believe me.

Once I stepped out, I saw a large bulletin board mounted in front of the elevators. To the right were a few closed offices, public restrooms, a couple vending machines and a small bench next to a pair of trashcans, one for garbage, one for recycling pop bottles and cans. Slate gray was the wall color and the floors were black, white and tan tiles like in an elementary school. To my left was a private office, belonging to a Captain Stroud of the homicide unit, but the lights were out and no one was at home. Across from the office was a desk with the Police Administrative Aide, a.k.a. the PAA. She was a young woman in her early thirties, definitely Hispanic and attractive.

I admit this is a problem I have; I get too easily attracted to members of the opposite sex. This glitch of mine has gotten me into trouble more than once, but only one time I fell in love with the wrong woman because of this and I won't ever let that happen again.

I told the aide I was there to see the Detectives and she called them on her phone. From around a corner Bishop came around looking very professional. We shook hands. "Thanks for coming in, Mr. Seraph."

"Like I told Sebastian I want to help and I'll do what I can. Where do we start?"

Bishop led me to a small interview room, which was slate gray walls and the abstract pattern of tiles continued on the floor.

The officers sat around a rectangular table talking, with four chairs surrounding the table. To the left was a large mirror, on the wall, which I suspected was a two-way mirror, which had become a cliché on television. I also noticed high in one of the corners above the mirror was a video camera. Bishop introduced me to Detective Wolfe, a very attractive white woman sporting a short black ponytail and thought, *Christ just what I need.* When I saw her engagement ring I became grateful. If I know a woman is dating or married I won't try anything and make a jackass out of myself. Call me crazy, but I do have a sense of honor in such things.

Sergeant Yagel, an African American, was an older officer who I figured had to be in his late forties or fifties, a big fella almost six foot four with graying hair and a short beard, and I noticed he had a hell of a grip when we shook hands.

The atmosphere was somewhat relaxed but I wouldn't say everyone was in a good mood, but since I was cooperating with the police, I was being treated with the same amount of respect I showed them. I knew the police weren't used to having someone with my family's last name help them, but then again I didn't have that last name anymore.

There was a tape recorder on the desk and I was fine with going on the record since I hadn't done anything wrong, well for the most part. There were notebooks and file folders; on the top one, I was able to read Dana's name upside-down and let out a sigh as I sat down.

Yagel and Wolfe were the ones in charge now since the case was now a homicide, but being that it began as a missing persons' case they were keeping Bishop and Tyger informed.

Yagel began the interview. "So how did you get involved, Mr. Seraph?"

I was surprised by his voice because it reminded me of James Earl Jones. "Sebastian reached out to me because he thought my family's connections could help find Dana or what might have happened to her."

Detective Wolfe took her turn. "Where did you get the idea about looking under the bed?"

"The idea came to me when I was headed home from my parents'. I've a similar bed frame and use it for extra storage. Since I still had keys to Dana's place, I thought I'd check things out."

This was something Yagel and Wolfe didn't seem sure about from the looks I was reading. Yagel said, "Seems like a big coincidence you should look there."

"Maybe Sergeant, but coincidences do happen." I then told them how I reached out the old man and how he and Aldrich put feelers out through the Arm's network. "I'm going to check back with them in a few days, if I don't hear from them first. Once I hear anything I'll call you right away."After about forty-five minutes, we wrapped things up.

Two things happened that struck me funny. First, Yagel and Wolfe were appreciative of my help and seemed a little surprised I accommodated them, but asked if I wouldn't mind talking to the Organized Crime Intelligence Division. They cracked a smile to let me know it was a joke. The cold stare I gave told him I didn't think it was funny.

The second thing was as Bishop walked me out she thanked me again and told me she finally got off that stake out detail since the regular officers were back on nights, and if I learned anything or needed some help I was to give Wolfe, Yagel or her a call.

"One other thing,," she said as we stopped at the front desk, "I know you're holding back something, Mr. Seraph." She looked me square in the eye.

Oh shit!

"You seem to have some pretty good instincts, but I know when someone's hiding something." Scared for a second that she somehow knew the truth I figured I'd tell her about Dr. Irons.

"I found out Dana had a sex addiction and she was seeing a Dr. Irons for help."

"How did you find out about this?"

Now I believe in being honest with the police, but I can spread the bullshit better than a politician. "Sebastian mentioned Dana had some problems and I found Dr. Irons listed in Dana's address book. Turns out she's a specialist," I said, trying to sound as cool as possible. Technically, I found Irons listed in Dana's address book, so I was telling the truth.

"Uh-huh," was her only response, and not sure what else to do I kept up the ploy.

I learned awhile ago when using a good cover story or lie, keep it simple and stick with it to show how committed you are when trying to convince anyone who's questioning you. I also forced myself to look Bishop in the eye which I think helped me convince her. "I looked Irons up in the phone book and found out she specializes in these types of addictions and that's all, except I was thinking of contacting her."

"That's not a good idea."

"Why?"

"We're grateful for your assistance, but we don't recommend citizens involving themselves in active police investigations."

Trying to sound innocent I just added, "Well not a problem, Detective, but if I hear anything else I'll call you immediately."

"Right." Although she seemed fine, there was something in her tone that told me she knew I was bullshitting. Bishop told me after my interview, they got a call from Sebastian who not only wanted them to stay active in the investigation since he felt comfortable with them, and was using his position in the Mayor's office to get what he wanted, but Bishop was able to talk Sebastian down.

* * * *

When I got to my car I felt relieved because I was afraid I'd run into Berriah, so not seeing him became the highlight of the week so far.

I had to figure out what my next move was. Even though Bishop gave me a warning, I had to plan this out as if I were playing chess. The problem was I have no head for strategy, unlike the old man who's a real chess player. Sometimes I swear he can see around corners. I'm definitely more guts than brains at times.

Even though I listened to what Bishop said, I felt compelled to keep going. The police were limited in resources and manpower since they had so many cases to look into, but I didn't have these problems. I knew the news already broke and word would spread eventually, so I wasn't worried about leaking out some info but knew I'd have to be careful at what I said.

I decided to drive to Addar's campaign office and see what I could find out. According to her diary, Dana admitted she'd been involved with someone at work and this maybe someone I should talk to, if I could find him.

Chapter Fourteen

I pulled out of the parking lot and drove past the station as I made a left on to Franklin, and made good time going past the Convention Center. Soon, I pulled into a parking lot near the law offices of Ables and Juda, all while trying to avoid a number of downtown drivers, commuters and bikers who don't believe traffic laws applied to them.

I swung into the little lot faster than I should have and almost nailed a Cadillac. I paid the attendant for a couple hours since I didn't know how long I'd be. My nearly empty wallet only reminded me of my equally low checking account and I reconsidered about calling in sick to work, or taking Sebastian's money.

I was surprised to find a spot because by mid-afternoon most parking places were long gone. The campaign office was across the street, kiddy-corner between the Convention Center and the lot and was next door to a bar. *What a great combo.* I mean what could go wrong and, for some reason, Nixon and Watergate came to mind.

I waited for traffic to pass then ran into the shadow of the three story building as a bus was roaring its' way towards me. Once I was across the street, I took off my sunglasses and leapt up on the curb to take a good look around.

In the center of the main window was a huge poster with a picture of Kingsley Adder and the printing was in red, white, and blue, showing the man to be strong and confident. Lining the perimeter of the window were white banners with red and blue stars and stripes. Looking at the man's picture I thought one word described him, polished. He reminded me of a young Sean Connery or Cary Grant, but with his thin moustache and black hair, Addar resembled a Howard Hughes clone to me. It was easy to see why the press had nicknamed him 'the White Knight'.

As I walked inside, I saw a lot of activity going on all over the place. At the front door was a secretary's station with a light-skinned African-American girl with short curly hair. She was bubbly and smiling, but when she greeted me, she sounded totally rehearsed. "Welcome to the Addar Foundation., Are you here to lend your support to the Senator?"

Taken a little by surprise at the amount of flurry around me I paused for a sec, "Ah…no actually I'm wondering if I can talk to someone in charge about one of your employees?"

She looked puzzled and asked if there was a problem so I leaned in close so only she could hear me. "This is a delicate matter, regarding Dana Tillis." Her face went blank then it became pale when she realized the seriousness of the matter. I played a hunch and asked her if she heard what happened and she just nodded. "Maybe its best I speak to your office manager," and she just nodded again slightly.

"Just one moment please."

"Thank you." I looked around as she called someone on the phone.

"The office manager will be with you in a minute."

I thanked her and tried to make the mood easier by politely smiling, but she looked uneasy, which was about how my stomach felt.

While I waited I read a flyer about the Addar Foundation and what they had done to help drug addicts in New York State and their plans for the future, but I couldn't concentrate and kept on repeating a verse from *Charge of the Light Brigade* to myself over and over to boost up my nerve. Tennyson's words didn't help.

Finally, a guy that looked like a rolling tool chest and had to be six foot seven at least, with short brown hair and slim glasses came over and smiled broadly. Then he stuck out a massive hand that was bigger than mine, which surprised me. "Hiya there, name's Sean Bruden. You needed to talk about Dana Tillis?"

We shook hands and I explained myself. "I was asked by the Tillis family to look into Dana's disappearance and even though we found her body the investigation's not done."

Bruden suggested we talk in private and I followed him to a small conference room. I figured he was at least four inches taller than me and outweighed me by a hundred and fifty pounds. As he led me in, I glanced around and could see about forty people in what was a call center in the office. From the snippets I could hear, it sounded like the callers were asking voters if they knew about Addar, what he stood for, the Addar Foundation, what they wanted from the next President and other political questions.

After we sat down at an eight-person table Bruden took off his glasses, wiped them clean and reexamined them as he offered me a drink. "No thanks, Mr. Bruden. I'm assuming you heard Dana was found last night."

"Yeah, I saw the news this morning and I was sorry to hear Dana died. We all liked her around here."

"I'm wondering if Dana had any friends or was close to anyone." I already knew the answer but I wanted to see what Bruden would say.

"Uh, well, I know she and one of the girls, Crystal Bell were pretty tight. I think Angie Eden went with her clubbing a few times. Other than that I'm not sure."

"What about boyfriends or any office romances?"

He just shook his head. "Nah, nothing I ever heard of, but you can't tell what happens after hours. I mean it's not like we've got any rules against employees dating."

"You think I could talk to those girls you mentioned?"

"I don't see a problem, but do you mind waiting for their break? I'll ask them in a few minutes."

"No, that's fine. I got to ask, can you think of anyone that had a problem with Dana or would want to see her dead?"

He just shook his head again. "Nope, can't think of anyone here who'd want to hurt her, but like I said you can't tell what happens after hours around here. I guess anything's possible. Mind if I ask you something?"

"Go ahead."

"If Dana's dead how come you're still looking into things?"

"Because someone's responsible, her brother asked me to find Dana and he was looking for some peace. The Tillis family's going through hell and I'm going make sure they get the peace of mind they deserve."

Bruden left me alone in the conference room while he went to get the girls once they were off the phones. While I waited, I skimmed a booklet about Addar and what he had done during his political career and what he wanted to accomplish in the future. As I read more on the guy I wasn't sure what to make of him, I mean he's a Democrat and I'm a Green Party member. In the big picture, I know the Democrats are little better the Republicans, but to be honest choosing between the two groups is like choosing between airline and hospital food. They'll both keep you alive, but don't expect a gourmet meal.

* * * *

A couple minutes after he left, Bruden lead the two girls, one a blonde with a bob cut hairstyle, and wearing a small nose piercing in her left nostril, and the other was the cute brunette with the glasses I saw in the strip of pictures from Dana's bedroom. *Holy Mother!*

"Mr. Seraph, this is Angie Eden." The blonde waved hi, "and Crystal Bell," who extended her hand which I shook, but Crystal seemed to be shell-shocked.

I knew Crystal and Dana had been good friends, but didn't know how close they were and I didn't read anything in the diary about Crystal. Also, I couldn't help but notice how alluring she really was in person and I felt those old feelings kicking in. I thought *Oh boy, here we go again.* I knew I had to get my attraction for the girls under control, but I didn't see that day coming anytime soon.

I explained the situation, repeating the story I gave Bruden, and they'd also heard the news. The girls agreed to answer my questions, which were pretty much the same ones I asked Bruden.

Eden told me in a casual manner, "Well, I heard Dana was seeing a couple folks, but I didn't know who they were."

Crystal shook her head looking mournful she said, "I didn't hear anything like that, and we were really close. I just can't believe she's gone." Before, her eyes were just welling up, but now that the words were out she fell apart and began crying.

I didn't know what to say to her and did the only thing I could think of, I passed her my handkerchief. Fortunately, I hadn't used it yet and it still smelled like the fresh garden scent detergent. "Here you go Miss Bell, its clean."

She took it without saying anything, while Bruden tried to console her by placing his hand on her shoulder. At the same time I noticed Eden placed her elbow on the table and was resting her head on her hand, she almost looked bored. I didn't like her attitude, but tried not to let it influence my thinking. I knew I had to be professional like Detective Bishop would, and couldn't let my feeling sway me about anyone or anything.

"Are you going to be okay, Miss Bell?"

Finally, she got herself under control. "Yes, thank you, Mr. Seraph."

"No problem and call me John." I tried to give her a reassuring smile, but I doubt it did any good. I wasn't sure what else to do because I seemed to have run out of questions and had a feeling I was waist deep and sinking fast.

Eden spoke up in a tone that made her sound like a kid who was annoyed at not being the center of attention. "I know Dana had been seeing some guys from a couple of the clubs we hit."

"Which ones?"

"We were regulars at Club Marcella, 67 West, the Crocodile Bar and the Soho Bar." A cold shot blasted through my guts like a shotgun round because my brothers, Mike and Paul, were private investors of the Soho Bar.

The bars on Chippewa Avenue, which is a main strip in downtown, was a major center for prostitution during the seventies and eighties, but in the late eighties and the early nineties the area had been cleaned up and legitimate businesses came in. Nowadays there were at least twenty bars along the drag that ran the gambit from the after work crowd for bankers, businessmen and lawyers like T.G.I. Fridays, to the bars Eden mentioned that were mainly for the college crowds. Most of them were loud, crowded, brightly lit-up, and overpriced for my tastes. The bar was legitimate but the Arm conducted business there from time to time. With my brothers being silent partners, it was the equivalent of having a pit bull with rabies guard your house. Trouble would stay away, but sooner or later your protection would bite you in the ass big time.

"Do you think she could have picked up the wrong guy and something went bad?" Eden asked.

I thought about that for a sec and answered. "Well, I guess anything's possible," then I stirred up the storm by adding, "the killer could even be working in this office." All three of them had unusual reactions, and I got the feeling no one considered the possibility before. The mood shifted to something cold and menacing.

I gave my phone numbers to Bruden and the girls and told them if they thought of anything else I'd be grateful if they called, and I saw something funny in the way Eden was smiling at me. It made me think of the way a cat eyes a bird. I'd a feeling she was holding back, but didn't have any idea what. As Crystal and Bruden went back to work, Eden came up close to me and made sure she wasn't heard by anyone else.

"You know I knew Dana pretty well, and I'm sure I can find out more about her dating habits than Crystal can." Then she placed her hand on my thigh inching it closer towards my crotch. "I bet you can be really appreciative."

I peeled her hand off and held it tight, while looking her square in the eye. I gave her my most serious 'Don't Fuck With Me' look. "You're right I can be very grateful, but till I find who's responsible I don't feel grateful."

It was the way she rapidly blinked her blue eyes that told me she got the message loud and clear and backed off. "If…if I hear anything I'll call ya."

I just nodded thanks without taking my eyes off her. It was here she realized I wasn't flirting or playing games. I wasn't just asking questions or butting into things that weren't my business. It was at that moment I realized something, I was now a predator and those responsible were my prey.

Chapter Fifteen

I thanked Bruden on my way out and asked him, "Is there anyone else you can think of who might be helpful?"

The big man just shook his head and scratched his short brown hair looking clueless. "I don't know, I mean Dana was friendly with a lot of folks here, but Crystal and Angie are the only ones I know of who she hung out with."

"You think I could ask around, see if I can find someone who might know something else?"

"Well half the staff's polling voters and the rest are sending out mailers, pretty much everyone's pretty busy."

"I understand. I don't want to get in the way, but I'm surprised the police haven't stopped by yet."

"The cops?"

I guess he never considered the police would bring their investigation to the office.

"Yeah that's right, I'm sure they'll be back here sooner or later and want to talk to your whole staff. This is now a homicide investigation so the police may even shut down the office for a few days and interview everyone here." A look of panic over ran Bruden's face at the thought of having to close up shop and explain things to the Senator of what happened and why and I figured this was a good time to play an ace I had. "Actually I might be able to do you a favor, so they won't bother you guys. I'm on pretty good terms with the lead detectives and if I talk to some of the folks here, I can pass on any info I get and they may be less likely to shut things down."

Bruden quickly pieced things together, and the expression on his face changed from a panic attack to seeing how helpful this would be. I learned if you want something from someone it helps to offer something else in return. In dealing with most folks it just comes down to the old phrase; Quid pro quo.

"Do you mind waiting a day or so? We got a lot of calls to make for the polls. Senator Addar wants to know if voters want to see him in the White House someday, and there's talk he may start his official campaign next year."

"Yeah, that's no problem. When should I come back?"

"Let me check the schedule. Give me sec." Bruden went behind the secretary's desk and picked up a clipboard. He ran his fingers over the pages, flipped them back and forth and finally found a date for me. "How's about Thursday, round four thirty? Seems we got a light day for phone calls, but most of the staff will be working on mailers."

"Sounds doable. Just out of curiosity, besides the phone calls, what else goes on here?"

"Thanks, Tiff," he said handing back the weekly schedules. "Well, down-stairs are the phone banks, where our callers do the polling. We got about forty callers at any given time calling not only in New York, but all throughout the northeast."

"All the states into which the Addar Foundation's expanding."

"Right. Upstairs we got folks who send out mailers, reminders, handle campaign contributions and deal with posters, bumper stickers and all that stuff."

"Sounds like the senator's getting ready to make his move on the White House now."

"From what I heard he's not quite there yet, but you're not far off."

Now my interest was piqued. "Really, what's the word?"

"Guess I'm not leaking anything really confidential, but according to Chalmer Bernard, the senator's campaign manager, the senator's planning on announcing his official candidacy in the next couple months. You got to keep this on the q.t. Okay?"

"Yeah, no problem. What do think his chances are?"

The big man just smiled broadly and shook his head. "Don't know. I mean anything can happen and he might not even make the primaries. The thing is he's done a lot of good work in the past, so he might make a good President."

* * * *

As soon as I stepped outside, I slipped on my sunglasses, my eyes readjusting to the light. A black stretch limo came rolling in cutting me off before I could cross the street. I felt a panic attack starting because I thought it was the old man's limo. On top of the fleet of cars, he also has a limousine he uses exclusively for the Arm's business, because it's a rolling armory. Family business, because it's a rolling armory.

When I saw the license plate wasn't the old man's I starting breathing again. The car stopped a half a car length in front of me, and a second later an intense looking black man wearing mirrored sunglasses, a black suit and an extremely short haircut came out of the front passenger seat, looked around, stared at me then went over and opened up the rear door. He leaned in and said something, then pulled the door wide open. Out came the White Knight himself, Senator Kingsley Addar, his wife Desiree, and they were followed by campaign manager Chalmer Bernard.

The couple was dressed about as well as my family usually does, with the senator in a gray suit and black tie and Mrs. Addar was in a violet dress. As polished as Addar was, I could see his wife surpassed him in this arena with shoulder length black hair done up with a French twist. I admit she's an attractive woman, very stylish and she reminded me of Jackie Kennedy, who was one lady I admired greatly.

When they got out of the limo the intense black fellow came over to me, joined by an equally extremely intimidating looking man who may have been Asian. The second bodyguard was yellow skinned, wore his black hair short and spiky. If one word could describe this man it'd be thick. His arms, legs, neck, chest and head were all majorly thick, not fat, thick and strong. He reminded me of Odd Job from the movie, *Goldfinger*. As they got closer I saw Bernard rushing the Addars inside the office, then in a voice that sounded like a tuba, the black guy asked if I had a problem.

"Not at all, bubba, I was just leaving."

"You got some I.D.?" Then his partner got uncomfortably close.

"Yeah I do, if it's any of your business." Even though 'Mr. Thick' was almost on top of me, I kept my eyes locked on 'Mr. Mirrored Glasses'. Neither of us could see through the others' sunglasses and I realized I was in the middle of a pissing contest. Dealing with these two was a hell of a lot more difficult than dealing with the old man's security. Finally, 'Mirrored Glasses' reached inside his jacket and pulled out his I.D. As he did I saw he was armed with what looked like the butt of the new model Beretta, and I realized these boys weren't playing games.

"I am Mr. Caleb, this is Mr. Hondoa. We're in charge of the senator's safety. Now who are you?"

Just then, Bernard slinked over and told the boys to stand down.

"My name's John Seraph."

"Sorry about this, Mr. Seraph, but our security people tend to take their jobs seriously." He extended his hand and I saw the man liked to show off that he had money. He kind of reminded me of some of my relations. Bernard was wearing a gold bracelet and a pair of gold and onyx rings on his right hand. I shook his hand and noticed on his left hand there was a gold Rolex and a simple gold wedding band, and he had a weak handshake. It felt clammy and I remembered what the old man said about a man with a weak handshake, he can't be trusted and was someone with whom you shouldn't turn your back on.

As Bernard waved the guard dogs off, he smiled broadly. The best way I could describe him was he reminded me of a combination of a weasel and a mole with greasy, slicked back black hair. "So are you here to volunteer your services to help out Senator Addar?"

I gave him the same story I told Bruden and for some reason he went white. "See the private investigator, Mr. Lee, wasn't making much progress and Sebastian Tillis asked me to look into things. I intend to do better than Lee did."

Bernard looked like he swallowed a ferret. "I have to get going. See you around." I crossed the street before he could say anything else, but felt his eyes on me. I knew he was wondering what I really wanted and what I was planning. My gut told me Bernard was hiding something and I wanted to know what it was.

* * * *

After I got to my car I realized I had options. The first, I could head home, take care of a paper that was due next week. The second, I could head over to Club Soho and see if I could learn anything, even though Bishop told me the police didn't want me poking around anymore, I figured since Soho fell under the area of the Arm's business, and since I was asked to check stuff out, that they couldn't, this was something that fell under Bishop's request.

* * * *

Fifteen minutes later, I was on Chippewa and trying to find a parking place. Unfortunately, it was up on Delaware so I had hike up to Delaware and Chippewa. Luckily, from that point, most of the bars are nearby. It'd suddenly become muggy outside or maybe I just imagined it and I began sweating a bit, either way I was glad when the breeze off Lake Erie picked up and cooled me off.

It'd been a long time since I'd been here, even longer than it had been since I'd seen my family. Club Soho is a nice bar, a Fisherman Wharf style building with patios on the ground and upper levels. I walked in and had to look around just to see what changes had been made. Most of the walls were burgundy, with some sort of modern art pieces that were white, silver and gold in color. The bar itself is all black with brass, high-back barstools. Behind the bar were three rows of three of red-lighted shelving units showcasing higher end liquor bottles on them. I think they're more for decoration, because behind the bartenders there were several liquor bottles. It's not a bad bar, actually kind of classy. I'd hang out here if I could afford it, and if I didn't know who some of the silent partners were.

It was still early and the bar wouldn't open until nine, but I could see the employees through the windows cleaning the place up from last night's bar-hoppers, and getting ready for another busy night. I walked through the front door and gave my eyes a minute to adjust to the sudden darkness. As I was looking around, re-acquainting myself, the hostess came over. "I'm sorry, sir, we're not open yet."

"It's okay, I'm not thirsty. My name's John Seraph, and I was wondering if you might have seen this woman," I said, then pulled out the strip of photos of Dana and Crystal and pointed out Dana.

As she looked over the photos, the pretty black hostess began shaking her head. "She seems familiar, but I don't think so."

"Damn."

"Sorry. Is she famous or something? I know I've seen her."

"Well, her name's Dana Tillis, she's been missing for about three weeks. Maybe you saw her in the news."

She seemed to be happy she knew who she was talking about. "That's right, but I've never seen her around here. But, I've only been here about four weeks. The regular hostess is on maternity leave, maybe she knows something."

"That's possible, but I don't want to bother her if she has a new baby. Is there anyone here I can talk to?"

"The assistant manager, Vince is here, so is Sammy one of our bartenders is here too. They've all been here a lot longer than I have."

"Can I speak to Vince then?"

"Sure, please wait here a moment."

As she walked off to get Vince, I wondered how much my brothers invested then suddenly I was a run over by an edgy feeling because anything related to the Arm makes me feel uneasy.

A minute later, the hostess came back with what looked like a would-be male model. Vince was a big guy, with black hair, a spray on tan I was betting, and an earning stud in his right ear. He looked like he could have snuck into an Angelo family reunionn "Thanks, Angie," he said, giving her a smart swat on her backside. *Asshole,* I thought, and from what I saw, Angie didn't like it. "Hi there, how I can help you?"

"I was wondering if you ever saw this blonde woman?" and showed him the pictures.

"Hmmm, damn. Bet she's a sweet piece," he said with a laugh. I fought a strong urge to slap him on the back of the head. "And the other one's not too bad either. Bet they'd make a great double feature."

I fought the desire to shatter his kneecap. "It's nothing like that. Dana Tillis has been missing for the past couple weeks, and I've been asked by her family to help find her." I thought it best not to mention finding her body. The news had broken, but I wanted to keep my involvement to a minimum, as long as I could.

"Hmm, she looks really familiar. Come with me." We headed over to the bar where the light was better. "Sammy, come here," he yelled to the bartender. Sammy was shorter than the both of us, with short spiked hair and three earrings in his right ear.

Great. Another pretty-boy, I thought.

"Ever see this blonde girl before?"

"Oh yeah, umm…vodka gimlets with an onion, and chocolate martinis."

"Not bad." My revulsion was replaced by a combination of amazement and astonishment.

"Yeah, that's how I remember the regulars," Sammy said. "Comes in handy."

"How well you guys know her?"

"I can't speak for Vince here, but just enough to get drink orders from and say hi. Pretty good tipper too," Sammy said, as he finished putting glasses away under the bar, then I turned to Vince.

"Well I, uh…saw her around the club just to say hi to." My built-in bullshit detector went off like someone pulled a fire alarm.

"Really?" I asked while staring Vince down.

"Uh, yeah. You want a drink or something? Sammy, get the man whatever he wants."

"Ah, no thanks, I'm not thirsty."

Sammy then broke in again. "Hey, wait Vince, I remember you taking her to the office last month."

"Really?" I said, with a predatory grin creeping across my face.

"Nah, you're wrong Sammy," Vince said looked somewhere between embarrassed and nervous. "I was never with her."

"Maybe you should tell me the truth Vince."

"Look, I don't have time for this." He started to get up.

I grabbed his forearm and slammed it on top of the bar, as he went from bad to worse. "Well, bubba, you better make time. Two things, the police are going be here sooner or later once they find out Dana was a regular. Second, I know the silent partners here." Vince then looked like I pulled out an Uzi and was about to start a shooting spree. "I don't think it's a good idea you keeping things from me." *Here it comes!*

"What do you know about the partners?"

"Michael and Paul Angelo are my brothers. You know who our father is?" He just nodded slowly as if he'd just got the death penalty. This was the other side of the coin I played with Bruden. With him I played up being helpful, now I implied an unspoken threat. In this situation either worked for me. "What do you know about Dana, and I want to know everything you boys know, now!"

Vince quickly told me how a few times when Dana went clubbing she started dancing with him, by pulling him onto the floor, using the argument 'giving the customer what she wants'. While dancing, Dana bumped and ground into Vince knowing what kind of reaction she'd get, and afterwards they crept off to the office and hooked-up.

"It happened about five or six times, once with one of the waitresses. She came into the office and without missing a beat Dana, only in a g-string at this point, went right over to her, kissed her and began rubbing the girl's tits and ass. Next thing I know I'm having my first three-way. Man now that was a night to remember," Vince said, smiling at his boast. I wanted to drive his forehead into the top of the bar. "But that was the last time."

"That's all?" I emphasized my point by added real pressure onto his arm. So much so, I saw the color of his hand change to red and figured I was cutting off his blood flow. Sammy just wisely kept quiet. The Angelo name can go a long way.

"Ahh...yeah I swear, Mr. Angelo." I knew he said that out of fear, not respect, so I let the prick go. He rubbed his arm to get the blood flowing again Vince told me one more thing. "You probably already know this, too, but your brother was banging that girl too."

Every cell in my body went into immediate shock. There was no way this bastard was telling the truth and I called him out on it. "You're lying!"

"Oh, come on, man. He was giving it to her more than I was."

My rage flared out of control and I grabbed Vince by his throat and drove his back into the bar. I don't like losing my temper, but when I do, it turns in Krakatoa. "What the hell are you saying asshole?"

"Take it easy man!" Sammy said to me.

I glared at Sammy, the look in my eyes said everything and he backed off.

While Vince was clawing at my right hand he was gasping hard, "Please...please man." he begged. "I swear it was your brother."

"Which one?" I hissed.

"Michael, Michael I swear on my mother! It was Michael!" I let go without realizing it. My head felt like it was full of Novocain.

"I'm going to look into this, and you better be telling the truth."

"I swear to God I am, Mr. Angelo."

"If not I'm coming back here and we're going to have another friendly chat."

"That won't happen." I believed him. Vince was too scared to lie to me.

"Two more things—get a better attitude about women. No more smacking female employees on their asses, no more banging clients, none of it." I paused for a moment and took a step closer, to make my point. "If I hear anything, I'll be back, and you don't want me back."

"Right, Mr. Angelo."

"Secondly, the name's Seraph. Remember it." I turned to leave and went by Angie at the door. I told her things should improve with Vince from now on, if not she could call me. I admit it all felt good, but this stuff about Mike left me feeling like a raw egg full of battery acid.

Chapter Sixteen

On the ride home, I played a Sinatra concert and hoped it'd clear my head. That wasn't the case this time. There was too much on my mind.

It was almost four when I got home; the winds had picked up and were blowing the seed pods that were hanging from the trees. The parking lot was full of them and sounded like a crackling fire when I drove over them.

I sorted my mail, most of it the usual junk. The only highlight was a letter from one of my few friends, Katsuro Ryuu. Kats and I became friends when I was still living with my folks, and he was working for the Yakuza. A couple years later Kats moved to San Francisco, and the only thing I'm positive of, is he can never go back to Japan. The reasons involve a girl named Yukiko, and if he does go home, it'll cost him his life. After Kats moved to the States he became a professional gun-for-hire, what some call an enforcer. The difference between him and everyone else doing this work is he has more honor, courage, and guts than anyone else. I know Kats is a descendant of an actual Japanese Samurai, and practices their code of honor, Bushido. I was really looking forward to reading the letter after dinner.

I sorted through the rest of the mail, checked my answering machine and found the light blinking. Charles Lee finally called back. He apologized because he had been on a skip trace going after a client's ex-husband in Albany. He wanted to talk to me about Dana's case and knew some of the facts from the news, but he was going to be in court for most of the week and asked me to call him on Friday. I wrote myself a reminder note, and got the feeling Sebastian would have the same results had he flushed his money.

I went to my bedroom, kicked off my cowboy boots, peeled my socks off then tossed them right into the hamper, then put on my beat up sneakers and headed to the living room when the buzzer rang to let me know someone was at the front door.

I went into the hallway opened the front door, and was blinded by the sun that just began its descent behind the apartments across the street. In front of me was a young woman I guessed was in her late twenties, early thirties. She had shoulder length soft reddish-brown, which reminded of the fall foliage we get around here. She was dressed smartly in a business suit of a tweed jacket, a pale yellow blouse and skirt, with knee-high boots. She smiled and stuck out her hand. "John Seraph?" she said, sounding like a college student.

Not sure what to expect I told her "Yes?"

"Mr. Seraph, my name's Bobbie Bedell, and…"

I held a hand up. "Bobbie?"

"It's Roberta. My father wanted a boy and he sort of got the last word over Mom," then she laughed softly as she handed me her card. "Mr. Seraph, I'm a reporter with the *Buffalo News* and I wanted to ask you about your involvement in the Dana Tillis case."

Shit! My stomach tightened and I felt myself becoming defensive. Mama always said that was a bit of a problem for me, my emotions tend to get me in trouble.

I finally remembered her name from her byline and knew she was a quality writer. Bedell was still new to the area having started at the News last year, but she was already making a name for herself in certain circles. "What makes you think I know anything, Ms. Bedell?"

"Three things." To emphasize her points, she held up a finger for each. "First, I know you met with Sebastian Tillis in his office Friday. Second, Saturday you two checked out Dana's apartment. Third, you were at the crime scene. I saw you there talking to the cops. Finally, you drove Tillis out of there."

I didn't see the point of trying to lie or stall her, then she took the initiative. "So you going to invite me in, or what?" Smiling warmly, she stepped into the foyer coming close to me. She pressed right up to me just like Caleb did, but this was a whole lot nicer.

I looked straight into her green eyes and was surprised by her confidence. She had guts—I'd give her that. "Why should I help you at all?"

"You have contacts most folks can't dream of. I know you're

Giovanni Angelo, eldest son to mob boss, Stefano Angelo." As soon as she said it, I felt my blood boil.

"First, that's not my name, and second, what's that crack mean?"

"Whoa, easy big fella, I didn't mean anything personal. I'm just saying you have access to info I can't get anywhere else."

Once I heard that I learned something about Ms. Bedell, she was one ambitious woman.

"I've a feeling that's why Tillis contacted you," she continued. "I found out you two were classmates and I guessed he asked you for help because of your father."

I also learned she's a smart reporter too.

"Whatever happens I am going write that you're involved in the investigation."

I'd an idea where she was heading. "So if I don't help out, you'll make it look bad for me?"

"I wouldn't say that, but there are two ways I can write the story."

I thought *God I love being right all the time.*

Her tone shifted. "Seriously, Mr. Seraph, I don't want to make any trouble for you, but I was thinking, if you gave me an exclusive, I can really make it worth your while."

I must have looked at her funny because I tilted my head out of reflex and Bobbie realized how that sounded and blushed. She quickly corrected herself, and I just smiled.

"What I mean is I can pay you for your information and I keep my sources confidential. You wouldn't even be named as a confidential informant."

I thought about what she offered and, to be honest, I could use the money, but it didn't interest me. There was a way I knew how she could help. "Come with me." I turned back to my apartment, and she followed on my heels like a puppy. Her face glowed with anticipation, Bobbie knew she was going to get what she wanted, but I wanted something from her in return. Not what she offered or implied, at least not right now if at all.

I said, as I shut the door, "Have a seat."

Looking around, she said, "Nice place, tasteful but not what I'd expected. I thought you'd have a large plasma screen and expensive furniture and all the kind of stuff most folks want. I never figured you for the South Buffalo type, in a small two bedroom done in Southwestern style."

I sat down across from her in the rocker "I guess you really don't know that much about me."

"I read what was in the archives and…"

"Sounds like you only got half the story. Maybe you're not the reporter you think you are." This is where I got on her defensive side.

"Hey, I'm a damn good writer, busting my ass in a tough field."

She became flushed again and I couldn't help notice her chest rising a bit in anger. I guess I knew which buttons to push if I wanted to piss her off.

"Easy little-lady, I'm just saying you don't know everything." I explained a lot to her, why I walked away, but didn't mention Fred. "Everything here I paid for myself, I didn't take any help or money from my family and despite a bunch of meddlers I'm related to, I haven't talked or seen most of them in three years."

"Till Sunday, right?"

"Yeah right, now if you want an exclusive I'll make you a deal. I'm still looking into Dana's case, even though Sebastian only asked me to help find her, but now I'm after her killer." Her eyes widened and she reminded me of a kid at Christmas. "When this is over I'll give you an exclusive, but I want something in return." Bobbie's mouth tightened up and she seemed to swallow her lips. "You've access to information I don't, and have sources I probably can't get in touch with. So I may have to reach out to get some 411. If I do, you give me a hand, but also I know you have to talk to the Tillis Family. Give them time to mourn. They're going through hell right now. Take it or leave it."

For a second she looked pensive. "Alright, you're on."She opened her purse and took out a card. "My editor might want me to talk to them, but I'll respect their wishes. Here's my numbers and email, so you can reach me when you need to."

She paused and knelt on the floor right in front of me and I was immediately entranced by her perfume. It was flowery and sweet, I knew it wasn't as expensive as the stuff my sisters wore, but it worked extremely well with Bobbie. I couldn't help myself with her so close before me I caught myself staring at her body. It wasn't that she had anything that really jumped out at a guy, but you could see she had it all in the right places. "Mr. Seraph, I need to explain something. I may have come off a little strong and flirty, but that's not the real me. I really want to do a good job, sometimes I get a little…hmmm overeager and sometimes that gets me in trouble."

I listened to her, but I caught myself looking over the curve of her neck, leading down to the slope of her breasts and then to the rest of her body. I pulled myself together. *Man I need a cold shower bad.* I stood up and took her hand as I helped her to her feet. In one perfect moment, we stared into each other's eyes.

Finally, I broke silence, "It's alright. I've done some dumb things too. One other thing, and this is serious, if you see any of my family members or anything that doesn't feel right let me know A.S.A.P."

"You think the mob's involved and would hurt me?"

"No, I don't think so, but I can never tell what my old man will do. Actually I'm waiting to hear from him or someone else, but sometimes things can get uncomfortable with him and my brothers." I didn't mention about Mike and Dana being involved. I still didn't want to believe it, and wouldn't until I talked to him.

I jotted down my numbers and email for her and, before I walked Bobbie out to the foyer, I told her since we were partners now she could call me John. She said I could call her Bobbie, but not Roberta. When we got to her car, I opened her door, and before she slid in, she thanked me. "You know you're a lot cuter than your pictures in the archives led me to think."

"Gee thanks. I'll keep you posted." As she drove down Arbour, I had to squint and look sideways because the sun was in the perfect position to blind me until I shaded my eyes with my hand. Bobbie honked her horn and waved her left arm out the window, and I don't know why, but I waved back like some goofy teenager saying bye to his girlfriend.

I spun around to head back inside then paused when I saw, at the corner of Eden and Arbour, a gold SUV with tinted windows. I never saw it before and didn't think anyone in the neighborhood owned it. I took a couple of steps toward it without realizing it. Suddenly the engine started up and it peeled out speeding towards McKinley Parkway. I heard the truck revving its engine and hauled ass. Even if I felt like running after it, there was no way I'd catch up. There wasn't any reason to think the SUV had anything to do with me or what I was doing, but I don't believe in coincidences.

Chapter Seventeen

Back inside a lot went through my head, and I felt a little drunk. There was plenty to sort out, including whether or not Bobbie was flirting with me and if so, was she serious or just trying to get my help? I knew it was a game a lot of women played when they wanted something. My sisters play it successfully, but I was never in this position before and I'd like to think I was a good enough looking guy, and Bobbie might actually be interested.

I headed into the kitchen and took the chicken TV dinner out from the freezer, tossed it into the microwave, then made a pitcher of ice tea. I doubled up on the scoops since I love a nice strong brew, then put it on the dining table and got a glass with a knife and fork. While I waited for the microwave, I turned the news on to see if there was anything new on Dana's case and tried to sort out what Dana's co-workers told me.

I wrote down everything I could remember and, as I looked over my notes my head was as clear as mud, and hoped things would look better after dinner.

The news didn't have anything new to report, which wasn't surprising. When I finished eating, I had the idea of calling Dr. Irons. I looked her up in the phone book, and wrote down her phone number. Her office is located on West Seneca over on East & West Road, near the Southgate Plaza, which meant she was about ten to fifteen minutes away from me. I decided to call her tomorrow, and find out what I could, if anything. Now I just needed a good story to go along with my call. I knew there were confidentiality laws about doctors and their patients, but I also knew it had to do with Dana's next of kin, so I might have to talk with Sebastian about this too. Then wondered how to tell a man his baby sister had a sex drive that could satisfy the crew of the U.S.S. Enterprise without him taking a swing at me.

I tried to watch the rest of the news, but couldn't and found myself daydreaming about getting Bobbie stripped down to her bra and panties. I think I needed the diversion from the mess I was in. I fantasized I was standing behind Bobbie, what it would be like to hold her in my arms, nuzzling her neck and massaging her breasts. I found her attractive, sexy and intelligent.

I was lost in the middle of my fantasy, which was hotter with each passing second and lost track of time, then violently thrown back to real world when the phone rang. *Sonuvabitch!* "Hello?"

"Hello, Mr. Seraph, this is Crystal Belle." I quickly recovered and came back to reality thanks to what felt like an icy tidal swell. I grabbed the remote to mute the T.V., which I forgot all about.

"Oh, hi Miss Belle. Are you feeling any better?"

"Yes, I am thank you. Mr. Seraph, I wanted to thank you for your kindness, and I was wondering if we could meet tomorrow. There's something I wanted to tell you, and I really wasn't with it today, plus this was something I didn't want to talk about in front of the others."

My curiosity was peaked. "Sure I understand if you want to talk about it now—I can listen."

"No, I'm a little busy and I still haven't eaten yet."

"Don't let me stop you. What time did you want to meet?"

"How about around one o'clock," Crystal said.

"Sure, no problem, I'll even spring for lunch."

"That isn't necessary."

"I know, but I'd like to."

"Okay, I'll see you then. Goodnight, Mr. Seraph."

"Night, Miss Belle, and you can make it John."

"Alright, night John, and it's Crystal."

I felt good about Crystal calling and I was extremely interested in what she had to tell me, but that would have to wait.

The rest of the night wasn't that productive, I had my notes scattered all over the love seat next to me while I tried to make any kind of sense of what I was looking at, but after awhile I finally realized I could be looking too hard. I had *The World's Wildest Police Chases* on then finally switched over to the History Channel, but I was bored with what was on.

I realized I couldn't get my head away from Dana. At first, I thought it was that I wasn't able to let go, but realized the mystery wouldn't let me go. It nagged at it me and nothing would stop it until justice was served, just like with the Honor's Club and Eddie.

* * * *

I headed to bed earlier than planned after another long shower and sacked out around ten. Instead of focusing on Dana, I forced myself to think about Bobbie and Crystal. They were the last clear, rational thoughts I had.

Chapter Eighteen
~ Tuesday ~

I got up around nine thirty and felt like shit. My head throbbed, my mouth felt like wallpaper paste, and all I wanted to do was stay in bed. That's what my body said, but my head ordered me to do the complete opposite.

I dragged myself into the shower where I stayed until the hot water started to get cold. Afterward, I wiped the steam off the mirror, looked at myself and tried to focus on the face I saw. For the first time I realized I wasn't the same person I was when Sebastian called me. I felt older, worn-out, and disheartened.

I dressed in my black jeans, black long sleeved polo, and black cowboy boots, then headed to the kitchen where I poured some orange juice and threw a raisin bagel into the toaster. While I waited, I called Dr. Irons' office and I asked to speak to her. Her secretary told me Irons was in session so I left a message for her to call me back A.S.A.P and gave the same story I told the Nicholas family, but added that I was the one who found Dana. I knew that would get a response.

I figured Irons must've heard about Dana by now. I also knew I was a step ahead of the police, but not by much. I didn't know how long my head start would last so I had to work fast, and was afraid Irons might tell them about the diary and then I could be in a real shit storm with the police.

After I ate, I wasn't sure what else to do since I had to wait for Sebastian's call about Dana's autopsy, which I figured already started. I was glad I wasn't going to be around for that.

* * * *

It was going on eleven thirty and I had some time to kill before meeting Crystal. I figured if anyone at her office asked why I was back, I'd lie and tell them Crystal and I had a lunch date. I learned awhile back it was best to have a good lie ready to go and to keep it simple. Actually, it was the truth now that I think about it.

It was bright and sunny out, but there were passing clouds and talk of showers and thundershowers later so I grabbed my suede jacket and did a final check, wallet, watch, keys, and hand sanitizer, all set. I stuffed the small bottle into my inside pocket of my jacket, locked up and checked to see if the mail came yet. Nothing yet so I headed out the back to my car, got in and drove around the block to the Baxter's store. I wanted to see if Dixie returned and how things were going with her sister. To be honest it wasn't that I didn't care about Dixie's sister. I needed the distraction.

I walked in and found Charles behind the counter slicing some Sahlen's ham for an old lady waiting at the deli counter, holding onto her walker.

"Hiya, Johnny, how's it going?"

"Not too bad," I said while looking around at the pop coolers right by the deli counter, and the three stacked chicken rotisserie ovens. Man I love that smell.

"Be with ya in a sec," he said, then turned back to his customer. After he finished slicing, weighing and wrapping up the ham Charles handed it over to the old lady. "Here ya go, Ma'am, anything else?"

"No, that's all, Mr. Baxter. Thank you." After she put the ham in her hanging basket, she shuffled down to the cashier.

"So, what's new?" Charles asked while he rewrapped the ham and wiped down the slicer. I told him everything that happened since we talked. "Holy Moses kid, I thought that was you on the news last night."

"Yeah, that was me, wasn't a lot of fun though."

"I bet." Then he came out from behind. "So you know the Tillis girl?"

I shook my head. "Never met her, but I went to school with her brother, and he asked me to help find her. He thought the old man might know something." We walked up toward the front and kept our voices low.

"So whatcha going to do?"

I shook my head. "Keep on swinging I guess. I mean I told the cops I'd find out what I can from the old man and I gave Sebastian my word.

Anyway, I'm meeting with a girlfriend of Dana's for lunch. I was at her office yesterday and something there gave me a creepy feeling. Something wasn't right, can't figure out what or why."

"Well, you've always been good at that sort of thing. I'm betting you'll figure everything out in no time."

I picked up a pack of breath mints at the candy counter, which is right under the cash register. "So Dixie back yet?"

"Nah, Ella's being a major pain in the ass for Dix and Mazy. It's almost like she can't do anything for herself when she gets like this. She actually orders them round, kills me when she does this shit. At times, she's perfectly normal, then other times Ella acts like a five year old. I mean she'll actually tell them what she wants and expects them to do."

For some reason I get this funny feeling when something doesn't feel or sound right. It's almost comes off like when a tuning fork is struck, and I can feel the vibrations coming off it. I don't know why or how it happens, but when it does, I sit up and pay attention.

I paid for the mints and got out of there. I had almost an hour to go, and thought I'd take a nice, slow drive downtown to clear my head.

I drove down Abbott Road, though the heart of South Buffalo going past the charter school, a number of local businesses, a number of well maintained two story homes, and a bunch of closed store fronts which seem to litter all of South Buffalo, whether on Abbott Road, South Park Avenue or Seneca.

I passed the Dog Eared Bookstore, turned onto the winding path that cuts through Cazenovia Park and got up to Seneca. From there I headed downtown. I drove past Seneca and Bailey going past an auto supply store, a lumber supply company and an adult entertainment store.

There was a fair amount of traffic out for a weekday morning, but once I cruised past the 190 onramp and the Seneca/Babcock intersection, I got into a rougher residential neighborhood and pretty much had Seneca to myself. I got downtown faster than planned, and parked in the same lot I was in before. To kill some more time I went over all the notes I brought with me, but I was almost at the point I could recite everything I'd been writing down.

It was just before one when I got out of my car and went to the campaign office, and waved at Crystal through the window. She smiled at me, and I liked it. I headed on in and waved at the secretary who was on the phone. I sat down and began flipping through a brochure I missed the day before. After Tiffany got off the phone, she asked what I was doing there and I explained I had a lunch date and promised I wouldn't be a pest.

After a couple minutes, Crystal came out with her jacket on, smiling and looking like someone without a care in the world. I couldn't help but smile myself because Crystal is really a beautiful girl, and someone I'd like to get to know a whole lot better.

Chapter Nineteen

We stepped out of the office and were forced to put our sunglasses on because the sun came out, despite the threat of rain and clouds. I asked her where she wanted to eat. "There's nice place over on Delaware, ever been to the King's Court?"

"Nope, good food?"

"The staff goes there a lot."

Crystal had forty-five minutes for lunch, so there was plenty of time to talk. When we got to King's Court, we decided it was nice enough outside to eat on their patio, even though it was still cool out. "Are you alright? You look a little cold. We can sit inside," I suggested.

"No, I'll be fine," Crystal responded.

I ordered the julienne salad and Crystal the Hawaiian Salad plate. We both had lemonade and split an appetizer of a combo plate, which consists of pizza logs, mozzarella sticks and real Buffalo wings.

The food was very good, and the company was even better. I figured the best way to start things was to ease Crystal into talking. I knew she wanted to talk, but I also knew I'd have to be careful and handle her with kid gloves since she seemed to still be a little shaky. I played it casual and asked Crystal about herself and found this a good way of getting her to open up.

"Well there isn't much to tell. I'm twenty-eight, from North Buffalo, grew up on Tacoma with my parents and two sisters. I'm the middle daughter and finally living in my own apartment on Hertel Avenue. I like being near my family, but I needed my own space."

"Believe me, I understand that."

"I've been going to U.B. for a couple semesters, but I'm still not sure what I really want to do, so I'm taking some time off to figure things out."

"So how did you meet Dana?"

"I started working at the office a year ago when they were hiring and she showed me the ropes. We became friends and went shopping, to movies, hit the gym, and of course, clubbing. Everything was fine, but she changed when we'd go to Chippewa. It was almost like Dana became a different person when we'd head out."

"How so?" I asked in-between bites.

"Don't get me wrong. I loved Dana, but there were times when she'd openly flirt with guys. I mean we could be out for lunch and she'd tease and caress a waiter or even once openly kissed another, and while doing it she began rubbing his crouch under our table."

"The worst came one night when we were at Club Marcela and I caught Dana in the ladies' room with one of the bartenders and another girl groping each other while the bartender was stripping them and himself."

"I get the picture."

She put her fork down and I could tell she was getting serious now. "I want to tell you why I fell apart yesterday."

"It's all right, Crystal, I don't need to know." I meant what I said, but I was curious as all hell.

"I really liked Dana, she was a good friend, but about a week and a half before she disappeared we had a girl's night out after work. You know dinner, movies. Afterward, we headed back to her place." I nodded, listening. She went on, "We popped in a movie and got to talking about nothing really important, and after a couple drinks Dana was getting silly. She wanted to show me some new 'toys' she had gotten and I admit it was a little embarrassing. I mean it isn't like I don't know about that stuff, but I never saw anything like the ones Dana had and …"

Crystal's voice sped up and her face began to flush so I saved her the embarrassment. "I get the idea," especially after having seen Dana's 'toy chest' first hand. "So what happened?"

Crystal tried to look at me, but she kept on glancing away as if she had a nervous condition or something.

"It's something I'm not really comfortable with."

"That's okay, if you don't want to tell me…"

She held up her hands almost as if in an act of defiance. I could see she was trembling and knew it had nothing to do with the weather. "No you don't understand I have to tell someone. I feel horrible about how I treated her. After we were talking about her toys for a bit she got closer and kissed me."

I listened as Crystal told me in her way, at her own pace. Eventually she got the rest out. "She surprised me, and my reaction wasn't the best. At first I was totally stunned and couldn't say anything, finally I asked her what she was thinking. Dana told me she had felt an attraction to me and believed it was mutual. I told she was wrong and she said she was sorry but still cared about me and that she'd be willing to show me things, after that I just left.

"The next day at work I ignored her and when she tried calling me I let my voice mail take her calls. This went on for about a week and half and I did what I could to avoid her. I just wasn't sure how to handle the situation." Crystal's brown eyes got weepy again and I reached for the clean hankie in my pocket, but she pulled out a small pack of tissues from her purse and gave me a sort of smile.

"This time I'm ready," she said and wiped her eyes. "Oh, by the way, I have this for you..." She dug around in her purse and pulled out my hankie from the day before. "I washed it last night."

"Thanks." Having forgotten about it, I stuffed it back in my other front pocket.

"I've had girlfriends who are bisexual or lesbian, but never messed around with them. I don't have a problem with that stuff. It's just, I like guys."

"Really?" I asked in a hammy voice and gave her a big cocky grin as a way to break the mood and make her laugh, which she did. "So what happened then?"

"The last time I saw Dana it was really awkward, and she actually cornered me in the ladies' room and tried to apologize to me, but I didn't want to hear it and went right past her." Our waitress came over and asked if we'd like any dessert. Crystal just shook her head and waved her hand in a stop gesture, and I didn't want anything else so I just asked for the check.

"Crystal, I think you should know something about Dana. Maybe I shouldn't tell you, but I think it's important you know she had problems." I felt peculiar, but after hearing her story, I thought Crystal needed to know the truth. I told her about Dana's addiction and her face was overrun with the same disbelief I felt when I heard about Dana and

Mike.

"I know it's a lot to take in, but you have to know Dana was sick. She had an addiction that ruled her life. It was the same as when an alcoholic can't stop drinking and this didn't have anything to do with her being bi or straight. From what I understand, it was a powerful compulsion over which she had no control. I just hope you understand she really did care about you as a real friend, and didn't want to hurt you. I guess in her own way she thought she could trust you and I know she wanted to talk to you about her problem. I think she didn't know how to tell you about her attraction or addiction and maybe coming onto you was the only way she could tell you these things."

Crystal wiped away a few more tears, but the look in her eyes wasn't the heartbreaking, doleful look I had seen. This time she had a more hopeful look that I admit gave me confidence.

* * * *

On the way back to the office, Crystal told me more about Dana, stuff she thought I should know. "People at the office, on several occasions, had heard Dana in the ladies' room pleasuring herself. Also, there were a rumors going round she'd been caught in the stall with one of the male workers, but no one knew who it was."

"Crystal, I need a favor. You've got to be quiet about Dana's addiction. I mean you can't tell anyone, not even your family."

"I promise, John, I owe her that much." It was here I was getting a clearer picture of Crystal's character, and liked what I saw.

* * * *

Clouds had moved in, darkened the skies and I could smell the rain in the air. I was curious about where the Addars were living since they spent so much time in Buffalo, and Crystal told me an office secret; Besides buying that home in the Northtowns, they rented out the top two floors at City Condominiums up on Main Street.

I knew the building a bit, because the old man's construction company did some of the work when the building was built back in the late 80's and 90's. It was at the start of the Theater District near West Chippewa. I also knew you had to have money to live there. Automatically, I looked up at the building as we reached the campaign office. It didn't give me a good feeling, and I felt uneasy from then on, as if they could look down on us, like raptors eyeing their prey.

When we got back to the office the limo was out front, and Hondoa standing there on alert, looking stern and granite like, like a gargoyle. I leaned down to Crystal and whispered, "I understand they can fix that look at birth nowadays." She laughed aloud.

I walked her back into the office, and Tiffany waved 'Hi' to us. "I really enjoyed myself and I want to thank you for your help."

"It's no problem, I had a good time too and glad you told me about Dana. I think I understand her better."

Crystal surprised me and kissed my cheek. "I had a good time too."

We both stood there for a moment smiling at one another, until we saw Bernard coming out of one of the inner offices.

When he saw us, he came over. "Hello, Mr. Seraph, I didn't think we'd see you back so soon. Still looking into things?"

"Nah, Mr. Bernard, I took Crystal to lunch."

"Really? Didn't know you two were friends," he replied with a smile I can only describe as reptilian. The creep reminded me of a combination of Iago and Claudius.

"Yeah, for a while now."

"How nice for you."

I turned back to Crystal and tried to play it cool as I could. "Well it was great, I'll call you later on, okay?"

"Uh, sure John, and thanks again," she followed my play, then kissed my cheek again.

The thing I wasn't sure about was if she was playing the role, or if she was really interested. I've never been good at reading women. To be honest, Chinese Algebra's easier to figure out than the so-called 'weaker' sex.

"Mr. Seraph, there's someone here who'd like to talk to you. Ah, he's in the back office and it is important."

My curiosity was peeked and I followed him back, but at the same time, my tuning fork went off. I didn't realize until this moment how short Bernard was. Now I'm around six foot two, maybe not the biggest bull in the barn, but I can look down on most, but Bernard, I figured, was at least a good foot shorter than me.

He led me to room where I'd met with Bruden, Crystal and Eden. As I headed in, I felt like I was being led to the electric chair. Sitting at the conference table was 'The New Royal Couple' as the papers called them, the Addars. As I walked in, my stomach tightened up and felt I'd just walked into a viper's nest.

Chapter Twenty

There was a part of me that wanted to get the hell out of there because I figured Addar was on to me, wanting to know what I was doing. I knew I had to watch it but also thought it might be a good idea to see if I could find out what they might know. If anything, I learned a lot with Aldrich as a tutor.

Bernard pulled out a swivel chair for me, but the senator was already on his feet and smiled at me as he stuck out his hand. His handshake was firmer than I thought it'd be. "A pleasure to meet you, Mr. Seraph, I am Senator Kingsley Addar and thank you for agreeing to see me so quickly." Alongside the Adders was a smartly dressed woman, wearing oval shaped framed glasses, her brown hair up with a pair of sticks that looked like chop sticks, holding a file folder, and resembled a New England schoolteacher.

"Nice to meet you, Senator and Mrs. Addar, of course." I extended my hand to the distinguished looking lady dressed in a dark blue business suit, sitting at the table near the wood paneled wall.

"Ah, pleasure, Mr. Seraph?" From her accent, I could tell she wasn't from Western New York.

"Nice to meet you, ma'am, how do you do?"

"Ah'll feel better after we get matters settled here, Mr. Seraph."

"Really, don't like Buffalo?"

"No, nothin' like that. Ah'm just anxious to go home. Ah'm sure you know how we feel."

"Of course, feeling at home is important. You've all been on the road for awhile now, right?"

"That's right," Bernard said. "Buffalo's a great city and the people have been incredibly kind to us, but it's not home."

"Yeah, that's right, you're from Rome, NY, right?"

"You've done your homework I see." Addar said, then he added "But so have we. Mr. Seraph this is Hope Abdi, our private secretary. Hope, if you will."

"Jonathan Seraph, legally changed name from Giovanni Angelo, born October 10th, 1970 to Stefano and Sophia Angelo. No known connections to your father's alleged criminal enterprises, but are reported to be close to your mother. Currently enrolled at Buffalo State College, majoring in English Education, while working on a minor in journalism, never married, have had several lady friends but engaged only once to…"

I heard enough and stopped her cold. "Point made." I became defensive, especially with my right fist balling up. Fortunately, I had it under the table.

The senator smiled. "Hope's amazing at her job, if there is anything we need to know she can get the information for us." Hope stood up, extended her hand towards me. I shook it but stared her down letting her know how I felt.

"I hope you're not upset with us Mr. Seraph, but we like to know who comes around to our office and why. After your visit yesterday we did a background check, partly because your story to Chalmer was a little too, um, dodgy is the word I'm looking for.

"So when we found out you and Sebastian Tillis were classmates and saw you were at his sister's apartment when she was found, Chalmer and I put two and two together," he added. I could feel the mood shifting.

"This is what I really meant, Mr. Seraph," Mrs. Addar said, "That por' girl. It's sucha shame."

"Did you folks know Dana at all?"

"Well enough to say hello to her here at the office, just like the rest of the staff," the senator said as he sat down across from me. "Every few days I do a walk through, thank the folks for their hard work, shake hands and talk to them, a little sports-talk, get their input on the issues. You know how it goes."

"Yeah, I mean it's a bitch when so many folks slam their phones down, or yell and swear at your workers. I know where they're coming from, I had a job in tele-sales a couple years ago and trust me the abuse gets really old, really fast." I then shifted gears, "Senator, I heard a rumor you're making plans for a possible run on 1600 Pennsylvania Avenue. Just out of curiosity I was wondering if that's true."

He smiled and looked almost completely innocent. "Well to be honest, Mr. Seraph, this is one of the many things we've been discussing," he said, glancing at his wife and staff. "I admit I am certainly interested, but right now, it may not be the right time for a presidential campaign. Now let me ask you something. Why are you still looking into Dana's death? I mean it's a police matter now."

"Yes it is, as a matter of fact I've been in touch with the detectives in charge, and they'll be around here soon. Like I told Mr. Bruden, I thought I'd ask a few questions and tell them what I could and not bother your office."

"Tha's very considerate of you, Mr. Seraph, but Ah'd think the police wouldn't want a civilian interfering in a murder investigation," Mrs. Addar said.

I answered smiling while gritting my teeth, "Yeah, normally that's true, but I've certain 'connections' the police don't have. So they're letting me see what I can turn up. Besides I gave a man my word I'd help, and I'm not finished." My smile dropped. "Hell, I haven't even started yet."

"Very venerable of you, Mr. Seraph, but Ah always felt a case of murder should be left to professionals."

"Yeah, like those guards of yours that ran into me yesterday. About as professional as they come." This wasn't going as well as I'd hoped because I could hear the contempt in my voice rising. Then it finally hit me; not only did they want to know what I knew, but nobody liked the fact I invited myself to the dance. So I figured the best thing to do was draw a line in the sand, and push a bit, just to see how much they'd take.

I got up by shoving myself away from the table. "Your boys were about as subtle as a train derailment. If they're the best you can get, I'd get a refund if I were you." I turned to leave, but the senator stopped me by putting his hand on my shoulder.

"Mr. Seraph, wait I am sorry if we seemed a little assertive, but we have to be extremely careful around here. You see my political opponents are always on the lookout for ammunition to use against me. As a matter of fact we've heard rumors that *Buffalo News* may be trying to get a plant in here."

As soon as he said that, my bullshit detector went off and prayed my face didn't give anything away. I knew I was going to have to talk with

Bobbie.

After that, we talked a little more and finally I made my goodbyes, anxious to get the hell out of there, and grateful my skin was intact.

* * * *

Outside I put my sunglasses back on, then turned back to take a last look around for Crystal through the large storefront window. When I saw her, I was hit with a bombshell, because I saw her talking to Caleb, who sat on the corner of her desk. He leaned in close to her, as if he didn't want to be heard by anyone. Then he placed his hand on her upper back as if he were really friendly with Crystal. I'd argue anxious and edgy were the best words to describe how she seemed, a definite change from lunch. He walked away and smiled, which was something I didn't think he was capable of, then gave Crystal a 'Gottcha' shot with his left forefinger and thumb. I'd no idea what they talked about, but seeing Caleb with Crystal left me with a sour stomach. I'd the feeling Caleb was reported everything to the Addars about what Crystal and I talked about at lunch, if she told him anything. I felt the same when I knew I'd have to tell Sebastian about Dana.

* * * *

I was about go into my car when Ms. Abdi ran over to the parking lot and didn't know if she was following me, so I stood there and watched her head to a red CR-V, which is when she saw me. She carried a large brown, shoulder bag on her right side that went along perfectly with her teacher themed outfit.

"Mr. Seraph, please wait!" she yelled as she jogged over. I figured I'd hear the lady out. "I wanted to apologize for back there. After you first showed, Mr. Bernard told the Addars what happened and he, not the senator, had me run a background check on you with Mr. Caleb. I understand why you may be upset over that, I just hope you can forgive me."

I looked into her green eyes and it seemed she played it straight. She looked straight at me, so I felt Abdi told me the truth. "It's no problem Ms. Abdi. I know you were following orders."

"To be honest I work for both the Addars." she said while shifting the bag from one shoulder to the other. "Besides working as the senator's secretary, I'm also Mrs. Addar's social secretary."

"That's got to be a handful of a job on its own. I mean the lady's in the society pages or on the news every other week."

"It can be." She had to use both hands to hold her bag.

"Here, let me," I offered while reaching for the bag.

"Thank you, after a while it gets to be a bit too much to carry while standing around, but I need everything in there when I'm out of the office."

We started walking towards her car, "I know what you mean. Most of the time I'm running around with a full bag of school books. If the job's that tough, why stick with it. I'm sure there's plenty of things you can do."

"It's exciting to be this close to such a powerful political figure. See, my father was an assistant to a few Washington lobbyists, and I grew up in those circles and always wanted to be on the inside. So when I got the opportunity to work for the Addars I took it."

"Sounds like a pretty good break."

"You're absolutely right. I believe Senator Addar has an excellent chance when he runs for the Presidency."

"So you think it's definite he'll run."

"Yes, I do. I mean Senator Addar's done great things, like the drug addict programs he and Mrs. Addar started and are planning on expanding throughout the Northeast and down the seaboard. And he'll do even better things once he is in the White House."

"Really, like what?"

"The senator is having me gather information about a National Health Care program for universal care."

"Seems I've heard that before."

"You're right of course, but this is something the senator is committed to seeing happen, unlike some of our former Presidents.

So he's already made up his mind, I thought. I noticed Abdi sounded more passionate with each second. I almost wanted to say fanatical. She was a real believer, committed to the cause, and the word zealot came to mind. I wondered how far she'd go to see Addar get into White House, and what role she saw herself in. "So I take it you're like the others and want to see this whole thing wrapped up A.S.A.P?"

"Exactly! I mean the senator doesn't deserve this sort of a problem. What politician needs a sex and drug scandal?"

"Who said anything about sex or drugs?" I tried to sound as innocent as I could, but I wanted to know how she knew about Dana's life and death.

"The rumors about Ms. Tillis' sex drive were all over the office."

"Maybe, but nobody said anything about drugs." I knew the police held back that info from the press and I sure as hell didn't tell anyone.

"It's those rumors again and..." I noticed her eyes began darting around a bit and she added, "And besides when you have a sex scandal you're bound to have drugs involved somewhere there too." She was really uncomfortable and I didn't know why. I felt Abdi knew more than she said but couldn't figure out what.

She took her bag from me, thanked me for my help and headed into her car. As I watched her pull out of the lot, I was left with more questions than I expected to have at this point.

* * * *

When I got into my car, I saw I had a voice mail on my cell, while I was talking to Abdi, Crystal called and told me about Caleb talking to her. I felt better that she told me.

"John, Caleb just talked to me. He tried to play up to me, being friendly. He claimed he was curious about you coming back two days in a row and tried to pump me for information. Also, this has me scared and I wondered if you could stop by my apartment after work. If you can make it the pizza's on me." She gave me her address and said she'd be home by five thirty. I had about two and half hours and thought it best to make a few calls and check in with Bobbie and the Arm.

Chapter Twenty-One

I stayed where I was and called Bobbie's cell. "Hiya, Handsome, sorry I can't talk. I'm covering a double homicide over on the West Side."

"No problem. Just call me back when you can. There's something I need to go over with you."

"Sure darlin', bye."

I admit at first I wasn't sure about Bobbie, but the more I thought about her the more I liked. It was still too early to make any real judgment calls about her, but it's been my experience a person is defined by their actions, not their words.

Next, I called Aldrich's cell, which went straight to voice mail. I guessed he was in some meeting, so I left a message for him to call me back. I needed to see if he turned up anything new, which I doubted.

I waited around in the lot for about a half hour and got bored fast. I was going blind from reviewing my notes, so I tried to clear my mind. It didn't work. I felt light headed, almost like I was buzzed from inhaling too much paint thinner. Of course, the way the sun heated up my car didn't help, so I planned to get out of there.

As I started the engine, Aldrich called back. "Jonathan, I am at my downtown office, your father is here as well. We need to talk to you immediately."

"Okay, Aldrich, I'll be there in about fifteen, twenty minutes."

"I'll tell your father."

If I'm lucky, I'll get hit by one of the street trains on the way over. I locked my car back up and walked the two blocks over to Pearl, then up to Main Street. Once there I headed up to the nearest streetcar platform, near Mohawk.

Back in '85, the City Fathers finished putting in a transit rail system along Main Street, which according to some was a great idea. Others saw it as a giant pain in the ass. Main Street was now cut off from all car traffic from the head of Main down by the First Niagara Center and the Naval Servicemen's Park to the Theater District, where Shea's Performing Arts Theater, the Market Arcade Movie Theater and Studio Arena at Pearl and Main are. And this is where Aldrich's downtown office is. The streetcars run only above ground for seven stops, then go underground for another eight stops, going about six miles down Main Street to the University of Buffalo. Passengers ride for free above ground, but need to pay if going further out. It's a nice way to travel is if you're downtown and you need to get around Main Street throughout the city.

I grabbed the next streetcar that came by, and even though there were about twenty seats available, I stood up giving my legs a chance to stretch. I was at the Theater District platform in about six minutes, and then did my best to avoid the rush of folks trying to get onto the streetcar. I put my sunglasses back on since the sun forced its way from behind some rolling clouds that moved in.

I walked up to Main and Pearl, and strolled into Aldrich's office, kiddy corner from the Artvoice Newspaper office. As I headed there, I kept looking over my shoulder at the City Condos Tower. I was uneasy, and felt like I had two snipers aiming at me, which wasn't hard to see, being I was in the line of fire between the Addars' apartment and Aldrich's office with my family there. I began to wonder if this is how ducks feel during hunting season.

I reached Aldrich's office, which was pretty small and plain when compared to his other offices. This plain red brick building, with large smoky glass windows, only had a gun metal colored, plaque style sign in the front next to some potted trees that told the public this was the Downtown office for Kaufman & Heyman Law Associates.

I headed in and went right past the staircase that led to the second floor and the offices. Aldrich and his associates had the building to themselves so I wasn't concerned about running into a lot of people. I went straight to the elevator than ran alongside the stairs. The lobby was cool thanks to the air conditioning and it felt good. I pressed the number two in the car and headed on up bracing myself for the worst.

In the mid sized, cream-colored waiting area were two of the old man's 'bodyguards'. Robert 'Car Wash' Lupo, and Richard 'Big Mouth' Madono in reality were a pair of the old man's top hitters, or button men as my Grandfather would say. They got up and I talked to the guys for a couple minutes since I really didn't have a problem with either of them.

I left them in the small lobby with the secretary after I told the redhead who I was, and she told me I was expected. She was getting up to escort me to the inner office when I stopped her. "It's alright, I can find it."

"Uh, yes, Mr. Seraph, it's the last door at the end of the hallway."

While I walked down the hallway I went past photos of Aldrich with local sports figures and politicians, past and present alike, Jim Kelly, Pat LaFontaine, the late, former Mayor Jimmy Griffin, and former Governor George Pataki.

I heard the old man talking to Aldrich from behind the closed door, and just before I reached the office I heard a third voice and cringed when I realized it was my brother Paul. *Oh Shit!* I didn't bother knocking and headed on in, as I told myself this wouldn't be any worse than Sunday night. I was wrong.

Besides Aldrich, who was at his L-shaped desk, the old man and Paul were sitting in front of Aldrich, Michael was there too and he was pouring himself a whiskey from Aldrich's bar. As soon as I saw him, my guts tightened up into one major knot.

This office was smaller than Aldrich's Northtown's office, but it was decorated with the same sort of awards, photos and men's ornaments placed out on the various shelves like a small brass and glass clock, a wedding photo of Aldrich and Wenona, some crystal sculpture and a pewter statue of Lady Justice with her scale off balance. It was almost a perfect twin of the one in the Northtowns. I guess she too was looking for justice to be served as well. I stood by the shelves, which housed Aldrich's large collection of law books. I wasn't sure if he actually used them or relied on Westlaw and the books were part of the decor.

Paul got up and grabbed onto my right hand shaking it vigorously. I forgot how much he looked like the old man, when Dad was younger, except he was a lot slimmer and had a full head of black hair to go along with his olive complexion. "Hiya, big brother how the hell have you been?"

"Doing alright. School's going pretty good. How you doing, Paul?"

"Like always I can use more money, but I got a sweet little deal going I got to tell ya bout."

"Furgettaboudit! All that's fuckin' piss ant stuff. I keep telling you, Paul, you want to make the big money, you got to quit dealing with that street level shit," Mike said over the clink of the ice cubes in his glass. "You're looking good bro, but looks like you're still doing your hair like a girl."

I saw he was still a cafone, really ill mannered, I returned fire. "Thanks Mike, you're looking good too. Is that an earring you're still wearing?"

"Yeah why?"

"Just wondering if you're using a tampon too?" I grinned as Mike's vanished. He made a gesture like he was going to start something in front of the old man, except Paul held him back. Mike had no problem dishing the shots out, but he could never take them. If he hated that insult, I knew he'd really love what was coming.

"Take it easy man, you know he's kidding," Paul said as he handed Mike his drink and tried to play peacekeeper. I gave Mike a look that told him if he was feeling lucky he should go for it. It wasn't the big brother-little brother shit we used to do, this was for real.

Paul then asked, "You want a drink John?"

I waved my hand back dismissing his offer. "No thanks. So did you learn anything new Aldrich?"

Aldrich cleared his throat, rose from behind his desk and brought a manila folder over to me. Opening it, Aldrich showed me an investigator's report similar to Lee's. "One of my associates in Washington learned the senator has had a serious addiction to certain drugs. We are unsure of what sorts, but there is serious speculation he may have a problem with drugs for an increase in his sex drive."

"Now that's an addiction I could get into," Paul said. We all just looked at him, mainly because of his poor taste.

I turned away from Paul who just didn't get it, and said, "I thought as much. There was a stash of drugs that looked like poppers at Dana's. I think he got her addicted to them."

Aldrich continued, "Your father and I had our contacts find out. It looks like Ms. Tillis made bus reservations to Santa Fe, New Mexico."

"I already know that. Sebastian gave me that info, and I'm betting they're faked."

"Whatcha mean faked?" Paul asked.

"The other night I went online and found out anyone can make reservations and print out tickets at home. According to the receipt

Sebastian gave me, it was printed just over three weeks ago, maybe even before Dana died, depending on the time of her death."

Aldrich was wearing a dark blue suit, but his jacket was hanging on a coat tree. "We found out one more thing. A woman fitting Ms. Tillis' description was seen at the bus station on the day the reservations were for."

"Hmm…" I thought about that for a minute with everyone watching me then said, "I'll bet either that was a fake Dana sent on the bus to give a false lead just in case anyone began looking into things, or there was a real passenger who resembled her."

"Perhaps, but I think we are all too grown up to believe in coincidence. Unfortunately, that is all we have been able to learn."

"Great, might as well have been nothing then."

The old man got up and gave me a troubled look. "Giovanni, we could only do so much. It is regrettable we cannot do more." He came over to the bookcase where I was still standing with Aldrich looking over the file. "You know the old saying about accepting one's limitations? It seems you have done all you could to help your friend. And now with the girl found this is a matter for the police."

I listened as he made sense like he usually did, but things were still nagging at me. I thought about all the doubts I had about myself when Sebastian first asked for my help. The funny thing is for a while, I thought was starting to make a real difference, and I wondered if I did all I could do. Besides there was one more thing to go over. "Maybe you're right," I said, then flipped through the papers Aldrich assembled. There was a report, which was complete with recent photos of the Tillis family. To be honest, this actually looked more complete than Lee's report, which still bugged me. "Tell me something, did your boys find out anything about a local P.I. Charles Lee?" I glanced at Aldrich and the old man.

"Well, ah…" Aldrich looked like he'd been caught screwing the babysitter, by his wife, but the old man never lost his composure, like always. "There were some indication Mr. Lee's report was not as through as it could have been."

"Really, how'd you know?"

He looked begrudgingly at me. "Our man talked to Mr. Lee and he told us everything he knew."

"Hmm, sounds like there's more to it than you first told me." My doubts began to disappear.

"Perhaps." He couldn't seem to quite look me in the eye. "When our man talked to him, he found out Lee had begun his investigation, but someone met with him and told him it would be in his best interests to stop looking into the girl's disappearance. They emphasized their intentions by breaking a number of his bones in his left hand and arm."

"How'd your man find out all this, same methods?"

"No, that was not necessary. As a matter of fact, we paid Mr. Lee generously for his time and trouble. Not only was he cooperative, but he told us he would like a chance for some payback."

"Hmmm, that might explain why he seemed to be ducking me. I called him earlier this week and at first, thought he was blowing me off. He gave me some story about being out of town on a skip trace, which may be true. But I can understand why he'd be gun-shy." As soon as I said it, the room got uncomfortably quiet, like in a funeral parlor.

"There's something else..." I turned to face Mike again, "I found out Dana was a regular at Soho. I also found out you saw her several times, Mike. I need to know if that's the truth."

"What, who the fuck's saying that shit?"

"Yeah, I tell you and someone gets the shit beat out of them. I don't think so little brother." Then I got right in his face. Don't get me wrong, Mike's my brother and I love him, but he's also a world class asshole who I will kick the crap out of some day.

"Even if that's true, that's none of your fuckin' business." He took out his gold cigarette case, popped a cigarette into his mouth and lit it. "Besides," then he stuck his finger into my face. "It's not like you tell me who you're screwin'."

Stay calm. My temper was rising again like at the bar. It amazed and disgusted me at the same time how people can simply disregard a human life the way they do. They make tasteless jokes, snide remarks, and rude comments not giving a damn about those left behind hurting, or the memory of the dead.

I quietly said to him, "Get your finger out of my face, or I'm going to break it, Michael." This was his only warning, and I wasn't kidding.

"Bull shit." He took two steps closer.

I quickly grabbed his finger with my left hand and twisted it hard enough to drive Mike to his knees. He landed on the beige wall-to-wall. What surprised me more than anything was nobody said or did anything to stop me. "Now tell me, were you involved with Dana, you piece of shit?" At first, he just grunted, so I gave him a little more twist.

"Alright, alright! Yeah we hooked up a few times! Jesus Christ let go!" His eyes were tearing up.

"Go on!" I spat out.

"We met at Soho then, we went back to my place about eight or nine times. Jesus John let go! Pop!"

I finally let him go. The bile and disgust built up again. I quietly just said, "I knew it." As I left him on the floor, I turned to the old man and Aldrich. "Dana wrote down she had been seeing one of the club's owners and only called him 'M'. This could be a major problem."

Paul, who was helping Mike to his feet, asked, "What do you mean?"

"Simple, the police are going to find out sooner or later with whom Dana was involved. When they learn Mike was one of her partners it's going to be ugly, for all of you."

"How's that?"

"They might see Mike as a suspect."

"What?" Mike yelled.

"I am afraid Jonathan is quite correct." Aldrich said from behind his desk.

Finally, the old man spoke up, "Giovanni, I understand what you are saying, but your brother has an alibi for the night Ms. Tillis died."

"Dad that's difficult, because the time of death and exact day haven't been established by the coroner."

"What motive would Michael have to kill her?" Aldrich asked.

"I'm betting the police and D.A. could make a strong circumstantial case, especially with his temper so well documented in the news." Mike glared at me knowing I was right.

"You do not believe that, do you Jonathan?" Aldrich asked me.

"As much as Mike and I may go at it, no I don't think you killed Dana, but the police are another story."

"So what are you going to do, son?" the old man asked.

"Keep doing what I've been doing, and hopefully get lucky."

After I finished the old man changed the subject. "Giovanni I am sorry we couldn't find out more, but I do need to talk to you about your brothers."

Hearing this Mike and Paul listened more intently, looked over at our father and me. "What do you mean, Pop?" Mike asked as he finally stopped clutching his fingers.

"Michael, I want Giovanni...how to put this...help you and your brother."

Mike shocked everyone when he erupted like that. "What the hell are you talking about!?" He stressed his point by slamming his glass onto the bar, shattering it and spilling his whiskey all over.

"Michael you will behave yourself at once!" the old man ordered as he went over to him. "This is why you cannot be trusted! I love you, but you are still a child! Giovanni is correct. You are nothing but a cacasodo." If we were surprised before, that redefined our shock. I admit I loved seeing this play out.

"Jesus Christ, Pop!"

Then the old man did something that added to the tension of the situation, he reached out and smacked Mike across the face.

"That is for the blasphemy!" He calmed down then turned to Aldrich. "I want to give you my personal apology for this insult, Aldrich." Then he turned back to Mike and Paul. "You are good boys, but the two of you need to grow up before I would trust either of you with family business. Maybe I've indulged you children too much. Michael your temper is part of the problem, and you still have a lot to learn. You have potential to lead someday. Paul, you don't use the brains the good Lord put in that head of yours. Your head is always in the clouds, thinking about someday, not the here and now. If either of you want to be given real responsibility someday you need to be more like Giovanni."

"Geez, Pop," was all Paul said because he was almost embarrassed as much as Mike was.

Everything was clear now. "So that's why you wanted me back, not to as you put it, help them 'pick up on my better traits'. You want me to help breed them into the next heads of the Arm. I should have known better." I turned to leave.

"Giovanni, wait!"

Then Mike jumped in, uninvited. "Despite what Pop say Gio, I don't need your fuckin' help! Fatti i cazzi tuoi!" He told me to mind my own fucking business.

"Mike, Vaffanculo, tu Fill'e bagassa. Sei un Ceffo. "

I turned back to the old man "I came to you looking for help, and the only thing you want to do is groom these two idiots into the next boss. I knew I should never have come to you. You know how I feel about this shit and you still tried to play me!" My temper rose again and my face got hot. When that happens my face gets really red. "I guess I kidded myself into thinking you might change!" The hate and venom I'd held back since this all began detonated at him in one enormous explosion. "I bet you're still fucking those bimbos, aren't you. Does Mama know, or she still in the dark about that?" Then I spat at him in his own language, "Una volta un ladro sempre un ladro." Translation; Once a thief always a thief.

It was the way the old man's face turned into an amalgamation of a beet and plum that told me it was time to get the hell out of there. I could still hear him yelling for me when I reached the elevator and at the street door. I forgot how loud that bastard could yell.

Chapter Twenty-Two

I sped away from downtown on the 190 as fast as I could. I didn't know how fast I drove, but I knew I hauled ass. For years when I'm really pissed off, I've a tendency to drive very fast, at least until I calm down or I see a police car. Stupid I know, but it beats the hell out of hitting people.

I headed up the Scajaquada and pulled onto Main Street, and finally slowed down. Thinking about seeing Crystal made me feel better and I calmed down. Eight blocks later, I made a left onto Hertel Avenue, after a fire truck flew down Main going the way I came.

Hertel's a scaled down model of Buffalo and what's been happening here. The surrounding neighborhood is a combination of apartment buildings and businesses, some open, but there are a lot of closed storefronts. In many ways, it reminds me of South Buffalo.

It didn't take me long to get to Crystal's and I found her building near the intersection of Hertel and Parkside. There were a lot of local businesses like a Chinese takeout, a dry cleaner, a few bars, some stores, a Rite Aid and a Walgreen's all right there. I could see why folks liked living around here. You could take care of all your errands in a few hours of just walking around. Most of the businesses take up the bottom floors of what are mainly two story buildings and in a large number of the buildings, the top floors rented out apartments.

I parked in front of a pizzeria two stores away from Crystal's apartment, fed the meter, and strolled around for a bit since I had about twenty minutes before she was due to arrive. The sky clouded up again and from where I was, the sun already began to vanish. I heard what sounded like a little rumble of thunder rolling through the sky. At first, I wasn't sure if it was a truck or helicopter, but the echoing booms told me rain was coming.

To kill time I hung around the Walgreen's, across the street from Crystal's apartment. As I browsed, I wondered how and why I got into this whole mess. I was satisfied with my life the way it was a week ago. It may have not been perfect, but it was mine and I was relatively happy. Now I'm stuck dealing with people I'd normally avoid. I wasn't comfortable with anyone, well except for Crystal, Bobbie and Sebastian. When it came to the senator's people and my family I felt like I was waist deep in a backed up sewer.

* * * *

I headed back to Crystal's. I'd given her enough time, and I didn't want to show up at her door at five thirty on the dot. I figured she'd need a few minutes to straighten up a bit since she didn't have time get ready. As I was leaving the store, I thought I'd be a good guest and picked up a small box of mixed chocolates. I may not know lots about the females of the species, but almost universally they all love chocolate.

I checked the mailbox of her building and found Crystal's apartment number. I headed up to the second floor and once upstairs I knocked on her door and glanced around. From what I saw, the landlords needed to add some more railings and lighting fixtures. The staircase and hallways weren't lit up like they should've been. All I could see in the dimness was a pale, sick shade of light green paint on the walls. It all made me wonder if the Housing Authority ever had to be called out for this place. For Crystal's sake, I hoped not.

I was about to knock a second time when I heard locks being sprung and the door opened. A smiling face greeted me on the other side, "Hope I'm not too late," I said as I showed off the chocolates and gave my best smile.

"Oh, thank you! That wasn't necessary, but I really appreciate it. Come on in, can I take your jacket?"

"Sure," I said as I unzipped, pulled the jacket from my shoulders and handed it over. I glanced around her small apartment. From what I could see, it was smaller than mine, but still a nice little place. Her front door had a small patch of tile in front of it, with a floor mat saying in bright colors 'Welcome Friends'. The coat rack was right there and Crystal hung up my jacket. To my right was the kitchenette. In front of me was the living room, with a brown carpeted floor, a shade of light green paint on the walls that was bright and cheery as opposed to the halls. There were three windows on the far wall that overlooked Hertel, and from left to right was an old fashion blacktop stove/fireplace, a beige couch in front of the windows with a potted plant to the right. Next to the plant was a plasma screen, in front of the couch was a small coffee table where some books were sitting and finally there were a pair of wooden high back chairs facing the couch.

It appeared Crystal had a thing for butterflies and deer. There were images, figurines and various curios around her place on bookcases, the coffee table and on the walls.

"Nice place you got here."

"Thank you. Ohh..." Crystal was a surprised when my hand sanitizer fell out of my jacket pocket and bounced off the tile.

"Oh, that's always happening." I grabbed it and stuffed the bottle into my pants pocket. "Since I started using this stuff I really cut down on the number of colds I get."

"Really?"

"Yeah, nice to see there's some truth in advertising."

"Have a seat. Can I get you something to drink?"

"No thanks, I'm fine." I sat in one of the chairs while Crystal ran back toward her bedroom.

"I just need to change, after almost nine hours in this suit I have to relax."

"Take your time. I've been there myself plenty of times." As I looked around and picked up a small ceramic deer from the coffee table, I realized Crystal had her stereo on and I was surprised by her choice of music. It was an instrumental version of *Bewitched, Bothered and Bewildered*. I yelled back to her, "So why did you want me to come over? I mean was there anything else you wanted to tell me?"

In what sounded like a rushed pant, Crystal yelled back, "No, not really. I guess it was that creep Caleb talking to me. He freaked me out a bit." A moment later Crystal came out wearing purple and white sweatpants and a white sleeveless t-shirt and sneakers and with her hair tied back making her look younger than she really was. "I think I just needed some reassurance, see Caleb and Hondoa run around the office like it's theirs at times and today Caleb really shook me up today."

Crystal then popped into her kitchen, picked up the phone and I heard her order a large cheese, sausage and pepperoni pizza, which sounded good to me. Crystal then came out with a bottle of white wine, a corkscrew and a pair of glasses. "Would you mind?" she asked as she handed me the bottle and the corkscrew.

"No problem." I worked on the cork while Crystal lit some scented candles scattered around the apartment then sat down across from me on the couch. I pulled out the cork, poured Crystal a glass and about a half glass for me, even though I really didn't want one. I did it to be polite, because I once heard you should never let a lady drink alone.

We talked for a while and Crystal told me more about herself after I pried a bit to get her started. "Well, let's see, my favorite colors are rose and teal, favorite song, *High Enough* by Damn Yankees. My dog, Farley." She reached to the coffee table and pulled back a framed picture of her with this black, monstrous Newfoundland dog, that almost took up the whole scene. "He's still with my parents since I don't have the room, but I see him every day or so."

I laughed aloud at the sight of Farley mugging for the camera. "It looks like he was pushing you out of the way."

"Yeah he was. He's really a big baby. God I love him to death."

"Never had pets on the estate, the old man and half my brothers and sisters are allergic to cats and dogs. Fortunately I don't have that problem."

"Sounds like you lucked out."

"In some areas, yeah."

"What's that mean?"

I braced myself and took another sip. "Well, I haven't seen my family in three years, until the other day. My old man keeps trying to recruit me into the family business."

"What's wrong with that?"

I then explained the whole story. Crystal took the news better I expected. "Oh my God."

"Yeah, tell me about it. That's one of the reasons an ex of mine broke up with me."

"Really?"

"Uh-huh, but not for what you might be thinking. She thought I'd have a better financial future with the family business a.k.a. the Arm, than as a teacher. After our last argument over that we stopped talking."

"I'm sorry, I've been there too."

"Really?"

"Yeah, my ex-boyfriend was cheating on me with at least three different girls. Then he'd have the audacity to get angry with me whenever I'd talk to a guy."

"Ouch, sorry to hear that."

"Don't be. Rich was an asshole."

I didn't realize how much time passed because when I looked at my watch it said it was almost six-thirty. Talking with Crystal was easy and restful. I hadn't talked like this to anyone in a very long time. It was different when I was with Charles and Dixie or Mama, with almost everyone else I felt like I had to be on guard, at least part of the time. With Crystal, I felt I could be myself totally open and free. I felt like this with only one other person.

I gave us both another refill which killed the bottle. *So much for one glass*, I thought when there was a knock at the door. "Great pizza's here," Crystal said.

"Well I didn't think it was for me," I joked then took another sip as Crystal got up to answer the door.

"Yes?"

From behind the door, we heard a heavy voice say "I got pizza for a Bell."

Crystal pulled a twenty out from her pants pocket and she started to unlock the door. Once the chain was off the latch the door exploded and a hulking figure shoved Crystal hard, back towards the chairs before I could do anything. I got up and spun around to face a man wearing a tan overcoat and Buffalo Bills' ball cap pulled down over his face so I couldn't make a clear I.D.

All I could see was this gorilla was about as bulky and broad as an armored truck. I charged at him, but two things kept me from shoving him into the hallway.

Once I reached him, he kneed me in my gut. I was so busy watching his upper body I never saw his leg bend up and nail my stomach. I saw shooting stars, and felt like I was going to cough up a lung as my eyes teared up. The second reason I stopped was he pulled out a snub nose .38 from his pocket and aimed it at Crystal while I was doubled over, coughing and trying to catch my breath. The bastard dropped me like a beer bottle onto a bar floor.

While down, I clutched at my stomach and looked at Crystal who was petrified. I read it in her face, and so did the intruder. He was a pro, but I've been hit worse by others and knew from experience once the shock was out of my system I'd be fine, if I lived that long.

He slammed the door shut and finally raised his face high enough that I recognized him, it was Hondoa, the second of the Addar's bodyguards.

"What the hell are you doing here?" I demanded.

"Don't move, either of you!" he barked, then grabbed my arm and pulled me right up to my feet.

"Now, get over by the couch, both of you."

"What's this about?" Crystal barked as she pulled herself to her feet, but Hondoa shoved his gun in her face as a reply.

"Crystal, do what he says," I warned. We moved slowly by the couch with the coffee table to my left in front of me as I faced Hondoa and the door.

Growing up the way I did, I saw many dangerous men, and some wore their aggression like a suit or a splash of cheap cologne as a way to impress others. Others liked to show off to the old man that they could be useful, or showed off to women because some like bad-boys. Mostly they were nothing more than real big talkers when it came down to it, and couldn't deliver.

Every so often, I saw something else, a look in a face or an eye that told me this person was a born killer. I'd seen it in Richard Madono's eyes. I'd seen it in Katsuro's eyes and it was in Hondoa's eyes too. I knew he was going to kill us. It was just a matter of time.

"I take it you got a problem, bubba?"

"Nothing personal, but I've a job to do," he growled. Like that would make either of us feel any better.

"Gee, thanks. Nice to know we didn't offend you personally." I knew I shouldn't push him, but sometimes my mouth goes into automatic overdrive.

"So you killed Dana?" Crystal asked while rubbing her arm where Hondoa shoved her.

"Me? No way, but your boyfriend's been making trouble and I've to get rid of him. You're just collateral damage. Sorry babe, wrong place, wrong fuckin' time."

I had to buy time because that was the only thing going for me, and if I was lucky, I could get him to tell me who was really responsible. Either way I was trying to figure out something that wouldn't get us killed.

"So if you didn't kill her, why us?" I asked as I tried to sound cool, but right then I brushed my hand against my pocket and realized my hand sanitizer was still there. I felt that 'POP' go off in my head, now I had something to work with.

"Orders, plain and simple." He pulled out a hypodermic needle from inside his jacket. "See, with you showing up at the office and telling people you two were friends, this sadly turns into a disappointing love affair that turns into an accident and suicide."

I turned just slightly so that I was at an angle, and not straight ahead face to face with Hondoa. This way I was able to ease my left hand into my pocket without Hondoa seeing. I had an idea and prayed it'd work. Once my hand was inside my pocket I palmed the bottle. As I began to speak, I used my thumb to pop open the snap lid, and hoped he wouldn't hear anything. I had to keep him distracted.

"Nice plan, but won't it look funny to anyone who knows Crystal or me?" SNAP. Once I got the bottle open my heart stopped beating for a second, but it felt a lot longer. "And since we haven't talked about each other to our families or friends, they might not buy your story." Crystal turned her head and looked at me like I was insane. "Just for argument's sake how are you going to convince anyone of your story?" I asked while I tried to crack a friendly, small smile trying to make Hondoa think he was totally in charge.

"You two have been really discrete, and when you came over to bang her, you brought this..." He motioned his left hand up and down pointing out the capped hypo. "...it's full of Cheese. There's enough to kill both of you, but the lady will die from an accidental overdose. In your grief, you shoot yourself. Simple."

I knew the bastard played for keeps because Cheese was a nasty sex drug. I turned to Crystal and tried to still sound calm, composed and comfortable. Believe me, not the easiest thing to do under those conditions. "Well at least he has the whole story plotted out, nice huh? Since you already said you were under orders, mind telling us who wants me dead?"

"Yeah right, like I'm going to tell you. Guess this will be one of those unsolved mysteries."

I turned back to face Crystal to try reassure her. When I thought it was safe I gave a slight, fast wink with my left eye giving her the sign to be ready. "Gee that's a shame, because I really wanted to know. What about you Crystal?"

"Well, I want to know the truth too." She looked at me like I was nuts, but answered, not sure what to expect. Truth be told, neither did I.

I bounced my head between the two talking, and tried to dance as fast as I could and said, "See man at least let the lady know before you do anything. Come on!" then before anybody could do anything I inched myself closer to the edge of the couch cushion and toward Hondoa. Knowing I was going to have one shot and I had to be close.

I pulled my hand out, extended my arm toward his face and squeezed the bottle as hard as I could. It sounded like a whoopie cushion being sat on as the sanitizer squirted up in the air. with all I had. Most hand sanitizers are great for cold prevention, but being over sixty percent alcohol, I figured I might blind the bastard. I was able to hit Hondoa's eyes, face and clothes, then I moved.

While he howled in pain, Hondoa dropped the hypo to the carpet, but kept his vise grip on the .38. It flayed around like a kite in a hurricane. A long time ago, I learned the key to a knife defense is to maintain control of the knife hand. This also applies to being up close with a gun when the shooter can't see. I grabbed Hondoa's right hand, and hit him with my knees and free hand before he could wipe his eyes clear. I don't remember exactly what he said, but I recall he swore at me in English and something that sounded Asian.

The other thing about dealing with someone who has a gun to your head, you may have to wait for your opening by buying time, but once you have your chance, break their trigger finger as fast and as hard as possible, which is exactly what I did.

The sickening break reminded me of fresh celery stalks and Hondoa dropped his gun while grunting in pain. Immediately he swung back with his hammer-like left. It was wild shot, which backhanded my head and left me seeing another explosion of fireworks. I knew I couldn't out muscle him, so I had to out think him.

Once my eyes cleared, I saw Crystal reaching for the gun at the same time Hondoa went for it with his left. "No, door!" I ordered to have her open up the door to the hallway. Once Hondoa picked up the gun and realized what I said he looked up at me as Crystal ran around us and almost pulled the door off its hinges.

Before anything else could happen, I grabbed one of the candles from the coffee table and squeezed my bottle a second time, and shot a stream through the flame, which set the bastard on fire.

The agonizing screams Hondoa made were like nothing I'd ever heard before, and hope to never hear again. Before he could drop to his knees and attempt to put himself out, or burn up the apartment, I ran around him and despite the heat, I dragged him into the hallway by the backside of his coat. Once out there I shoved him over the wooden banister, and he crashed down the staircase in a fiery, smoking, screaming thud. On the floor of the foyer, Hondoa sent up a column of black smoke to the second floor that was joined by his shrill screams. The gloomy hallway was suddenly lit up with an orgy of red, yellow and orange glows and a column of heat that rose up to the ceiling.

Suddenly I heard doors beginning to unlock, and I knew Crystal's neighbors would be curious to see what happened, so I dove back into Crystal's and shut the door before I was seen.

"You okay?"

Her answer was she rushed me and almost collapsed in my arms. We were both shaking and out of breath.

"Someone will call 911, but we better get out of here, fast!"

"Why?" Crystal stammered out in her state of shock. I held her face in my hands gently in part to calm her down and in part to make my point. "We should call the police."

"We will when we're safe. I never thought something like this would happen, but since it did you're in danger. Till this is finished I'll make sure you're protected, because it's my fault."

I grabbed my jacket after I told Crystal to grab whatever she needed for a few days. I saw she wasn't happy about what I said, but she knew I was right. I blew out the candles and turned off the CD player while she ran to her bedroom and packed an overnight bag. I picked up the hypo and shoved it in my shirt pocket, and finally I grabbed the .38, opened the cylinder and dropped the bullets into my hand and the gun in my pocket.

"Ready?" I asked.

"Not really." I knew Crystal was confused and in a state of shock, but I meant what I said, this was my fault. These bastards brought the fight to her door, now I was going to protect her.

We braced ourselves for what was in the hallway and we got out through the back of the building. As we snuck out, we could see the hallway was full of black smoke and Crystal's neighbors wondered what happened. I couldn't hear Hondoa screaming anymore, and didn't know if he passed out or died. To be honest, I didn't care. We drifted past everyone, and it was here I caught the sickening stench of burnt, human flesh I didn't get before.

Once outside, in the rear of the building I tossed the gun into a dumpster after I wiped my prints off, then I threw the bullets down a storm drain. I got Crystal into my car and peeled out, avoiding an approaching ambulance coming down Hertel in the opposite direction. Once inside my car I think I finally allowed myself to be in that same state of shock Crystal had been in. Now I just had to figure out where I could hide us.

Chapter Twenty-Three

I kept my eyes on the road, and made sure we weren't followed. I don't know what was going faster, my heart rate or my speed. I learned a long time ago if you have a tail, a high-speed chase is a good way to wind up in a crash. Basically, losing a tail comes down to one thing, driving like you're a moron. Making a right turn in the left lane, hit your signal either way and go straight ahead, speed up, slow down, and make wild turns. Just keep driving like you went to grade school wearing a crash helmet until the other guy makes a mistake.

Fortunately, I didn't have to do any of this, if Hondoa had backup they stuck around long enough to watch him go up like a can of sterno and left us alone.

The orange streetlights that are all over the city started to come on and the only thing worse are oncoming headlights that are so damn bright they're like the lights at the airport. I was forced to put on my nighttime driving glasses, because oncoming headlights hurt my eyes.

Crystal curled up in the passenger seat with her feet tucked up under her. She'd tossed her gym bag in the back seat when I rushed her into the car. From the glances I got from Crystal she was frightened and not just of what happened, but of me too. I couldn't blame her.

"Are you okay?" It was the only thing I could think of to ask. I wasn't sure because she just sat there, seemingly catatonic. I knew she was alive, breathing, blood flowing and wasn't burned. Crystal was there, but at the same time, she wasn't. I didn't know what to say and any idea I had sucked. "I didn't think anything like this could happen, and never imagined you'd be in danger." I couldn't remember what I said back at her place, but I think I repeated myself. The quiet between us was frightening, and I didn't know what to do.

We were on the thruway headed back towards South Buffalo, thanks to pure instinct more than anything else. I ran on automatic pilot and if I lasted much longer, I knew we'd end up in an accident. The only noises were the radio playing something I couldn't tell, and cars that rushed past us. I remember I wasn't speeding because we didn't need to draw attention to ourselves.

Out of instinct, I followed the same route I take when I head home from school. I went past Buff State, eventually reaching the Skyway, pulled off at the Tift Street exit and headed into the heart of South Buffalo. The only thing I could think of was home. Finally, Crystal spoke up, "Where are you taking me?"

"I'm not sure, yet." To be honest I was just grateful she spoke. "I got to pick up a few things from my apartment, and then get you to a safe house."

"What about work?"

"Forget it. I'm betting whoever sent Hondoa, is in your office. They either killed Dana or had it done on their orders."

"No, wait a second John I need my job and …." she started to protest but as soon as she did I pulled over as fast as I could and turned to look her in the eye. The driver behind blasted his horn at me for my half-ass maneuver, and I couldn't blame him.

"You really want to go back there after what's happened? Hmm? Crystal you set one foot in that place and two things are going happen, first whoever sent Hondoa is going to know he dropped the ball and we're alive, if they don't already know what happened. Second, you'll be exposing yourself and sooner or later they'll try again. I won't risk your life." I took her hand in mine and just held it, but at this point, I couldn't look at her, because Fred came to mind. Sometimes when I can't sleep, Fred's ghost comes to me and the last thing I needed was another haunting my conscience.

"Crystal, you're not a prisoner, but if you don't come with me I can't protect you."

"What about going to the police? You said you've been in contact with them."

"Yeah, once we're safe I'll call them and let them know what happened. I know they'll want to talk to us."

"Why don't we just go to them now?"

I had a very good reason for not going to the cops now, "There's something at my place I got to get first to make sure it's safe."

"What's so important you have to go home first?"

Oh shit, time to confess. "I've got Dana's diary and I have to make sure nobody else gets it." To say Crystal was shocked was an understatement, but she seemed to take the news well, all things being equal.

"How did you get it?"

"I found it when I found Dana. It was locked in her hope chest, and I don't think this is something she'd want her family to know about, believe me. I read most of it and wish I hadn't. This is how I found out about her problems."

"I see." Crystal turned her head away from me again as she absorbed the info.

"I know I should've handed it over to the cops, but I've got a feeling the key to finding Dana's killer is in it. After Hondoa's visit I don't know who we can trust anymore."

Traffic passed on South Park Ave, and almost mechanically I locked my hands around the steering wheel as I admitted something else to Crystal, which was almost as hard as admitting my guilt. "Listen I know you're scared, but so am I. I don't have a plan, I'm not sure who we can trust or turn to. Hell, I don't even know about my own goddamn family. Half of them should being doing hard time, and I wouldn't put it past some of my brothers to sell us out to anyone looking." I closed my eyes and laid my head on my left fist and for the first time in a very long time, I felt overwhelmed.

After what seemed a long time a warm spark shot through me when I felt Crystal's hand on my right hand.

When I looked over at her, she gave me a look of understanding I wasn't used to. "Well maybe we can figure out who is really responsible, together."

I couldn't help but smile at what she said and her trust in me. "Alright, together." We were at my place in two minutes.

Chapter Twenty-Four

We swung in my parking lot and I led Crystal to the back door cautiously. Not that I was paranoid, well maybe a little, but when I got out I didn't hear any of the normal sounds South Buffalo has at night, no dog walkers, nobody was sitting out on their lawns or in the backyard from what I could see or hear, absolutely dead silence. It was even quiet on the other side of the fence and Abbott Road, which is almost always busy with traffic, nothing but unnerving silence. For a moment, it seemed as if Crystal and I were the only people on Earth. It felt like we were in graveyard, unnerving was the only word in my vocabulary for how it felt.

I walked Crystal to the back door of my building, and I tried to let my senses tell me what I couldn't see. Our footsteps on the blacktop, some night bird a couple blocks was crying out, then almost miraculously traffic passed by on Abbott and I finally heard somebody pulling into the Baxter's parking lot.

I didn't feel right until I got us inside and finally relaxed, but I only put on the light in my kitchen/dining area. I figured it was best not to advertise our presence just in case. I told Crystal to have a seat while I checked my answering machine and tossed my jacket over the loveseat. There were a couple messages and while I pressed the rewind button, I offered Crystal a drink. She took me up on a glass of ice water and after I got it, we listened.

The first message was from Sebastian, he called to tell me about Dana's autopsy. "The M.E. finished and he discovered Dana died from what looked to be a massive failure to her respiratory system and heart failure. Also it turns out she was pregnant, about fifteen to twenty weeks."

"Jesus Christ!" was the only thing I could spew and Crystal only closed her eyes in disbelief. Now I was madder. Crystal and I could look at one another with a silence that engulfed the room. She put her hand on mine and we shared the bad moment together.

Sebastian continued, "A full toxicology report should be in by the end of the week. Once I hear anything more I'll call you."

The second call was from Bobbie, she called back to tell me she had to write up her story as soon as she finished interviewing the police and neighbors involved in the homicide she covered. "Sorry handsome I couldn't get back to you sooner, but I've been interviewing a lot of folks today and I've to wrap the story up to make the morning edition. The deadline's at eleven, so as soon as I'm done I'll call you back. Bye sweetie."

"So who was that?" Crystal asked.

I wondered why she sounded so territorial, but explained who Bobbie was, how she introduced herself and what she wanted. I mentioned our deal and that I still had a lot to talk to Bobbie about.

I needed to see what she may have found and I needed to find out if she had any idea about someone showing up from the news undercover in the campaign office. I don't know if Addar and his people told me the truth or jerked my chain. Things reached a whole new level for me with Hondoa's visit, not only did I know things more dangerous than I thought, but I also knew I made progress. Someone ordered Hondoa to kill Crystal and me, which meant I made somebody nervous, and I have to admit the thought made me smile.

"I'll be right back. I have to get some stuff from my room. Have a look around," I told Crystal as I headed into my bedroom and grabbed my gym bag from the closet, stuffed it with a couple days worth of clothes, my better pair of sneakers, and then I went to the bathroom to grab my toiletries. I headed back to the bedroom and hesitated because I knew what I was thinking could make things go from bad to worse.

I pulled my mattress and box-spring partly off the bed which exposed the inside of the brass frame and the three support cross bars that held everything up. I was nervous, but since Hondoa and his people brought the fight to me, I sure as hell wasn't going to be caught off guard again. It was clear I was going to have to do something major to protect Crystal.

I pulled out my sawed-off Lupara shotgun and I honestly forgot how heavy it is despite its small size. It was about two years since I used it target shooting. After I put the shotgun down I reached for the box of shells I store next to the sawed off, then pulled out a cherry wood box. I opened it up and looked at my second gun; a five inch Mateba auto-revolver, nickel plated, wooden handle and it's one of few hybrid automatics out there. The Mateba isn't a true automatic in a traditional sense. It uses the energy from a fired round to rotate the cylinder and cock the hammer for the next round, technically making is a semi-automatic. Basically that means it has the speed of an automatic but the power of a .44.

As I held the Mateba, I used my thumb to turn the cylinder, which made a soft clicking sound with each rotation. Using the hand sanitizer was just dumb luck and it worked, but I couldn't count on luck. I needed to fight back and this was it. I sure as hell didn't want to resort to violence, but I was being forced to and I wasn't taking any more chances.

In the box, I also keep a gun cleaning kit, various tools for repairs and four speed loaders. Under the mattress next to the rounds for the sawed-off was a box of .44 rounds. I'm most comfortable with the .44's because they give me more control and penetration. My brothers and most of the guys that work for the old man prefer full automatics like a Smith & Wesson 9mm or the Glock, because they carry thirteen to sixteen rounds compared to my six. In a city like Buffalo, bullets can ricochet off cars or buildings, I've heard of it happening a lot. The Mateba can give me enough power when I need it, and only having six rounds forces me to be a better shot and to be in control. When I was eighteen, Aldrich arranged for me to get carry concealed license, like he did with the old man and my brothers.

The last thing I pulled out of from under my bed was a pair of black leather gloves, now to most they look like regular driving gloves, but these are special. They're my SAP Gloves, which are usually used by law enforcement because there's eight ounces of steel sewn into each glove, in the area for the knuckles, but because my hands are bigger than most, I had to have these specially made. It'd been awhile since I wore them, but they still felt great.

I admit I wish I could have some major backup like Katsuro, but since I was on my own I had to bring out everything I've got. This whole ugly mess evolved into a junkyard fight and I was going to do anything to come out on top.

I packed up the case for the Mateba and the rounds when Crystal came into my room. "Nice place you have here John. Omi..." It was the way she just froze that told me she wasn't comfortable with guns. Looking at each other, it was an uncomfortable moment for us.

I put on my shoulder holster then opened up the box of .44 rounds and began loading the cylinder.

"Is that necessary? Why can't we just call the police?"

"Trust me I know what I'm doing. First, we don't know who's involved. Hondoa worked for Executive Defense and so did Caleb, which means they're professional mercenaries. I did some research online and found out E.D. isn't just a bodyguard service, they get hired out as guns-for-hire, but on a military level. So bringing a body bag or whatever else they needed to Dana's isn't out of the realm of possibility. Now these guys are working for a U.S. senator, and we don't know how high this whole thing goes or who's ultimately responsible."

"You think the senator's responsible?"

"Don't know. He's got the money and influence to pull off something like this, but I don't see any kind of motive here, yet." When I finished I put the safety on and slid it into my holster. It felt heavy and odd hanging there on my left side. It'd been a while since I wore it and the straps cut into my sides, but knew I'd get used to the feeling after awhile. I tossed in my cell phone charger on top of everything and zipped up the bag. "All I know is I'm not taking any more chances. Next person that tries to kill me, I'm pulling the trigger first, this is war." I looked Crystal straight in the eye and slowed things up a bit. "Now I can drop you off at the police station on South Park or take you to the main percent downtown where the detectives in charge are stationed, but I have to tell you I know there's a few corrupt cops out there. My old man has a couple on his payroll and there's one cop, who hates me, big time.

"My point is if the old man has cops on his payroll and God knows who else, I can only imagine Addar and his people have similar arrangements. I don't want word getting back to that cop or anyone like him. I know it sounds paranoid, but believe me I've heard too many stories from the Arm to know bad things like that happen."

"What about going to my parents? I mean my dad's smart, maybe he can come up with an idea or two." I shook my head, because when Crystal was packing I thought about her family being nearby as an option but rejected the idea of taking her there.

"If Hondoa's people were ready to kill us, they'd be willing to slaughter your family. It's bad enough you're in the middle of this, I won't endanger their lives."

"I didn't think of that. Alright I'll go with you, but where are we going to hide if we can't stay here?"

"I've been thinking about that, there may be a place out by the airport."

I put my mattress back in place, grabbed up my bag, stuffed the gloves in, grabbed the shotgun and turned out the light. As we headed back into the dining area, I told Crystal about some of the safe houses the Arm used in Buffalo and the suburbs. I knew about them for a long time, ever since I was a teenager, but never been inside any of them. There were a few times when the old man crashed at them for this reason or that, but never for that long.

The one in mind was at Aero and Wherle out near Amherst, by Erie Community College's North campus. The place was a small six room house that had been abandoned by the Arm for a while now, at least that's what I heard. It was the best I could come up with and I doubted anyone would look for us there.

The final thing I did was get the diary from where I stashed it in my linen closet.

Crystal and I headed out the backdoor as I carried my bag and shotgun in one hand. I opened the backdoor and tossed the bag inside then placed the Lupara under our bags, just in case we got pulled over by the police for some reason I didn't want anyone to see I was carrying. I opened Crystal's door for her then shut it as soon as soon as she got in, then I walked round to my side, and suddenly I was overrun by the feeling we were being watched.

I looked around in the darkness and tried in vain to find an enemy who wasn't there. After a tense moment I was positive we were alone, confident my paranoia ran into the red-zone, and finally I got into my car and pulled away from home, not certain I'd see it again.

Chapter Twenty-Five

It took us around twenty minutes to get to the safe-house and it was almost nine-thirty by the time we got there. We took the thruway, went past Walden Avenue and made our way up to Union Road. From there I got onto Wherle Drive and headed into a residential neighborhood. Finally, we drove past the backside of the airport and near the golf-ball like weather-radar tower I turned onto Aero. Just past the nice two-story country home was the safe-house just as I remembered it, dark, small, gloomy. Now that I was looking at it may have been worse than I remembered.

Crystal didn't say much on the ride out, but neither did I. I think we both were still in shock after what happened, but since we left her apartment, I knew she saw me in a different light, and to be honest I knew I'd changed too. I also knew I had more of my father in me than I ever admitted to anyone, even myself. This was a part of me I hated, but it's something I can't do anything about. Perhaps it was a part I needed to survive.

"So are we just going to sit here?" Crystal asked.

"Sorry, it's…it's just been awhile since I saw this place. We should be safe."

We headed toward the front door. "What are you looking for?" Crystal asked while I glanced back and forth at the bushes in front of the living room window.

"There's a fake rock here, somewhere. You know, one of those hide-a-keys."

"I was expecting a major security system or something from the way you were talking."

I bent over towards the bushes that needed some major trimming, and began going through the bigger rocks that were lining the area. I tossed aside the real ones until I found the fake one.

"Yeah, that's what a lot of folks think. Most would never figure to get inside a place like this all you'd need is just a key." Finally, I felt cold plastic instead of stone. "I think this is it," then picked up the phony rock. I popped the rear panel off the back, dropped the key into my hand and put the fake back. I went up the three steps to the storm door then unlocked the front door.

Crystal started to follow me up the steps as I tried to find the light switch. Finally, I pulled out my keychain which has a small light on it. I squeezed the two sides and the bright blue light sliced through the dark. I passed the light back and forth until I found the light switch on the wall next to me, flipped it and saw the dump for the toilet it really was.

The air was musty and against the far wall was an old-fashioned ceiling-to-floor lamp with three swivel lights attached on the pole. The walls had fake wood paneling, totally in the style of the late sixties and seventies. There were hard wood floors that had seen better days. The only furniture in here was a brown and tan patterned couch with three good legs, a crummy old rectangular coffee table and a TV stand that was cleared out of everything except dust, just like the rest of the house. Two steps away from the living room was the dining area where there was a beaten up old wood table that still had all four of its chairs. They looked in pretty good shape and there were a number of playing cards scattered on top of the table with a cardboard poker set.

Between the living and dining areas was a small bathroom in serious need of cleaning. From the looks of the place, I doubted the old man or anyone else cleaned while they were using the hideout. It was so bad I couldn't tell what color the tile on the floor or walls were supposed to be.

The kitchen had linoleum flooring that used to be white I'm assuming, but now was yellowed and filthy. An old gas stove was there, but wasn't hooked up. No fridge and half the white cupboards were opened and empty, I figured the rest of cabinets were the same. Finally, the bedroom off the kitchen was a mess, with a beat up bed, small dresser and nightstand by the bed. There weren't any sheets or blankets on the mattress, but I doubted they'd help because of the holes and springs poking through. I could only imagine how bad it'd be to sleep on.

After looking around, we stood in the living room and I saw Crystal became uneasy again. She held her sides and when I reached out to put my hand on her shoulder, she bolted away like a frightened colt. "Don't touch me!" and she back stepped into the wall that lead to the bathroom.

All I could see was this frightened woman ahead of me and knew this was her breaking point. "Crystal, it'll be okay. We'll only be here a short time, I promise."

"John, that isn't it, I mean yes it is but not entirely!" She paced around back and forth like a caged tiger that was agitated beyond belief.

I couldn't blame her for freaking out. This was a lot for an innocent, hell this whole thing would've been too much for some members of my family. Crystal yelled at me and waved her arms around like a maniac. I stood and let her get it all out of her system. I grabbed onto her and hugged her as she tried to hit me. There was no way she was going hurt me by pounding her fists into my chest, but I knew she needed a release. I wrapped my arms around her and tried to calm her as best I could. "Believe me, I know this sucks," I told her as she began crying. "I'm sorry you got dragged into this. I promise this will be over, soon. Once we know who's really guilty, we can get back to our lives."

Crystal was in a pretty bad state and right now I was doing all I could, but it wasn't enough. One of the things that pissed me off was that whoever was responsible affected other people's lives. It was bad enough they killed Dana, someone who needed real help and tried to turn her life around but didn't have the chance, but now they were coming after an innocent woman.

* * * *

Crystal calmed down and we looked into each other's eyes as I held her gently and stroked some hair away from her face. I admit I really wanted to kiss her, but it wasn't the right time. "I give you my word this will be over soon, and Crystal, I never break my word. Never have, never will."

"I don't understand why we are caught up in this whole thing. I mean once you found Dana that should have been it for you, why are you still looking into this mess?"

Guess it was time to be honest, with Crystal and myself. "Too many times I've seen people get away with all kinds of things because they have money, power, and influence, whatever. They tell anyone who'd listen "I'm not responsible", and it makes me sick. This is one time I can do something about it."

* * * *

We looked around to see what was left behind, and what we had to work with. In the bedroom, Crystal checked the closet and dresser to see what was there, and I flipped the mattress over and saw the bottom was in better shape, no holes or springs sticking through so I figured Crystal could sleep on it. In the closet, Crystal found some old sheets, a couple pillows and a couple blankets. "Great, maybe this is a sign things are turning around," I joked.

Crystal made the bed and I suddenly realized how hungry I was and asked if she was too, which she was since we never got our pizza. I headed out to the car, picked up our bags and the shogun and brought everything into the bedroom.

"I'm going to get us something to eat before everything round here closes up." I tossed the bags near the bed and laid the Lupara down. "I won't be long and since nobody knows we're here everything should be okay."

I opened up my bag and pulled out the shotgun shells. I saw her green eyes widen with apprehension, part fear, and part wonder. "Don't worry I doubt you'll need this but its insurance." I double checked to make sure it was loaded, shut the breach and locked it up. "It's really easy to use. Simply flip the safety here," and I showed her where everything was, "aim and pull the triggers. You can fire both barrels at once if you need to. Trust me if you do it'll stop anyone. Flip the lock, open the breech up and replace the rounds, lock it back up and you're ready." I saw an uncomfortable look on Crystal's face and tried to reassure her. "I just don't want to take any chances, it's like taking a condom on a date, I'd rather have it and not need it, than need it and not have it." This made Crystal blush and laugh at the same time. "I'll be right back." I came in closer and when we were less than a foot apart I lifted her chin and looked straight into her eyes. "So what do you want?" She seemed a little surprised at my approach and blushed again. "I mean what would you like to eat?"

"Think you can get me a turkey sub?"

"Yeah there's a Subway up on Union. I'll get us some other stuff too. Also, I'm taking the key with me and don't worry I'll lock up." Then I gave her a quick kiss on her rosy cheek that smelled like lilac. Funny I didn't notice her perfume before.

* * * *

In a half hour, I was back with two subs, one turkey, and one tuna. I also picked up a dozen cookies. Half were chocolate with M & M's, the other half were oatmeal raisin, which are my all time favorites. I also stopped at the Mobil station and picked up some bottled water, a couple bottles of pop, a couple bags of ice, a bunch of snacks and before leaving I grabbed some of the paper coffee cups by the front nearby the coffee pots since we'd need something to drink out of.

When I got back I found Crystal had done a bit of cleaning. The kitchen was a little more humane, the bed was made, the dining room table was cleared off and some of the papers and debris scattered about she'd picked up. Crystal found some garbage bags, paper towels and a few cleaning products under the kitchen sink while scrounging. After bringing everything inside, I pulled the car into the garage and shut the door. I figured it was best not to advertise we were here. On top of avoiding the bad guys, I didn't want the local cops snooping around. It'd be hard enough to explain our being there, but also I didn't think the legal owners would appreciate it, especially because my old man is the actual owner of the property.

* * * *

As we ate, we examined Dana's diary and Crystal truly began to understand how big a problem her friend had. We read how many people Dana had been with, how many times and in Dana's own words she had a quite a track record.

The list was really something, which included but was not limited to a bartender from Club Marcella, a waitress from T.G.I. Fridays, a cab driver who picked Dana up at the airport when she came back from a business trip last year. There was a pizza delivery guy, a parking lot attendant at the First Niagara Center. From her sex addicts group Dana had been with two different men, one twice and one once. A woman she'd been with three times, and finally she'd slept with Dr. Irons' secretary, a student assistant four times. I guess they really clicked, and of course Vince, and my little brother.

Dana realized how much trouble this would bring her so she switched from strangers and her therapy group to coworkers. It was here Dana started using code names, maybe as way to protect herself, or whoever she slept with. I wasn't sure why she gave the nicknames here and nowhere else. Maybe she realized she was playing with fire in this situation.

According to the diary one of the guys Dana saw was someone she named Bigby. Bigby was the one some heard with her in the ladies' room, but nobody saw or would admit to seeing. This also was a temp thing, a quick fix when Dana's urges got out of control.

Someone named Caesar became a regular thing. They'd been involved for more than five months and for Dana it was getting serious. Caesar told her all the right things and had some big plans for Dana, but he never got around to what they were. According to Dana, it was Caesar who started her on the poppers and she loved the rush the drugs gave her during sex, which was one of the reasons she hadn't been able to stop herself. Caesar also paid for most of the pricy dresses and the fur I found in her closet. She wrote of how Caesar cooled things a bit over the past few weeks and Dana had no idea why, although around the office when they could steal a moment here or there they took it.

After Caesar hit the brakes, Dana found a few other officemates to play with. One fella who was nicknamed Bull, according to Dana, wasn't the best. There was a girl called Angel who was pretty good by Dana's standards and enjoyed the poppers Caesar brought. About a week before she died Dana, Caesar and Angel were able to get together and have a three-way in her apartment. After that Dana listed her most recent partner as someone she nicknamed Cole. He hit on her at the office and she got turned on almost immediately and they made plans for the next night. That was the final entry. The whole thing left Crystal and me uneasy and I put the diary aside after we finished eating.

I'd taken the bags of ice and put them in the kitchen sink and left the pop sitting in the ice. I figured if anything we should have cold drinks. Then I checked on the bathroom and saw the toilet seemed to work fine, but when it came to the sink, I turned on the water it took a minute to clear out. First brown, rusty water oozed out of the faucet until the water cleared out the crap and finally cold water ran free. I did the same with the shower and it was a repeat, but after a few minutes, we had clear water running. Now if our luck would just keep holding.

Chapter Twenty-Six

Around eleven, Crystal finally fell asleep in the bedroom and at first, she was concerned where I'd crash. I told her I'd be in the living room, despite the fact the couch was off center.

When we said goodnight Crystal thanked me. "John I know you're trying your best to help me and trying to figure everything out. I know this isn't easy." She was calm and rational now, and seeing her like this made me want to kiss her, hold her and try to make both of us forget any of this shit was happening. But I knew I couldn't go there, at least not yet.

"Once we get this settled and stop who's responsible I'll make it up to you, I promise."

Crystal came up close to me and whispered, "Oh I know you will," turned around and waved goodnight to me as she shut the door. She seemed to be coping and I was grateful, but I just stood thinking *La donna e mobile.* Which translates to, *Woman is a fickle thing.* Truer words were never spoken.

* * * *

I double checked the windows and doors, and made sure we were locked down tight. I turned off most of the lights after Crystal went to bed. I knew this was hard on her because violence wasn't something she was used to. Growing up I'd seen it firsthand. The old man never laid a hand on my mother, but every once and while one of my brothers would get out of line and they'd get popped a good one. Only once did he lose it with Michael, because he mouthed off to Mama and the old man laid into Mike like a Marine Division. When you get shoved into a wall hard enough to knock paintings and ceramics to the floor, you know you just had your bell rung.

After I made sure we were secure, I went into the living room and stretched out on the couch as best I could, but I kept both guns within reach and filled all my speed loaders. I kept the box of shotgun rounds and speed loaders in the corner behind me, away from the living room window where I could get them in a hurry, without exposing myself and the guns were lying on the floor next to me with safeties on.

I flipped through Dana's diary again and while I was re-reading the entry about this 'Cole', Bobbie finally called back. "'Bout time," I said aloud and I realized I sounded pissed off and tired at the same time and she picked up on it.

"You okay handsome?"

"Been better." Then I asked if she heard anything about the Hondoa or the fire.

"Yeah, there was a story that came over the services. Channel Two's reporters were the first ones there, why?"

"Let's just say I was there and know a little about what happened."

"I've a feeling you know a lot more than just a little."

"We can talk about that later."

"Part of the exclusive?"

"Yeah, part of the story. What did you find out about Senator Addar?"

"Mostly what's already out there, nothing new really." Then Bobbie read off what I'd already printed out off the net.

The disappointment in my voice was apparent. "Thanks anyway. It was worth a shot."

"Hey, I'm not done big boy, I learned from a girlfriend who's a reporter on the *Washington Post,* there's been some stories when he was in Washington last year. Addar was having some sort of problem last time the senate was in session."

This definitely got my attention, "Your friend know what sort of problems?"

"Nothing specific, there's the normal gossip of drugs and booze."

"What sort of drugs?"

"Amyl nitrate." It was the sound I made that told Bobbie I was onto something. *Holy Shitballs!* I thought. My tuning fork went off as if it were a real one jammed in my shoulder. "That means something to you?"

"Yeah, turns out someone got Dana hooked on poppers. You

confirmed what my old man's lawyer dug up, from a different source."

"Really, that's something." Then it sounded as if Bobbie was scribbling down some notes.

"You're writing this down?"

"Yeah, I wouldn't be doing my job if I wasn't."

"Just remember our deal."

"Don't worry, John, I keep my word, otherwise my credibility would be shit in this town. I won't print anything till you give me the word."

"Okay, just making sure."

"I don't blame you. I know how some sources can get."

"Yeah, me too."

"I bet, especially with your family."

"What's that mean?"

"Don't get mad, John, but I've read some of the old archives about your Grandfather and Father. There were a lot of unnamed sources."

Maybe it was because I was tired and not just physically, but for some reason I got defensive and told Bobbie some info I know she didn't read in the records room at the News. "Let me tell you something, when I walked away from my family, a lot of people saw the old man not doing anything to me as a major sign of weakness. Others saw it as an opportunity, and tried to move into Buffalo and take over."

"What happened?" In Bobbie's voice, I could read her emotions, part fascination, and part fear, just like Crystal acted before.

"They were buried somewhere near Model City up in Lewiston. You know, near the Tuscarora Indian Reservation."

"My God."

I then let Bobbie know the cold reality of my father. "Believe me God didn't have anything to do with it. He could've killed me, but didn't. It's happened before in situations like this. I know what a first class sonuvabitch he can be, but there are times…well you get the idea." Then I realized I was ranting. "Bobbie I'm sorry I'm just tired. I'm just sick of all that shit. The old man and Grandpa were the ones who went into 'the family business'."

"It's fine, John. So what happened tonight?"

"Well, I'll tell you I met someone at Dana's office the other day, she agreed to talk to me and one of Addar's bodyguards tried to kill us."

"Oh my God! Are you okay? What happened?"

"We're fine, but to save us I had to set him on fire. It was the one bodyguard Hondoa. What did the reports say?"

"The latest reports are he had third degree burns to around forty-five percent of his body and a broken leg."

"Yeah, that'd be from me shoving him down the staircase."

"Jesus, John, how bad was it?"

"Bobbie, I swear he was going to kill us. Believe me this isn't something I'm proud of, it was him or us."

"Who's this 'us'?"

"I told you it was one of the folks from Dana's office." Then she giggled a bit in that same soft, sweet tone she used back in my living room. It sounded like she was trying her flirty charms again, and I was too tired to really fight them. "Well "us" is me and Crystal Bell."

"Really? So where are you now?"

"I got Crystal out of the city and we're locked down tight in a safe house."

"Did you call the cops?"

"No, my first thought was getting Crystal someplace safe. I'm the one who got her into this, so I had to get her out."

"That's really something. I mean why not call the cops?"

I then explained about Berriah and not sure how many other cops, if any were bought. "If it happens with the old man, I'd bet it happens with Addar and his people, too."

"Makes sense. So what's your next step?"

"Not sure, but I'm thinking I'm going to have to chase the bear into his cave."

"What? What's that mean?"

"I once read about how native peoples who hunted bears in winter and what they did, was they'd chase the bears into the caves, right into their dens. What I mean is I'm going to have to let the whole office know I'm still alive and fighting mad to see what kind of reaction I get. I think Dana's killer is in that office, and definitely connected to Addar. Should be fun to see."

"Really?" The surprise in Bobbie's voice rose up and she almost shouted so loud I had to pull the phone away from my ear.

"Yeah, I'm also thinking whoever sent Hondoa to kill us, is going to be pissed off if they aren't already."

"From what I heard Hondoa's expected to make it, so you may be right, but whatever happens just be careful, please."

"I'm planning on it." I had to admit I was surprised and touched, then Bobbie turned smart ass,

"Yeah because if anything happens to you I lose my exclusive." Then she began laughing.

"Gee thanks."

"I'm teasing you, sexy. Really, do be careful."

"Thanks." I noticed something changing in Bobbie's voice.

"I'd hate to see you get hurt or worse. So you have any idea when you'll know who really did it?"

"I still have some things to work out, but maybe in a day or two."

"Are you serious, John? I mean have you told anyone you're that close?"

"No, and you can't tell anyone, either."

"Don't worry about that. I told you I'd wait until you gave me the whole story, but what I can't figure out is why anyone would want to kill Tillis."

"I think I know from something I read in Dana's journal."

"Whoa!! How did you get that?"

"Found it when I was looking through her apartment, with her brother's permission. It was before I found Dana." Technically, I was telling the truth, even though it was by ninety seconds. I had a feeling Bobbie took more notes and started to write her story so I changed subjects to get her off track. I'm not opposed to reporters doing their jobs, but I don't like getting played. "So get your story off to the presses?"

"Huh, oh yeah. It'll make the morning edition, was another shooting over on the West side."

"Drug related?"

"Cops aren't sure yet, but they think so."

"Sounds like you earned your paycheck for the day."

"Why do I get the feeling you're teasing me now?" she laughed.

"Maybe a little, so what are you up to now?"

"Well to be honest, I just got home and right now am about to strip off all my clothes and take a long, hot shower. Sound good to you?"Back to the teasing with one hell of image in my mind, I knew I'd have to deal with Bobbie on this other level sooner or later, if I lived long enough.

"We can talk about that later after I figure out who killed Dana."

"Sure it's a date. Seriously just be careful, okay?"

"That's the plan, pretty lady. Once I figure everything out I'll call you but right now I got to get some sleep. You have a good night

Bobbie."

"Night, good-looking."

* * * *

After I hung up, I plugged my phone into the charger and set it aside by the ammo on the floor, then turned back to the diary. I tried to re-read Dana's words but I kept going over the suspects and realized how many I had, with just as many motives. For some reason Bobbie's nicknames dashed through my head, one after the other. Then suddenly my tuning fork went off like a gorilla hit it with a baseball bat. I grabbed a piece of a paper and wrote down the nick names of Dana's partners from the office and thought of who might want to see me stopped and wrote their names down too across from the nick names.

There were Bigby, Bull, Angel, Caesar and Cole, five names, five possible suspects. With some of the names, I thought Dana got a little cutesy. I wrote and re-wrote the names down playing with them, in different ways, and started wondering if Dana had some sort of code like the guys who make book for my old man.

Bigby, Big B, B, BIG B. They all looked like personalized license plates to me and then something hit me. Maybe Dana was really being cutesy and having fun, the way Bobbie did with me.

Bigby could also be a way to describe someone like big Sean Bruden, Big Bruden. It made sense why he'd lie to me about being personal with Dana. If Bruden had sex with Dana, he had a number of motives. Sex, jealousy, lust, revenge and maybe love.

Ever since I was a kid there was something a little different about me. Where most people would see things one way or another, I see them from a totally different point of view. There's a saying about looking outside the box, my mother says I live outside it.

Once I realized Bigby could mean Bruden I thought about the other names and it really hit me. Each name represented a character or physical trait about the person she wrote about. Once I broke the code, I started scrawling down the rest of the names and thought about what the variations could have meant.

* * * *

After enough time and some more Diet Pepsi, I broke the code. Bigby was Bruden because of his height and weight I assumed, anymore than that I didn't want to think about. Bull was Bernard, he was a born bullshiter. Angel was the easiest to figure out, with her being Angie

Eden. Cole was a play on the word coal for black and he was Tyrone Caleb. That left Caesar, and when I realized the truth, a cold chill shot right through me.

There's a line in Shakespeare's *Julius Caesar* where the Emperor, drunk on his own power, says, *"I am as constant as the North Star."* I thought it an apt line for who Caesar really is. I had already suspected it from the drugs and the reports I had gotten from Aldrich and Bobbie, but this was something even the police could use as probable cause. I finally confirmed Dana's secret lover was Senator Kingsley Addar, and once I realized this I knew this was going beyond ugly.

Chapter Twenty-Seven

Here's what I knew. Dana Tillis had a number of affairs with strangers, friends, and co-workers, even my brother Michael because of a sexual addiction that had become so strong a compulsion she couldn't get a handle on it. She had been introduced to poppers, which added to her problems. Dana was pregnant, and died from heart failure and respiratory problems, which I'd bet everything I knew was drug induced.

Akiro Hondoa tried to kill Crystal and me and admitted he was under orders, but never said who gave them.

From reading Dana's diary I knew she had not only been involved with a number of coworkers, but gave them nicknames, then after figuring out her code I had an idea who Dana been sleeping with. Even though that part of the puzzle was almost solved, I still had a few more suspects to look at and the motives were piling up like a trash pile at the dump.

I knew Hondoa and Caleb were hired guns, but just because they were paid by Addar that didn't mean the senator was behind everything. Although he had plenty of motives, which included political gain, possibly worried about blackmail, fear of exposure and definitely protecting his career. I don't know how many of his supporters would be willing to vote for a candidate who was hooked on poppers.

Of course, Addar had a lot of folks who I bet were willing to protect him like Bernard. Besides protecting the senator, he'd want to watch out for his own career and was looking out for his own gain and from what I gathered the man was an ambitious piece of shit.

After talking to Hope Abdi, I was convinced she was more protective of Addar than others on his staff. She was ambitious and

149

would want to make it to Washington D.C. alongside the senator. Her devotion seemed to border on the fanatical from what I saw.

There was Sean Bruden, he was having sex with Dana in the office but could he have taken it to mean more than it really was? Of course, that question could be asked about everyone too.

Jealousy, lust, sex, revenge were also good motives not only for the big man but for Eden too. Not to mention she had an attitude problem the size of the Erie Basin Marina. I've known women like her who thought they could get by on their looks and sex appeal. She could've seen Dana as a possible rival. Then there was one thought that kept coming back to me and I hated it. Could Crystal somehow be involved?

Between the diary and Crystal's account, I knew Dana made a pass at her, but I began to wonder if Crystal could've been homophobic. She asked me to show up to her place and I could've been the real target. She could've set things up with Hondoa, if she was involved. I didn't want to think about it but I had to consider it.

Finally, the cherry on top, my brother Michael. I liked this idea about as much as thinking Crystal was involved. As much as I didn't like Mike at this time, I hate to think he was wrapped up in a murder like this. Mike's done a number of lousy things over the years, I know he's guilty of assault, being part of a protection racket, working with the old man's hijacking and racketeering. I don't think he ever actually killed someone, and if he did I seriously doubted he'd use drugs to cause an overdose to do it. It wasn't his style.

Sex, revenge, ambition, rivalry, jealousy, lust, gain, love, blackmail and fear all real motives for murder, each one as old the Bible and seen in most of the works of William Shakespeare.

I started to go nuts because there was something I missed, but had no idea what it was. I knew there was something or someone I overlooked but I didn't know what and I hated it. This was like writer's block. I knew what I had to do; I had a general idea and made some progress but now was stuck and not sure how to go on.

I couldn't sleep as everything rushed around in my head like a Texas twister. The facts bounced back and forth and ripped through the same material over and over. Eventually something hit me like a beer bottle in a bar fight and I felt my tuning fork go off again. Thanks to Dana's diary, I made a comparison Addar to Caesar, but I thought *What if I thought of the wrong play?* Instead of *Julius Caesar,* it should have been

Macbeth. Now I realized there was one other suspect I overlooked, who had as much motive as any of the others.

Chapter Twenty-Eight
~ Wednesday ~

The night passed but I didn't get much sleep thanks to the lop-sided couch. Except for the crickets, it'd been a very quiet night and to be honest I was grateful. I had the time I needed to think of a possible way to get the proof I'd need. The problem was it was going to be a hell of a gamble.

It was after seven and dawn just broke. The sun was hidden thanks to the cloud cover above us. When I went outside in the front yard to stretch my legs, I smelled rain in the air. I figured it was only a couple hours before we had a downpour here.

When I got to the kitchen, I heard Crystal in the bathroom running the shower. Guess she didn't get much sleep either. I pour myself a pop and used some of the half melted ice, while I tried to come up with my next move and wished I had a hot cup of tea or orange juice to help me wake up.

Like I told Bobbie I had to chase the bear in its cave, which meant I was going to have to head back to Addar's office to see what kind of reaction I could get out of the folks there. The only question was what to do with Crystal? I wasn't going to leave her alone and for a minute. I was tempted to take her to her parents but quickly dismissed that idea.

I kept wishing Katsuro was here, if he was I knew Crystal would be safe.

After Crystal finished up in the bathroom, I jumped in quickly to fully wake up with a hot shower, and shave. The hot water felt good and at least for a few minutes it took me away from everything and everyone. Even though I admitted to Crystal I was scared, I didn't tell her how scared.

I wished I were a little more like my brothers. With them full, fledged Arm members they were used to the violence that crept around my family for the past three generations. Some of them knew instinctively they could throw down on someone and put two in the back of their skulls before the victim had a chance to blink. Most of my brothers were able to walk into a business and if they didn't get what they wanted they had no doubts about breaking up someone's property or bones either without any regrets.

After I cleaned up, I changed into my blue jeans, black T, and dark blue long sleeved shirt and headed into the kitchen to talk things over with Crystal, who was dressed in a rose colored blouse, faded blue jeans and suede cowgirl boots. Her hair was flowing free, covering up the temples on her glasses. She scrounged through our leftovers and opened up a bottled-water while I rolled up my sleeves.

I had one idea, after the day before. I really didn't want to do it, but had no choice. I called Aldrich's offices and only got the answering machines, *Shit!* I thought, so I was forced to leave the same message three times since I didn't know what office Aldrich would be out of today. I told him to call me A.S.A.P

"I'm going to have to back to the office alone."

"Two things, why can you go back there and not me? Second, do you want me to stay here?"

"No, if my friend Katsuro was here, you'd be beyond safe, the man's part samurai, part hit-man. I'd bet he's the most dangerous man on the planet. To answer your first question nobody will expect me to go back to the office." Then I finally admitted something out-loud to myself that I've had in the back of my head, "Besides, Crystal, I'm expendable, you're not. I think I know what we're going have to do."

For a minute Crystal looked taken aback then said, "Are you talking about calling the police?"

"No, but I will soon. I still have a bad feeling about calling them. What I'm thinking is I'm going to have to call my family again."

"All right, if you think that's best."

"Not really, but we don't have a choice."

Crystal came close to me again, placed her hand on my face. "One thing though, you're not expendable." That did make me feel better about myself.

We weren't in any real hurry because I wanted to wait and hear from

Aldrich before I did anything else. While we waited, we talked over options. "We've two choices and I'm not crazy about either, so we better talk them out."

"What do you have in mind?"

"Either I can leave you here by yourself, which you know I don't think is a good idea. Or I take you someplace else you may be able to come up with. The second option is if I can get some help with my family, and I have someone watch over you."

"What about what you said last night, about not trusting your family."

"That still stands to a point, but there's an old saying about dealing with the devil you know. When I go to Addar's office, I can't worry about you walking in there with me. What do you think?"

"Why not?"

"We know Hondoa is just a gun for hire, but I think Caleb's the one who actually killed Dana."

"You really think so."

I then explained about Dana's code and what I came up with, what the names meant, who they represented and Dana's last entry. "She mentioned a Cole, now the name could be a play on c-o-a-l which is another word for black."

"Seems logical," Crystal said as she reached for some of the cookies.

"What I can't figure is how Hondoa knew we were meeting." I kept an eye on her reaction, because the idea of Crystal being involved oozed back into my brain like an oil slick.

"I'm not sure, John. When I called you back there wasn't anyone behind or near me."

"What about those desks you sit at?"

"What about them?"

"Well I noticed you all sit at double sided desks, four terminals on each side, so there could be eight people at any desk, right?"

"Right, but like I said I was the only one sitting at my desk, and Caleb was already gone when I called you."

"Do you all sit at the same terminals each day or bounce around?"

"Mostly we sit at the same spots, unless somebody new comes in."

"You know who sits on the other side of your desk?"

"Yeah there's a couple guys, Charlie who flirts with me, Chad's married and pretty nice, a new girl Reba, nice but really shy and Angie."

I knew it and I thought *God I love being right!* "Do you know if she was sitting there when you called me?" The look on Crystal's told me she didn't know, but the idea never occurred to her which wasn't a surprise. I learned sometimes folks never think of the obvious and need someone else to help give them a clearer perspective.

"My God, you think she overheard me and told Hondoa?"

"It's possible. Even if it wasn't him, I'd lay even money on her ratting out to someone. According the diary Dana had a three way with her and Addar and when I first spoke to you, she made a pass at me."

This got a curious look out of Crystal. "So was this a pass received?"

I laughed a little at her joke and came back with one of my own, "Ah, no, actually it was intercepted, out of bounds." I gave my best smart ass smile. "Seriously you know her better than I do, you trust her?"

Crystal got kind of quiet and had a look that told me she was far away. "I don't know. I mean she never did or said anything to make me think she wasn't trustworthy, but now..."

"I know what you mean. I used to think the same way about people I thought I could trust. My point is I wouldn't put it past her. When I talked to the two of you, as you cried I saw something in her I didn't like. She looked bored, almost as if since she wasn't the focus of the conversation she didn't care what anyone else talked about."

"Now that I think about it she is like that at times. Last year we threw a baby shower for one of the girls and all the focus was on Gina naturally, even some of the guys were there helping out. When everyone was paying attention to her Angie seemed to be sulking."

"Hmm, says something about her character or lack of. I'd be careful around her." The reality of everything and what I asked came over Crystal like being hit by the spray from Niagara Falls.

"So if you can arrange it where will I go?"

"That's one of the things I'd have to talk over with Aldrich. The old man's estate would be perfect, stone walls, armed guards, electrified gates and enough anti-spying tech to keep out and frustrate the FBI."

"Think your father would let me stay there?"

"Don't know, we don't have too many father-son moments, and we didn't part on the best of terms yesterday. All I can do is ask."

Crystal put her hand on top of mine and we looked into each other's eyes, suddenly I realized we said things that needed to be said in our silence.

"I know it's just so hard to go into hiding."

"You're not giving up anything. This is just a temporary retreat to save your life."

"Okay, John, I'll go." I leaned in lowering my head as Crystal did at the same time, we stared in one another's eyes and just then my cell rang.

Normally my cell is set on my ring tone, but after the week I was having kept it on vibrate. The caller I.D. showed Aldrich's office number and I answered immediately. "Jonathon, I'm surprised to hear from you after yesterday."

"I know I'm surprising myself a lot these days. I need some help and…"

"I think it is best if you let things calm down before…"

"Aldrich, shut up and listen! I don't have time to fuck around and play games with you guys. Did you hear about a burn victim on Hertel last night?"

"Yes, the story was on the news and in the papers. Why?"

"I did it." Three words no relative of mine ever said. I laid out the whole story for the Consigliore and got to the end. "Crystal needs to be protected, and not from anyone who'd sell her out. This whole thing's getting too personal."

Despite the fact, I knew I shocked him Aldrich was still frosty and professional. "You have always had that 'gift'. That is why your father wanted you to be in charge. The funny thing is somehow I always knew you would never go for it. It was never in your nature. Even when you were in high school, I knew that was the case. Somehow, I knew you were really the best of us, Jonathan. Bring Ms. Bell here, I will make the arrangements. She will be safe."

Aldrich is a lot of things, but like me he keeps his word. That's one thing we have in common. I knew Crystal would be just fine.

* * * *

Less than an hour later Crystal and I were at Aldrich's Northtown office, and as we walked into the building my head twitched around like I'd had ten cups of coffee. I had the Mateba out and all the speed loaders in my jacket pocket. *Better safe than sorry.* I thought.

I don't think either of us felt safe till we were upstairs in Aldrich's office. Once there I made the introductions and Aldrich being Aldrich, he came off very charming, but then again he always brought out this face when he met women. "I called your father, explained the situation and he agreed to send help. Anthony and Beauregard will be here within the hour."

"Good, at least it's not Michael."

"Why not?" Crystal asked.

"Anthony and Beau are level headed but after the blow up I had with Michael I didn't think it'd be a good thing. Plus Mike's a horn-dog, I can only imagine what he'd try if got within five feet of you."

"I see."

"We will take you to a very safe condominium we have across town," Aldrich explained, "If you want or need anything while you're there, we will arrange it."

"That's great, but I really should call my parents."

"Please feel free." Aldrich picked up the headset to his phone and offered it.

While Crystal talked to her mother, and tried her best to explain things about the fire, and told a whopper about helping out a girlfriend for a few days, Aldrich asked me my plans.

"I'm going downtown and let everyone at Addar's office know that Hondoa couldn't get the job done. Even money says someone already knows, but I thought I'd kick over the hornet's nest and see what happens."

"Sounds risky, not to mention foolish, and dangerous."

"I know, but I have to see their reactions and see who I can piss off big time. Once that happens I'll have a better idea of who's involved." I did have a question that had me confused. "One thing Aldrich, why am I getting this help, after yesterday?"

"After your father learned you were almost murdered he authorized that you were to receive any help you need."

Stunned wasn't the word that described how I felt. I didn't know what to think. For the first time since this started I went totally blank. I figured after my last meeting with him, our relationship went from bad to worse.

After Crystal finished her call I told her I was heading out. "Aldrich and the others will take care of you, and without having to worry about you I'm hunting them."

She grabbed onto me so tight I thought I my lungs were going to pop like balloons. "Please just be careful."

I held her hand in mine and gave my best cocky grin. "Trust me, I know what I'm doing." Then I kissed her cheek. "I'll see you when this is over" I said to Aldrich as I shook his hand firmly.

Aldrich placed his hand on my shoulder then said "I give my word, Miss Bell will be safe. You just take care of yourself, son." His words stopped me cold. I honestly forgot how much he cared.

I headed out as they watched me and I felt them stare at me as I reached the elevator. As I walked away, I overheard Aldrich reassure Crystal. "Do not worry, Miss Bell. Jonathan is the smartest, bravest and most resourceful man I know. If he doesn't have the tools he needs, he improvises. He does not know how to lose." I couldn't help but smile at that and hoped she believed him.

When I turned around I saw they both were still standing in the glass doorway, I gave one more cocky grin, but once the doors shut it went away and I thought of Tennyson's *Charge of the Light Brigade and the 600.*

Chapter Twenty-Nine

A half hour later, I was back downtown and ready to fight. It was almost eleven and the skies hadn't opened up yet, but it was gloomier. I felt a big storm coming, and took it as a sign. When I pulled into the lot again the attendant asked me if I got a job in the area since I came back three days in a row. When I paid him, I told the kid I was sort of working, but it was a temp thing and I wouldn't be around for long. It was the truth. While I sat across from Addar's office all I could think was *A mali estremi, estremi rimedi,* or *desperate times call for desperate measures.*

When I got out of the car, I double checked the Mateba and the speed loaders were still in my inside pocket, and finally put my gloves back on. I wasn't planning on starting a fire fight or beating the shit out of anyone, but I wasn't going go in like a lamb to slaughter. I put on my sunglasses, locked the car up and zipped my jacket up so no one could see I was carrying.

Just then a cold wind picked up and cut its way through downtown. I recited quietly, "Cannons to right of them, cannons to the left cannons in front of them, volley'd and thunder'd." Facing off against potential killers wasn't something I wanted to do, but I admit there was part of me that couldn't wait to see all their faces.

I walked in and said hi to Tiffany again, she asked me if I was there to see Crystal again. I told her not today. I stared right past her looking for any one of Dana's partners and once I saw Bernard talking to Abdi, I flew right by Tiffany and thought, *Targets in sight.*

"Mr. Seraph, I'm surprised to see you. Crystal isn't in today or do you like it here that much you keep coming back? Maybe we can get you a job doing something someone with your talents won't find boring."

The bullshit was in his voice and his welcoming, gracious attitude was a Halloween mask. "Well that's flattering and maybe I'll take you up on it after I finish the job I'm on now."

"Making any progress?"

"Actually yeah, I know who Dana was involved with around here and I know who had a motive to kill her." For someone so composed Bernard looked like an eel had been shoved down his shorts, Abdi didn't look that much better.

"Well that's really something. So you think you know who's responsible?" He tried to cover up his surprise at seeing me. He did a lousy job at it. "Yeah, I'm getting there, but I was wondering if anyone might know why Hondoa would try to kill me."

"What! Are you serious?" Bernard asked. I admit the look on his face read shock to me, but this was a guy who'd made his career in politics so he knew how to lie. Abdi also seemed surprised but that could've been faked too, right now I just wasn't sure how to tell the difference. I was dealing with professionals at lying and I couldn't help but wonder who was better at the game, the politicians, Aldrich, or the Arm.

"I'm very serious. The asshole held a gun on me and planned on killing someone else too, so I'm sure you can imagine I'm more than a little pissed off."

"I can't believe it, Mr. Seraph," Abdi said and wore a look of skepticism, so I emphasized my point.

"Believe this I've got evidence of what your boy was planning."

"Why haven't you gone to the police yet?" Bernard asked. I took off my sunglasses and looked him straight in the eye to get my point across loud and clear.

"You know about my family, and if there's one thing I picked up from my old man, it's that we take care of our problems ourselves. We don't run to the police. This is the one way, really the only way to make sure things are handled right." I tried to sound like the old man, making myself out to be more dangerous than I really was. I was mad and could feel my rage slowly simmer to a slow boil. This was more dangerous than my temper exploding like a bomb.

"That sounds ominous, Mr. Seraph. Are you positive?" It felt like Bernard got too sarcastic for my tastes and didn't get my message. I took three steps right up to his chest, getting right in his face,

"Believe me I know exactly what I'm saying." I had locked my eyes into Bernard's and I kept them locked there, until he finally started to look way too uncomfortable. He squirmed in his two hundred dollar brown loafers, and pulled at his necktie, trying to loosen it, while I stood there like my name was Wyatt Earp.

"So anyone here know why he would want to kill me?"

"Mr. Seraph, I doubt what you are claiming occurred," Abdi said.

"You better believe it lady, like I said I've got the evidence. I settled up with Hondoa, now I just need to find out who's the chicken-shit that gave him his marching orders." Out of the corner of my eye, I saw the Addars, and for the senator it must've been casual Wednesday. He wasn't wearing his sports coat, his sleeves were rolled up and his tie was askew. The lady was wearing some sort of light green blazer and matching skirt, and she had on a yellow blouse under the blazer.

They came towards us and I turned my head to face them. "Mr. Seraph, good to see you again. How can we help you?"

"How ar' you doin'?" she asked.

"Well, senator, I'm here to find out who wants me dead." I repeated myself and at first got a look of a deer caught in headlights of an oncoming big-rig.

"This is a man I have trusted with my life and my wife's, maybe involved in this mess?"

"Right now I'd lay even money on it, as much as I'd bet whoever gave Hondoa his marching orders is around here too."

"Ah cannot believe Mr. Hondoa is involved in tha' girl's poisionin'." Mrs. Addar declared.

"I can't believe I'm hearing this. You honestly think someone here has anything to do with the Tillis girl's death?"

I looked him right his face and said it straight out, and cut through the bullshit. "Yes I do." Addar finally understood how serious I was. "When I find out who's involved I'll kill the bastards. By the time I'm done with them they'll have wished they confessed everything to the police."

"Now wait a minute, son, it's one thing to come in here and say these things, but it's another to threaten any of my employees."

"I'm not used to having someone try and kill me and a friend of mine. Like I told Bernard here, in my family we settle matters ourselves. We don't let the cops fight our battles. I don't take prisoners, I don't negotiate and since nobody else around here seems to give a damn I'm going to make sure justice is served."

My temper got the best of me and knew I'd better get out of there. I turned to leave and Addar tried to stop me. He put his hand on my shoulder. By this point we'd attracted a small crowd, some were suspects, but most were office staff, some approached, others stopped talking or making calls, either way everyone was watching the show. I began to feel like Custer at the Last Stand so I knew it was time to leave.

As I put my sunglasses back on, I stared down Addar. "Just remember I know who Dana was involved with, I know she was killed by someone in this office and there isn't a goddamn thing anyone here can do to stop me. See, I'm going give onto Caesar what is Caesar's." I headed for the door when the senator tried to stop me again.

"Wait a minute..." was all he got out when I hit the sidewalk, but I was surprised to feel a hand on my shoulder pulling me back.

Caleb grabbed tight to my jacket, "The senator was talking to you, he wasn't done." He looked at me like he thought I'd back down. The look in his eyes reminded me of a Great White Shark, with black dead eyes, like a doll's eyes.

I gave him my coldest stare. "I'm done with him, now move your hand." My gut told me I was looking at Dana's killer.

I wasn't a killer like Madono or Kats, but there was a part of me that wished I was. To take an unregistered .22, come up behind Caleb when he was out and put two in head. I knew that would do it for certain. The .22's wouldn't penetrate his skull, but the bullets would ricochet around like a spinning top, ripping apart his brainpan, but that wasn't me. I wanted someone to suffer in jail and pay for taking two lives. Caleb was just like Hondoa, a gun-for-hire, but they weren't enough for me. It was going to be everyone or no one.

All I said was, "Move your hand." When Caleb didn't I jerked my upper body away from him and he reached for me again. I grabbed his right hand and arm with my left, and saw he didn't expect me to react. I pulled the S.O.B. towards me, hard and swung my right fist into his jaw. I knew I did some damage because my punch knocked him on his ass. Caleb may have been ready for a lot of things, but getting eight ounces of steel rammed into his face, with an oversized fist wasn't one of them. He dropped to the cement right away clutched his jaw in real pain. His eyes welled up then I added a finishing touch by swinging my right foot into his gut.

* * * *

By the time I reached my car, Caleb was being tended to. As I pulled out of the parking lot and made a left I passed by the office, with it on my right, and I couldn't resist. I honked my horn then waved 'Bye-Bye' out the window. If there's one thing I'm really good at its pissing off the wrong people.

Chapter Thirty

I headed home because I needed a few hours of sleep before I collapsed. I knew I couldn't get any leverage over Caleb, which meant I couldn't get him to flip on his bosses. I meant what I said about having evidence though, since I still had the hypodermic. I was on the fence about turning it over the cops or saving it for whoever gave Caleb and Hondoa their instructions and inject the damn thing in their heart.

I figured the best thing was call Detective Wolfe, or Sgt. Yagel. I knew they wouldn't be happy I didn't call them from Crystal's apartment, but I had to keep them in the loop. Best to get it out of the way, and I called but they were out handling another homicide, so I left a message for them to call me A.S.A.P

I crashed on the loveseat after I hung up my jacket, but decided to keep my holster on. I was right. I'd gotten used to it. I tossed the gym bag and the Lupara on one of the chairs, and the only thing I could think of was sleep. Exhausted didn't even begin to describe how I felt. *To sleep, perchance to dream-ay, there's the rub. For in that sleep of death what dreams may come when we have shuffled off this mortal coil.* Hamlet's words were the last clear thoughts I had cause I passed out as soon as my eyes shut.

* * * *

I usually never sleep on the loveseat because it's too short and narrow for me, especially since I flop around like a trout yanked out of a lake. I didn't sleep well. I had a bad dream with the Addars, their people, my family, even Sebastian whirling around me like a psychedelic pinwheel out of control.

The insanity ended when I saw an image of a young woman. I don't know who she was, because she was in front of a bright, glowing light. I had to learn her identity, but before I could find out who she was a thundering bell went off. The echoing clang went through my skull and I could feel it the front and back of my head. The bells became louder and more violent until I finally woke up to my cell phone ringing.

I pushed myself up and forgot I was on the loveseat, so when I rolled I fell on my back. Just glad I left the safety on.

From the floor, I grabbed my cell off the one end-table and saw it was Bobbie. When I picked up, I must've sounded like I swallowed a ferret because Bobbie wasn't sure she got the right number. "John, that you?"

I cleared my throat then I let Bobbi know it was me for certain. "Yeah, I just woke up."

"Good, I was calling to make sure you're alright. So what happened?"

"I got someone to look after Crystal, while I crashed. What time is it?"

"Almost four."

Christ! "I thought I'd be asleep for a couple hours, not half the day."

"Are you alright?"

"Yeah, it's just that I was up all night making sure no one would surprise us."

"You know you had me worried."

"Didn't mean to scare you." Then I remembered what I needed to speak to Bobbie about. "By the way, do you know if anyone from the News tried to get in Addar's office?" I could almost hear Bobbie swallow her lips when she let out an Eeek. "Well?"

"Why ask?"

"Addar told me they thought someone tried to slip their way in and I thought you might have heard something at your office."

"Did you get any names?" Bobbie's asking told me she knew something.

"No, just a few rumors."

"I'll tell you, one of our undercover reporters tried to get in. A contact made up some false credentials, driver's license, social security, even credit cards, the whole package. He went to office in disguise and has been waiting to hear. I don't think they're going to call back."

"I'm willing to bet they knew your friend's cover was phony. Bobbie listen to me, this is some serious shit we're in. If Addar's people are as good as my old man's they may know it was your friend, but you could be in danger too, since you're covering this story and they're suspicious of the News. Where are you?"

"I'm at the office. What are you talking about?" Her tone changed and a touch of fear was there now. "Are you serious, John?"

"Yeah I am. Now listen, Addar's security man Caleb is a pro I'm thinking if my old man's people can find out all kinds of shit, these guys can too." I'd wanted to keep Bobbie from panicking. "When you left my place, there was an SUV parked nearby, I never saw it before. When I headed toward it, the driver peeled out. Now whether it has anything to do with you or me I don't know. I honestly don't think they're onto to you, but promise me you'll stay at the office until you hear from me."

"You're not kidding are you?" She sounded nervous and I think she finally realized this wasn't a game.

"No I'm not. There's security all over the News, people have to sign in and there are cameras all over the place. You stay there and you should be safe. Right now armed guards and witnesses are your best friends."

"John, I can hear something in your voice." She was right. I was planning something now that my head was clear, and since I hadn't heard from the police yet, I couldn't sit back and wait for Caleb's boss to make the next move. I already set things in motion, but now I had to prime the pump.

"If my idea works, we'll all be safe, Dana's killers will be caught and you'll get that exclusive."

"And if it doesn't?"

I let a moment of silence say what I couldn't. We both knew this whole thing was risky and I could die. Either way, I knew this was going to end tonight!

"It's four now, you've got to promise me you'll stay where you're at and wait for me to call you, okay?"

"John what are you up to?"

"Just promise you'll do what I ask. If you don't hear from me in eight hours, I want you to call Aldrich Kaufman. He's my old man's lawyer. He knows what's been going on and he'll know what to do. Tell him everything that's happened, everything you know and give him Dana's diary."

"What?"

"I'm going to hide it under a trash dumpster that's around the block from me. It'll be under a grocery store's cardboard container, the green, recycling type."

"John, you're scaring me. Can't you wait?"

"These bastards are playing for keeps. They've money, power, and influence. They think they're above the law and everyone else."

"John, whatever you're thinking call the cops first!"

"I'm going to. I'm not suicidal but I'm not running anymore."

"What are you going to do?"

"Get the proof needed to hang them all. "This morning I went into the bear's cave, now I need to draw them out."

"What do have in mind?"

"Letting them know I have the diary and using the right bait. I know this isn't going to be easy, but at the very least I'm expecting Caleb to try and kill me."

"You seem to be taking the idea pretty calm." Bobbie got upset with me and I figured she thought I wasn't taking things seriously. It took me several minutes to convince her I thought my way through this plan. She promised to do what I asked, but only if I'd call the police.

"I told you that was already part of the plan. To draw them out I'll mention Dana's diary when I call Caleb, who, being the good soldier boy I know he is, will pass the message up the food change."

"Alright, John, I don't like it, but I'll go along with your plan." Then she changed her tone from worry and concern to flirting and playing again. "Besides I still need your exclusive and believe me if it gets me the front page, I'll give you something special."

Hello! If I wasn't awake before, I was now. "Really, any clues as to what that'll be?"

"Well I know you'll just love it. Bye cutie"

Tira de più un pél de figa che un carro de bò. There's a crass translation, but essentially it means "Woman has a great power on man."

Chapter Thirty-One

After I talked to Bobbie, I called Aldrich's cell to find out where he hid Crystal and how she was doing. "Miss Bell is quite well, Jonathan. We have her in one of the out-of-the-way safe-houses near the Eastern Hills Mall. Actually it turns out Miss Bell is quite the poker player. She has been beating Beauregard and Anthony all afternoon. I believe they're out over sixty dollars."

I laughed so hard I coughed. My brothers were decent gamblers, but I was always better than them, especially at Texas Hold'em and Blackjack. The thought of Crystal beating them was just too good and after the week I was having I needed the laugh.

"Well maybe you should tell the boys to quit while they still have their watches, jewelry, and clothes."

"Sound advice. I assume you would like to speak to Miss Bell."

"You're right, Consigliore." I kept laughing. Half a minute later I heard a very relieved Crystal on the phone then I had Crystal put me on speaker phone so Aldrich could hear a fast rundown of what happened and my plans.

"First, there's a reporter at the *Buffalo News*, Bobbie Bedell, whose been helping me get some information I need. I got a feeling she could be in danger too. She's at the paper right now, I told her to call you if she doesn't hear from me by midnight."

"Jonathan, what are planning?" I heard the alarm in Aldrich's voice rise a couple octaves and knew his concern was for real.

"I'm taking the fight to them. If Bobbie calls you, she'll have a copy of Dana's diary with my notes. I figured out who Dana was sleeping with and if word gets out any plans Addar has for the White House will be dead before they get started. He wouldn't make the primary for county dogcatcher.

"Aldrich, if things go bad, you and the old man will know what to do. If I can't finish things tonight I want you guys to work with Bobbie, and promise me you'll protect her and Crystal and no matter what take the sons-of-bitches down."

"John, call the police, please!" Repeating Bobbie's demand, Crystal begged, but it almost sounded like she was giving me an order. Didn't know the girl cared that much.

"That's part of the plan, kiddo. I'm going to try to get a confession from who's responsible and have the cops there. If they don't show I maybe up a creek."

"Do you have a 'boat' at least, Jonathan?"

"Yeah, but after what happened at Crystal's I'm bringing everything I've got to the dance."

"I take it you have an idea of who is behind it all."

"Yeah, I do, and no matter what happens, I already know when the story breaks not only is the shit going to hit the fan, but there's going to be a ton of pissed off people."

"Jonathan, have you thought this whole situation out?"

"I could've told Sebastian 'No way' and Dana would still be stuffed under her bed, leaving her family still wondering what happened to her. You know what happened when I didn't do the right thing before Aldrich, that's not going to happen this time."

* * * *

After I told them my plan and who I suspected, they wished me luck and I said goodbye. After I hung up, I couldn't help but think this could be the last time I talked to them and the thought put me on edge.

After Fred died, I had a long time to think things out, especially after Mama talked to me and I finally realized I wasn't going to live forever. In time, I learned to accept my own death. I didn't know where or when it would happen but coming to terms with the inevitable and accepting them brought me some peace. I know it sounds a little crazy, but there really is something to this. I'm not looking to die, but I'm not afraid to die, and I honestly believe that's the difference between me and them. It gave me an edge. I think Katsuro felt the same way since he was a student of Bushido.

After I cleared my head with cold water and gave myself a final once over in the bathroom, I looked at my reflection and told myself,

"All right you sonuvabitch, nothing to it but to do it."

I picked up the diary, all the notes I made, and wrapped them up in a plastic wrap and tossed the package in a pair of plastic shopping bags, which I tied up one inside the other, I drove over to Charles and Dixie's store.

I pulled in straight for the rear of the building. The recycling bin was by the fence, and I slid the package underneath. As I walked back to my car I prayed nothing would happen to it. I brought out my cell and called the campaign office. I knew the place was open till eight o'clock and someone would still be there.

When the receptionist picked up I asked to speak to Caleb. She told me he wasn't there but could call forward me to his cell if I liked. I told her to go ahead. A minute later, I heard the baritone voice pick up, "This is Caleb."

"How's the jaw?"

"Seraph, you got some balls man."

"And you and Hondoa don't have any brains. Otherwise I wouldn't have to make Korean Barbeque."

"That makes two I owe you mother-fucker."

Awhile back I learned if you piss off an enemy, you can get them not thinking right, and they're more likely to make mistakes, so I figured what the hell and I primed the pump some more. Besides, it was fun pissing the bastard off.

"So how's your boyfriend, regular or extra-crispy?" I swear I heard his teeth grinding in total rage. "Seems to me he got off lucky, I could've killed him."

"Next time I see you, you're dead." Now I've enraged a lot of folks, having driven some absolutely fucking nuts. Knowing how to get to them and pushing the right buttons, but this is the first time I ever got someone so crazy they actually threatened my life.

"You done pissing and moaning, yes, no, I really don't care. I'm calling you to deliver a message."

"What?"

"You heard me stupid. You get to play mailman, and tell your bosses—your real bosses—I know who killed Dana and if they want to deal with me tell them I'll meet them at Forrest Lawn at five thirty. If you can't remember the message I'll be happy to text you. Want to give me your number?" Either he had better self control than I thought or he immediately called the Mastermind because he just hung up on me.

Chapter Thirty-Two

I was betting a lot on a hunch, and the only thing I was positive of was who I'd meet at the cemetery. Caleb would be around somewhere, but he wouldn't be the one meeting me. If he was the good soldier boy I suspected him to be, he called the one who signed Dana's death warrant. I made the meeting for five thirty. Hopefully it didn't give them enough time to plan anything. It wouldn't give time to plan anything.

There were a number of roads and paths, and it was a public place so I figured he'd just try to either shoot me. One of the reasons I picked Forest Lawn was I could see them coming. There was no way they could sneak up and I knew I'd have to grow an extra set of eyes since I didn't have anyone watching my ass.

* * * *

It was just before five thirty when I got to the cemetery and Forest Lawn's something amazing. It's about four blocks from school and there's over two hundred and fifty acres filled with over one hundred and fifty thousand residents buried there. Some of the more famous residents include President Millard Fillmore and his two wives, the Senecan Indian Chief Red Jacket, Frederick Cook who discovered the North Pole, and singer Rick James.

The landscaping is stunning, even in the middle of winter people still take the official tours that circle the grounds with the monuments and memorials like the statue of Red Jacket, the Birge Memorial, and the Three Graces statue in the middle of Mirror Lake which is where I parked.

* * * *

I swung through the Delaware entrance and went past the office, then followed the signs until I got in front of Mirror Lake. I parked on the section of road between the lake and Scajaquada Creek. There were a number of visitors touring the grounds so I kept the Mateba in my shoulder holster with my speed loaders in my inside jacket pocket. The hypodermic was still in my shirt pocket, and I put my gloves back on.

I noticed it got colder or maybe it was just my imagination. It looked like rain clouds were coming closer to the city. It felt like late November instead of spring and even though I wanted to zip up my jacket I thought it was a good idea to keep it only half zipped, just in case.

I thought I'd clear my head and get an idea of the area since this was my first time to the cemetery. This may not be the home court for either side, but if I have a lay of the land it might give me a small edge, and I was ready to take any advantage I could get. I set my cell to vibrate and double checked to make sure the battery was fully charged.

My plan was to use my cell to record the confession I was praying to get. I got the phone ready to record and I was positive if they got me, I'd get them one way or the other.

I walked around Mirror Lake, headed towards Main, then to Delavan, angling down towards Delaware and back around to Scajaquada Creek right near where I parked. I could see why people from all over came here, the grounds were beautiful and I'd like to come back when I could relax and take the official tour after this was ended. My mind drifted as I looked at some of the incredible tombstones and memorials, some reaching as high as twenty or thirty feet high.

There were fresh flowers and wreaths at one grave and the white and violet arraignment made me think of Bobbie and Crystal. Both as beautiful and delicate as the flowers, and both were competing for my attention. The violet ones reminded me of Bobbie, so vibrant and full of life, where the white ones full of purity and innocence represented Crystal. If I made it through this, I knew I'd have to deal with them.

There were visitors nearby and I could hear traffic build up on Delaware. It was rush hour and I began to wonder how long I'd wait around. After After five minutes, I began to feel like a clay pigeon and got a little antsy. I looked back and forth and all around for any sign of trouble.

I may not have seen any trouble, but I felt it coming around the bend like an oncoming train. I checked my watch and it was was now five thirty on the dot. I tried to keep an eye on both driveways, which was difficult since they were on opposite ends. Every time a car came by one of the roads, I acted like a dog when a FedEx truck made a delivery. I was anxious and knew I had to stay frosty and calmed myself down by taking some deep breaths and thinking about the girls again. It helped, a lot.

While I thought about where I could take Crystal or Bobbie, I turned toward Delaware. For some reason my gut told me this was the way Caleb would come from. It was while I looked over a marker of a local soldier who had been killed at Gettysburg, I noticed a maroon town car that crept towards me from the Main Street side. It pulled around one side and parked across the road from me, in the opposite direction.

As soon as the engine turned off, I reached into my left jacket pocket and turned my phone around so that the microphone stuck out and I held it in place after I hit the record function.

I couldn't see inside the car because the windows were tinted, and stood ready to dive out of the way of anything that came at me, but didn't have to because the driver's door opened."Good evenin', Mr. Seraph."

"Well, I'm glad to see Caleb can take orders and not just from you Mrs. Addar."

Chapter Thirty-Three

Despite the attractive, smiling face that looked at me, I felt the evil came from it. Like always, Mrs. Addar was dressed immaculately. Her makeup and hair were perfect, as if she just came from the salon and was ready for a night on the town.

My teeth clenched as I stared her down. For that one moment, the only sounds were coming from the cars that passed on the surrounding streets.

"Mr. Caleb passed on a message you wanted t'speak t'someone from the campaign. Ah'm 'fraid t'othahs ar tied up, so yah stuck with me, which is probably for th' best. Ah' can understand why ya may not want to come back to the office, especially after yah last visit."

"You're right. My stomach is only so strong."

She laughed softly as if I was joking. She laid on her own brand of Southern sweetness, but I knew it was just bullshit.

"He was right. I wanted to ask you face to face why you wanted Dana dead. I figured you had at least five motives to kill her, so that puts you near the top of my suspect list." Her acting was better than I thought but it wasn't unexpected. She had that same fake surprised look that was a trademark of my sisters when they got a gift from the old man they knew was coming.

"Ar' you serious, Mr. Seraph? You Italian gentlemen have some peculiar sense of humor." Then she let out a bit of a giggle. I stood quiet.

"Actually I don't have much of one these days thanks to you and your people." I knew I had to speed things up because I wasn't sure how much recording time I had on my cell. "I know there seemed to be plenty of folks at the office who had a motive to kill Dana. The biggest one, protecting your husband's career, but the one thing I wasn't sure about is if he was involved. He had plenty of motives coming from their affair. We're looking at possible blackmail, saving his ass, and I doubt your foundation will survive a major scandal. You can ask Jim Baker how well things went for him and the PTL after he touched Jessica Hahn in the right place."

She faked a shocked look that could have won her an Oscar. "Ther' is no reason to be vulgar, Mr. Seraph, besides, Ah' know Kingsley nevah' slept with that girl. She might 'ave been an office slut who was foolin' 'round with the staff, but she was certainly beneath my husband's notice."

"I know for a fact Dana saw the senator. As a matter of fact I also know your husband has some serious problems of his own, including a sexual addiction and using different types of drugs to help him get his rocks off."

She started to head back toward her car, acting angry and disgusted. "Ah' refuse to stand here and listen to yah insultin' accusations, 'specially after everythin' we 'ave done for the people of this state, and…" Her self-righteous indignation was the final straw for me.

"Save it. I am in no mood to hear your lies! I got the whole story from Dana herself. She wrote down everything in her diary, who she saw, how many times, how good they were in bed, even the number of times she climaxed. Everything was written down including your husband's addiction and how he got Dana hooked on poppers. Their pillow talk included how he wanted to promote Dana to his personal staff." I saw it clearly, now she was pissed, now was time to play my last card.

"And I know you were involved because of what you said at the office." Her look of Southern Belle sweetness began to change to confusion and after I made my point her face changed colors, she went from porcelain to crimson in a heartbeat. "In front of witnesses you said you didn't think the police would want me looking into a murder investigation, and that Dana was poisoned. How'd you know all that?"

Here's where I caught her off guard.

"Ah' must 'ave heard 'bout the murder at the office."

"No, I never told anyone Dana was murdered, and the cops sure as hell wouldn't have said anything either. I know your people are good at digging out information, and even if they found out Dana had been murdered I doubt any of them could find out Dana had been poisoned!"

"Yo' not joking are you?" She still tried to sound innocent as she shook her head. "Tha' isn't real proof. Besides, from what I understand Dana was seen at the bus depot."

"Yeah, that's was a nice touch. You had me wondering about that until I found out anyone can order tickets online from Greyhound and print out the receipts, which you had planted. I'm betting you had Abdi or Eden play decoy just in case anyone started looking into things, and when that happened you had Caleb and Hondoa visit Mr. Lee. Just curious, did you have them work him over or was that their idea?"

She kept up her 'Little Miss Innocent' act, but I got to her and we both knew it. "Abdi fits Dana's general build and a wig would disguise the hair."

As I made my case, I tried to keep my eyes and ears open for any cars that came by Mirror Lake, and were right by where the path that surrounded the lake forked. "I guess I should say you had all this done, because you're not the type to dirty your hands with intimidation or murder, that falls to Hondoa and Caleb. Plus I know Angie Eden overheard Crystal inviting me over, and then she told your goons. That's how Hondoa knew where we'd be when he tried to kill us. He told us he was working on someone's orders, your orders." Okay I admit that was guesswork, and it was a bluff, but it seemed to fit with her character.

"Well this 'as been entertainin', Ah' 'ave to admit, droll but entertainin'. Just out of curiosity, why do yo think Mr. Caleb did what you claim?"

"Dana's last entry mentioned a date with a man she called Cole, who she knew from the office. She developed her own nicknames for her partners, using nicknames she thought were cute I guess. Cole's a synonym for c-o-a-l, another word for black.

"Once I cracked the code I figured out who she'd been seeing and I'm only guessing how Caleb approached her, but he must've done some flirting with her after you all found out about her addiction. Offering her another chance to have another sexual high was something she literally couldn't turn down. By the way, how'd you find out Dana had the same addiction your husband has? I'm just wondering if he confesses everything to you or do you spy on him through Bernard, Caleb and Hondoa?"

"Yah're being ridiculous, Mr. Seraph."

"Am I? I know Dana had also seen Bernard once, I guess he wasn't that good. You could've gotten the info from that weasel, but it doesn't matter, the point is you found out Dana was your husband's new playmate and he gave her money and gifts and the new job offer. By the way, Caleb isn't as good as you'd think. When he injected Dana he left signs he'd been there, even though he cleaned up good, even removing some pictures of Dana and your husband from her bedroom mirror." Another bluff I admit, but I knew some pictures were taken and the look on her face told me I was right.

"The sonuvabitch got her into her bedroom, seduced her and when the right moment came, he shot her up. Dana must've fought back, and when did he tore her charm necklace off and it fell to the floor. The charm wasn't anything big, just a key, but it was the key to her hope chest and that's where I found the diary."

Now I played my big hand, "Once word spreads, rumors or not, your husband won't have a prayer in hell of making the primaries. His supporters will leave skid marks running from you people." Like I said the old man's a chess player where you have to think three steps ahead of your opponent, and it's not something I ever picked up on. I'm a poker player. It's where I've learned to bluff when holding nothing more than a pair of twos and a hell of a stare down. If that's not good enough you kick over the table. Here's where I started to walk away.

"Mr. Seraph, stop. Ah'm not saying yah're right about what y've said, but what would it take to keep you from talkin' to anyone or the press, sugah?"

"Are you talking money?" I turned back to face her and saw she kept pace with me. I looked down into her blue eyes and the Southern Belle returned.

"Ah'm positive somethin' could be arranged to reach an agreement, darlin'. Y'all find Ah can be extremely accommodatin', and to answer yah question, yes Kingsley and Ah have an open relationship, discreet but open." She then came a little closer and smiled at me the same way Bobbie did when she'd knelt on my floor.

"I see, well I been known to play ball from time to time." *Now if she'd buy it, even for a minute. Please buy it.* "So tell me something whose idea was it to leave Dana stuffed under her bed?"

"Tha' was Caleb's idea. Th' man is good at takin' orders, but he cannot improvise ta save his life. He lef' the body ther', not thinking it'd be found. When he realize' tha' was a huge mistake ther' was no way he could go back and dispose of it."

"You mentioned an agreement before, so what do you have in

mind?" Just as she was about to answer I saw something in her face she couldn't hide, or change.

Out of pure instinct, she glanced behind me then looked back in my eyes. Automatically I turned my head and saw a gold SUV parallel us, after that all hell broke loose.

Chapter Thirty-Four

I turned back to face Addar one more time and saw a glimmer of evil clearly in her eyes. I'd seen it before in some of the guys who work for the old man. She cracked a sick smile knowing what was coming. I spat out in rage at her. "Chi cento ne fa, una ne aspetti!" It means *'What goes around, comes around,'* and I meant it.

The SUV was the same one I saw when Bobbie came over. I knew they'd try something, but didn't think a drive-by was something they'd consider with so many potential witnesses out here, who I suddenly noticed seemed to vanish. I guess Addar and her people were more desperate than I imagined.

The SUV came up the road behind me, made a right, then another right and finally came towards us as it built speed. As this happened I saw the passenger window open and Caleb pulled something out. I wasn't too clear what it was at first because I hauled ass.

I ran off the path, away from Addar and pulled the Mateba from my shoulder holster. I turned, aimed and fired at the SUV's engine. I must've been way too excited or nervous because with one squeeze I fired off three rounds almost instantly. The rounds echoed throughout the cemetery as if we were in a canyon. It'd been awhile since I used my gun and forgot sometimes when you squeeze off a Mateba you can fire two or three shots almost automatically.

I must've hit something because the SUV screeched to a stop, diagonally cutting off traffic in both directions as steam erupted from the radiator. I ran towards a memorial that looked like a small, gray Washington Monument, which was the only protection I could find. From behind the monument I heard the doors open and a pair of running

179

footsteps coming closer. The only thing I could think of was do the unexpected. I headed left, with the lake to my right. As soon as I turned I saw the driver was Bernard and it looked like he had a .38, and I knew Caleb was armed, and figured Bernard wasn't as a good a shot as Caleb.

While I moved, I saw Bernard was closer and he aimed at me, with Caleb about twenty steps behind him, since he had to run around the SUV. I stopped, turned and fired at Bernard. The look on his face gave the whole story. He instantly dropped to his knees and the color in face drained, while he held onto his gun when he fell over face first into a fresh plot.

That's all I could see because Caleb took a shot at me that grazed by my head and all I heard was a 'thweep' and realized he was using a suppressor. I figure he was rushing and that's why he missed.

I headed back towards toward the road, swerving back and forth so he couldn't line up a shot. I lost sight of Addar but was more focused on staying alive. I headed behind a mausoleum and realized my heart was pounding and I was short of breath. My knees were shaking and I tried to calm down. It wasn't easy, since I wasn't used to people trying to kill me or killing anyone myself, but I got use to both ideas, fast.

My back was to the mausoleum and I clutched my gun to my chest. I figured Delaware Avenue was at least two hundred feet ahead of me, and knew there was no way I'd make it to front gate. If I ran for it, Caleb would pick me off. I listened for him or Addar, but passing traffic made it hard to hear anything. I wasn't sure when or if the cops would show, but I knew one way to attract some attention and get them there faster.

There were two shots left and knew I'd have to move once I fired, which is just what I did. I turned towards Scajaquada Creek and so the sound would echo like thunder, but I didn't want any collateral damage so I aimed where I didn't see anyone and fired twice.

I headed for the other side of the mausoleum while I reached for one of my speed loaders and once on the opposite side I moved towards the front, slowly. From where I was, I could see the cars and lake to the left but I didn't see Caleb or Addar. Wasn't the most reassuring feeling I had, and I reloaded as fast as I could. Now that I had a feel for the Mateba again I knew I wouldn't waste any more rounds. I headed back toward the path surrounding Mirror Lake as quickly and quietly as I could but as I did, I caught a flash of Caleb coming around the building in the corner of my eye and he took his shot.

All I remember was hearing two more 'thweeps', being struck by something and yelling out loud in extreme pain. I twirled around and tripped on my own feet when my legs tangled up on each other. I fell hard on my chest with my gun still in hand and under my chest. *Oh God, I'm dead!* I thought. Hot blood ran out of my upper back and the pain was worse than I could've imagined. Tears stung my eyes as the sting exploded throughout my upper body and I didn't know how long I had before shock would set it, or if I'd pass out from blood loss.

I lay still to let my body tell me what I needed to know. After I calmed down and realized I got nailed in the shoulder, but that was it. Then I heard two sets of footsteps coming over the blacktop. They stopped. "Is he dead?"

"Could be, the fucker was running pretty fast. Doesn't matter, he'll be dead if he isn't already."

"Good, switch guns wit' Bernard an' tha' be th' end of it."

I'd heard enough. While they were talking, I cocked the hammer as quietly as I could.

"Do it before th' police arrive an' we can leave."

I screamed in pain when I rolled over and fired three times at Caleb's chest.

By the time I pulled myself straight, I saw Addar was running, I rolled left and unloaded the rest of my rounds at her. All the rounds rumbled throughout the cemetery and I figured someone had to hear the volley.

I knew I hit her because of the way she screamed aloud and hit the ground. I was breathing rapidly, but I didn't feel anything. It may have been because of the adrenaline rush.

As Addar tried to drag herself up, I pulled myself up thanks to a cross shaped tombstone, then I looked back to see Caleb was dead. I rolled the prick over and saw there were two holes in his chest and one through his neck dead center. I just looked in disgust at him, then spat at the body out of disrespect. "Chi pecora si fa, il lupo se la mangia!" Which in English means *'Those who make themselves sheep will be eaten by the wolf.'* I bent over and pulled out the hypodermic and put it in Caleb's hand to get his fingerprints. I put it back in my shirt pocket and would give it to the police when they'd question me, at least this would form the link between the attempt on Crystal and me and these bastards.

I knew what I was doing, but I figured there was no crime in framing the guilty.

Addar limped along, with her left leg dragging behind her. She left a bloody trail and I followed as fast as I could, reloading my gun. Somehow, she reached the SUV and used it to pull herself along.

"Freeze goddamnit!" I shouted and thumbed back the hammer. She kept on going, not bothering to look back. I lined up my shot and finally Addar glanced over her shoulder. With my rage at the boiling point, I took two more shots and hit what I aimed at.

I sounded like a cop when I yelled again, "I said freeze!"

Addar appeared to be in a new state of shock when she realized I put two through the windshield and not her head. She fell back to the ground and finally realized it was over.

I came over to her and she wasn't the same woman she'd been when she arrived. Her hair was to one side, makeup ruined by sweat and tears, blood pumped out of her left leg, just like my shoulder. I looked down at the sight, and let her know I had four shots ready for her to try something stupid.

"Was it worth it? Three people are dead, one in the burn ward, you're going to prison."

She couldn't look at me, but the contempt in her voice said volumes. "You don't 'ave any proof. It will be yah word 'gainst mine that I had anythin' to do with Tillis."

I felt for my phone and thought, *Thank God.* I pulled it out and showed her I'd been recording.

"Chi e causa del suo male piange se ste sso." She looked baffled, so I translated. "It means, He who has created his own evil cries over the same. You know it as 'He who has made his bed must lie in it.'"

* * * *

As we waited for the police to show up the final verse of the Six Hundred ran through my mind. *When can their glory fade? O the wild charge they made! All the world wondered. Honor the charge they made, Honor the Light Brigade, Noble six hundred.*

Chapter Thirty-Five
~ Friday ~

Buffalo General Hospital

Things went better than I hoped. I'm alive and so are the girls. Desiree Addar is under arrest and the Tillis family have their closure.

At the cemetery, after I had Addar down, I waited until the police showed up and made sure she didn't go anywhere. Of course, she couldn't argue with my Mateba, but once she pulled herself together Addar actually thought she could bribe me. I told her she was responsible for a lot of suffering and she was going to pay.

I guessed right and someone heard my shots and called the police. About a minute after everything settled down four police cars with lights and sirens going nuts sped into Forest Lawn from all sides.

I knew what was coming, so I put the gun and cell, which was still picking up everything, down on the hood of the SUV, and I extended my arms out to my sides.

I told the first officer my permit was in my wallet and didn't move till told do so. I was shoved into the side of the SUV and patted down. I understood they had to secure the scene, so I didn't have a problem with what they were doing.

I told them about my shoulder wound and once everything was secure and they saw I was unarmed, they called for ambulances.

We both started to get some first aid and Addar immediately played her cards pretty well. She told the police how she was lured out to be ambushed, how I'd harassed her husband and finally threatened blackmail and would implicate him in Dana's murder unless I got a nice pay day. Bernard & Caleb were killed trying to protect her from me.

I have to admit she was pretty good at slinging the bull. I guess being a Washington Wife gave her the skills. I gave my side of the story and told the police to contact the Mayor's office and Sebastian, Sgt. Yagel and Detective Wolfe and finally I showed them my cell phone and pointed out the hypo. I also explained that I did shoot Caleb and Bernard in self-defense.

After a painfully long time Wolfe and Yagel showed up with a pair of ambulances, and I repeated my story to them.

Both Addar and I were treated and taken to Buffalo General. Turns out I was hit twice in the shoulder, but never felt the second round. Guess I was full of too much adrenaline and fear. After the EMT's saw me, I felt the pain, big time. I don't think I'll be looking at guns in the same way again. I also cracked a bone in my leg when I tripped over my own feet. If anyone asks, I just tell them I fell over a headstone and leave it at that. The truth is too embarrassing.

Eventually everything was straightened out and the cops knew who was responsible once they heard my recording.

* * * *

By Wednesday night, everyone was contacted. Addar was sent to the jail ward and I got a private room thanks to the old man, who surprised me by telling the hospital he'd pick up my medical bills. I also found out from the nurses the old man left a couple of his men to make sure I was safe.

Wednesday night and a chunk of Thursday were a blur between the painkillers, the exhaustion and me sleeping like Rip Van Winkle. I'm not clear about a lot but I remember I had a number of visitors. The first were Sebastian and Nicole.

They were very grateful and apologetic. He kept on saying he had no idea any of this would happen. I told him it wasn't his fault. They didn't stay long because they saw how wiped out I was, but I told him everything was okay between us and he seemed relieved and has the peace he and his family needed. We're going to get together after I get out of the hospital. Maybe I can get the three-hundred dollars then.

* * * *

Later on my doctor asked if I was up to a surprise visitor; Senator Addar wanted to talk to me. The red flags went up. Even though the man looked professional, he also looked like he aged about a decade since I last saw him. It looked like he hadn't been getting much sleep, was pale, had a bad case of five o'clock shadow.

"I just came from seeing Desiree and I can't tell you how sorry I am for everything. I had no idea any of this was happening, I guess I was too focused on my career."

"You've also been preoccupied with your problems."

"You know about those?" I just nodded. "Well there isn't any point in denying it anymore."

"I read about your addictions in Dana's diary and I want you to know I won't be telling anyone anything." The man looked uneasy, "I know everything but this won't make my Facebook page. Your foundation does a lot of good and I don't want to see people who need help get hurt."

"I appreciate your discretion. I know I am far from perfect, but I never wanted to hurt anyone. I really wanted to help people. I knew Desiree was always ambitious and sometimes her aspirations got the best of her. Actually, I knew she'd always seen herself as the next Jackie Kennedy and used the Foundation to keep herself in the limelight."

"I know about your promises you made Dana, how serious were you about them?"

"I meant everything I told her. I wanted Dana with me all the way." Addar sat down in one of the chairs at the oval table in the room. "I'd like to explain something to you, Mr. Seraph. See, I still love my wife even after what's happened, but Dana and I were like kindred spirits. We connected in a way Desiree and I never could."

"I think you should know Dana was pregnant." The temperature dropped like an anchor in the room. Addar was solemn and stunned, I'd hoped he already knew the truth but I guess Dana either didn't have time to tell him or she didn't know how to let him know.

"Desiree and I tried for a long time, but she can't have children. Do you know what..." I knew what he was trying to ask and I shook my head.

"Looks like she was about two months along."

Quietly he said under his breath, "A baby, oh God." After a minute in total silence, Addar finally pushed himself up, and dragged himself over to my bed and stuck out his hand. We shook and left things off at a comfortable understanding.

"Mr. Seraph, I'm not holding you responsible. I know you did what you had to do. After talking to the police, I know Desiree was behind everything, with Bernard. I never fully realized how driven either of them were. From what we've gathered they both saw themselves as the 'power behind the throne' as it were. How's your shoulder?"

"It'll be okay. Caleb was a hell of a shot. I didn't even know I'd been hit the second time till the doctors told me."

"I'm not that surprised, I mean Caleb and Hondoa were hired because they were professionals. To be honest I'm amazed he didn't hit your head."

"Sometimes it's better to be lucky than good."

He smiled trying to make light of the situation. "Well looks like you very lucky."

"Yeah, but my shoulder wishes the rounds hit my head. Those pain killers seem to wear off too fast."

"I know, I snapped my leg skiing about ten years ago."

"So what are you going to do now?"

"To be honest I don't think I'll stand a chance in primaries after all this, and I don't think I deserve to go on to the White House. I'm thinking about turning my attention to the Foundation. I can set up an office here in Buffalo and offer jobs to all the campaign workers. They deserve to keep their jobs and this is all maybe for the best."

"That's great, but I meant about Mrs. Addar."

"Oh that, ahhh I can't answer that. It's too complicated."

"I understand that all too well."

As he turned to go, the senator turned back. "By the way I meant to ask where in the hell did you learn to shoot like that?"

"My old man. Once I was old enough, he started taking me to the gun range when I was twelve years old. Mama wasn't happy about it, but he usually got his way. He insisted all his boys know how to shoot. He saw it at as one of those ways to make his sons manly men."

"Well I could use someone of your talents. If you ever need a job, let me know."

* * * *

After the senator left, I fell back asleep thanks to the drugs, but later on the old man and Mama came by to see me. Most of the family came with them, but I noticed Mike and Connie were not among them.

The old man decided the visits would be in shifts and he and Mama were first. I have to admit after the way things went I was surprised by his generosity.

"Giovanni, I have to tell how proud we are of you," he told me. "Aldrich wanted to be here but he had to be in court and he's contacting the police to see when you can get your gun and cell phone back. From what I understand the authorities need to make a copy of your recording."

Then Mama handed me a wrapped up box. "Speaking of Aldrich, he sent this along."

I opened up the card, which read, "Jonathan, you've done us all proud son. I know you were admiring this at my office and thought you could use one yourself, but you make your own justice. Wenona and I will see you soon. Aldrich." Inside the box was a copy of his statue of Lady Justice. I set it out on the night table next to me and the scales were perfectly balanced.

"That's beautiful. Aldrich always had good taste."

"Yeah, Mama, the man sure knows the score."

"Yes, he does Giovanni," the old man said, then continued, "There is something we need to discuss..."

"If you're talking about me joining the Arm, furgettaboudit, that's not going to happen, ever." He got very quiet and listened as I told him I knew he was using me to owe him a favor and tried to draw me in, with watching over Michael and Paul as a legit excuse. "I'm my own man and make my own decisions, the same way you and Grandpa did when you two chose this life. Mama once said to me to make her proud, well I can't do that if I work for you." We stared at one another, but it wasn't a stare down and it wasn't uncomfortable, it was a moment of full realization. It was a moment he comprehended everything. I stood on my own, up to him like I had to.

"Of course you are right, son. Sometimes I get so focused on the big picture, I lose sight of what is truly important. Besides, after this incident, I do not think you would be allowed in the organization." I was confused then he reminded me why. "You didn't break the tenth commandment, but you came close enough." There are 'rules' to the Mafia, what some call their Ten Commandments, which are thought to be guidelines on how a good, respectful and honorable Mafioso should live his life. To be honest I didn't have a problem with breaking all ten.

We talked some more, and before my folks left we talked about me recouping at the estate, which I didn't think was necessary but thanked them for the offer and thanked the old man for picking up the hospital tab. I was going be here for another four days at least, but after that, I'd head home.

Before they left the old man gave me one more huge surprise. "You know if you recover at home, you and your mother won't have to meet for lunch this month."

I was stunned, we'd been so careful about meeting and I never saw any of the old man's boys around. It's possible Mama was followed to our lunches.

He just smiled at me as he left and said, "What Giovanni? You don't think I know what goes on with my family?"

* * * *

After an hour or so and seeing almost everyone, the drugs kicked in again and I got drowsy. Before I fell asleep, I called Bobbie, told her I'd give her the exclusive on Saturday. She was glad I was all right and we talked for a while, then she said she'd see me Saturday.

Next, I called Crystal giving her a full rundown of what happened and let her know I was okay. She was back home and safe. Crystal also told me she'd stop by tomorrow too.

Like Bobbie, Crystal was happy to see I was all right and grateful. I knew both girls were safe, and talking to them set my mind at ease. For the first time in a week, I could fully relax and get some sleep I really needed. I recalled an old saying, *Chi trova un amico trova un Tesoro,* or *He who finds a friend, finds a treasure.* Guess in my case that makes me doubly lucky.

Epilogue
~ Saturday ~

After I saw Aldrich and Wenona, Crystal, Charles and Dixie, who I had pick up the package and hold till I got home, I gave Bobbie her exclusive.

Early Saturday evening a nurse brought me a dinner of roast beef, mashed potatoes, green beans, apple cobbler, milk, apple juice and tea and I remember thinking, *Thank God I wasn't stuck with tea, toast, chicken broth and lime Jell-o.* After I ate, I had a visitor, one I saw for a second time that day.

"Hi there."

"Glad to see you're still all right."

"You know I'll be fine. I didn't think I'd see you till tomorrow or Monday."

"I know, but after everything that's happened I wanted to make sure you're really okay not just physically."

"Well I'll be home next week."

She came over to the bed. "Can I see?" Surprised by the request I just nodded, leaned forward, pulled up the gown and she ran her hand over my bandages.

"The doctors says I'm responding to the antibiotics well, but I'll feel a twinge every once and awhile. Has something to do with a shock to my nerves."

"John, I want to really thank you for everything you've done."

"I know but I didn't want take a chance you or anyone would be hurt."

"I appreciate it all, and I wanted you to know how I feel." Then she kissed me and it was really nice.

"I have something special for you."

189

"Really," I said with my cocky-grin, "the nurse could here anytime. Quick lock the door." I laughed out loud.

She blushed and laughed, "Not *that* wise-guy." Then from her purse, she pulled out a pin. "I got this a long time ago from my Grandmother." Out of a small envelope came a metal pin of an angel. Head high, wings extended, sword in one hand and shield in the other.

"It's beautiful,"

She slipped it into my hand. "I want you to have it."

"What?"

"Grandma told me this guardian angel would watch out for me until my real angel here on Earth would take over the job. I think that's happened. I know you were just watching out for me and making sure I was safe."

"Are you sure? I mean it's a special gift."

She looked me with those warm, caring eyes I noticed right from the second we met. "You don't have to wear it, but I think you deserve it."

I didn't know what to say, so I kissed her again, and this time it was even better.

"It took me some time, but I finally figured out the joke about your name. Angelo and Seraph, angel and seraphim, cute. I guess it's your way of staying connected to your family."

"Yeah, but that's our secret."

"Well I won't tell anyone."

I caressed her beautiful face and stroked her hair. "Oh I know you won't," I said and kissed her again.

THE END